PENGUIN BOOKS

HALF LOVE HALF ARRANGED

Itisha Peerbhoy continues to live in deep regret that she didn't become a zookeeper. However, being able to write this book has done a considerable amount of soothing, elating and pep-talking to her animal-poo-deprived nerves. She lives in Bangalore, travels to Bombay as often as she can to visit her childhood home, and channels her inner Delhiite to any 'Southie' who will listen. This is her first book, and she is currently working on her next. She would love to hear from you at ipeerbhoy@gmail.com.

ITISHA PEERBHOY

PENGUIN BOOKS

PENGUIN BOOKS
Published by the Penguin Group
Penguin Books India Pvt. Ltd, 7th Floor, Infinity Tower C, DLF Cyber City,
Gurgaon 122 002, Haryana, India
Penguin Group (USA) Inc., 375 Hudson Street, New York, New York 10014, USA
Penguin Group (Canada), 90 Eglinton Avenue East, Suite 700, Toronto, Ontario,
M4P 2Y3, Canada
Penguin Books Ltd, 80 Strand, London WC2R 0RL, England
Penguin Ireland, 25 St Stephen's Green, Dublin 2, Ireland (a division of
Penguin Books Ltd)
Penguin Group (Australia), 707 Collins Street, Melbourne, Victoria 3008, Australia
Penguin Group (NZ), 67 Apollo Drive, Rosedale, Auckland 0632, New Zealand
Penguin Books (South Africa) (Pty) Ltd, Block D, Rosebank Office Park, 181 Jan
Smuts Avenue, Parktown North, Johannesburg 2193, South Africa

Penguin Books Ltd, Registered Offices: 80 Strand, London WC2R 0RL, England

First published by Penguin Books India 2014

Copyright © Itisha Peerbhoy 2014

ISBN 9780143423089

Typeset in Requiem by R. Ajith Kumar, New Delhi
Printed at Replika Press Pvt. Ltd, India

A PENGUIN RANDOM HOUSE COMPANY

For Sumera Peerbhoy,
who kicks ass

1

O<small>H CRAP!</small>

I clapped my hand to my forehead.

Goddammit! Did I sign out at work today?

I tried scrabbling for my phone, thought of the cops and the fines I'd have to pay for talking on the phone while driving, and decided to keep going.

I do this often. I forget to sign out at work. Then, I spend the rest of the evening cursing myself, my origin, my birth, the very sage from whom my line had descended. He must have been the absent-minded one, the one who forgot his condom.

At least I have enough to talk to myself about. I was near home, anyway. (This was not particularly uplifting, because I live with my parents.)

I'm thirty, single, and still feel obliged to tell my mother about my 'gynee problems'. I'm also 10 kilos behind on my goal weight and, in some quiet moments, I can hear my boobs racing towards my toes.

I'd better do my deep-breathing and centring exercises. Because soon I will be home, and it will start: 'You're-thirty-now-why-won't-you-get-married-it's-time-you-settled-down-cry-cry-wail-wail-oh-god-what-did-I-do-to-deserve-this.'

And *then* they will nag.

It's not like they're the typical Hindi-serial parents. My mother gets along with my grandmother; my dad doesn't spend his life behind a newspaper, nor does he conduct pujas attended by 10,000 people. It's just that all my friends are married: friends, cousins, friends' friends, and even some friends' children. At the rate it's going, it won't be long before thirteen-year-olds will want to stop having online, phone or camera sex and get married—just to spite me.

The thing is, it's not like I don't/didn't want to get married. I just haven't met anyone I could; at least not since Slime.

Slime and I started seeing each other in the eleventh standard. Then, after nine years, he told me he didn't want to marry me. I was so crazy about him, I didn't even screw around when I went to study abroad—and there were at least three, super-hot blonde guys who hit on me. But I was all, like, I have a boyfriend back home, and we're going to get married and have babies and live happily ever after. Turns out, he didn't think we'd last—you know, in the long run.

I was a nine-year-long learning experience. And now I'm thirty and listening to how even my 'fat friend' Tish got married.

Tish is really fat. Like an-entire-Oprah-episode-dedicated-to-her fat. But at least she's married. And that somehow negates every other way I might be a better person than her. At least I'm only 10 kilos overweight—now.

'Rheaaaaaaa! Rheaaaaaaaah! Is that you?'

In a perfect, sitcom world, I would say, 'No, Mummy. It's that guy who stole your bag last week. He found the house key and dropped in because he hasn't been nagged in, let's see, THE LAST FIVE MINUTES.' I mean, who was it going to be, except me? Well, in all probability, it could be my (smug, married) older sister, Pia, or my (irritating, curse-on-mankind) younger sister, Sia. It's true that the rhyming thing holds great merit in my family, and my parents chose a winner. We can rhyme for generations. There's still Gia, Diya, Mia, Leah, Affia and Keeya to go. And who knows, maybe even a Malaria.

My mother considers herself very 'upmarket' and 'kewl'—words she learnt when MTV first came to India. She wears Nikes with her salwar-kameez and, three times a year, she wears jeans with my dad's button-down shirts. She says things like 'sove' when she means 'suave', and thinks her accent is really high-class. Once, in a train, she told this Haryanvi guy that her 'Punjabi accent was ironed out by Irish nuns. We were trained till the twelfth standard, when class dissipated.' The Haryanvi contemplatively ate his gujiya and nodded. It was also this Irish-nun-imparted accent and a medical degree that enabled her to nail my dad—a 'second-generation English speaker'—who had left Dhi Punjab with only six bush-shirts to his name, but who now owned a metal-pipe factory and supply unit, was a member of the local Freemasons society and golfed with rich people.

'*Beta*, I got a nice watermelon. I'll juice it?'

My mother would juice cars if she could.

'No, mother, can't I just eat it instead? It's healthier, right?'

'Oops, beta, *kya hain na*, I juiced it already for Sia.'

Aaaaarghhh!!! How *annoying* is that!

'Maaan! Why can't I just eat watermelon when I want to, ya? You know I'm gymming! You could have left some of it, no?!'

What's the point in getting annoyed? The problem is, I'm not supposed to be still living at home. I'm supposed to be married, making things like rocket-and-feta salad with my husband; and owning a sparkling fridge that houses exactly one apple, a piece of ham and a carton of milk—not lifting shiny aluminium plates off aluminium *degchi*s with seemingly identical contents. I'm supposed to have a house with red walls, rubber-wood furniture and beanbags, and be saving for a trip to Morocco. Not living in a house with plump, rose-printed cushions and a fat sofa with velvety, red-and-beige upholstery, hearing about my aunt's niece's cousin's holiday to 'abroad'.

I put my bag down and gave myself a few more minutes of self-pity before my mother charged in and yelled at me for leaving my 'stuffs' around. I felt like those school experiments where you grow mustard seeds on cotton wool. Initially, it comes up really well. But when the time comes to transplant it and put it in mud so it can grow to its full potential, everything goes to shit. How much longer is it going to be gobi-aloo-dahi-pulao at mealtimes, no talking on the phone after nine, and my mother banging my bedroom door down every fifteen minutes, I thought. I'm thirty, goddamit. I make major decisions at work, have a cabin of my own and a team reporting to me—and still, when I come home, my mother asks me if my pee is pale yellow or 'darkish *jaisa*'.

I walked into my room, with its tattered Michael J. Fox poster and the one-eyed frog that Slime gave me in the ninth standard, and slammed the door. I never thought of doing it up, because with every new I guy I'd meet, I was convinced it would end with us falling in love and getting married/moving in together.

Potential Husband No. 1: Dhir was my mom's best friend's son. Whenever Auntie was visiting, he'd come over to pick her up and hang around till she was ready to leave. Then he began coming up to my room to check out my computer. Then he started showing me some websites he thought were cool. We got along pretty well, neither of us noticing that his mother was taking longer and longer to leave. In a week or so, he dropped the pretence of being there only to pick his mother up, and began to come straight upstairs to hang with me. For once, my mother didn't find a million excuses to barge in without knocking. She and her best friend would hold hands and giggle every time we passed them.

One day, while leaning over the back of my chair, Dhir leaned over an extra inch till his chest brushed my shoulder and the tip of his hair touched mine. A second later I was falling into a deep, sweet kiss, with Dhir's left arm wrapped around my shoulders, his fingers brushing my breast.

We lasted all of two weeks. At the end of which he posted a picture of his girlfriend and him on Facebook with the caption, 'Me and my best girl'. Hint: It wasn't me. It had been four months since the day he first came up to my room.

Potential Husband No. 2: Shaan was plump, wore glasses and had the same gym timings as me. He seemed stable and sweet and dependable. And I felt sorry for him. It turns out, however, that I needn't have: Shaan felt sorry for me for six months, after which he decided he should be with someone who actually did lose weight at the gym.

Somewhere in between was Rohit. Rohit was my older sister

Pia's ex. They'd had this really intense relationship where she used to write his name on her forearm with a permanent marker and would sleep holding one of his T-shirts. Years after they had broken up and Pia was fighting Dad so he would let her marry Ant, I ran into Rohit online and we began chatting for hours. We had so much in common, movies, music, games—we loved the same things. He told me that he'd always thought I was pretty and that if he hadn't been seeing Pia, he would have asked me out. He was so comfortable to be around—he knew my whole family; he was familiar with all our friends—it was just like falling in love with a childhood friend. Just as I had begun to work up the courage to tell Pia about Rohit, he asked me if I would talk to her and convince her to go back to him.

I stared at the frilly bedspread, the desk splattered with childish stickers, the tiny disco-ball hanging at my window— each a symbol of my unmarried-ness. My single-ness.

I wanted to be married, but frankly, where were the options? I'd done what I could by not being terribly unmarriageable: I had nice skin, was working my way into size-eight jeans, and when all my friends started smoking, I didn't, because my mother said the reason Dimple Kapadia looked so bad in *Dil Chahta Hai* was because she was a smoker and 'smoking will turn your lips black and small like those Japanese dancers who look so scary'. Considering my mother had been called a 'white beauty' in her 'haydays', as she kept informing us, I didn't want to challenge her wisdom.

I sighed.

'Hello, room. Here I am. Thirty.'

And here you are, room. Pale blue with Minnie Mouse curtains, and a collection of Akshay Kumar DVDs.

My head felt hot and compressed into a tightly wound ball of nerves. What does Tish have that I don't? I began to think of all the weddings I had gone to over the years. All my friends, pink-faced and shiny and decked out in red, white or pink, looking around them half overwhelmed, half proud. And I hated them all. Hate them!

2

My RIGHT FOOT WAS on fire. That's how I knew it was morning and time to get to work. My bed is near the window, and the Minnie Mouse curtains have kind of shrunk so they don't cover the entire window. So every summer morning, when the sun is high enough in the sky, it gets really hot and my right foot begins to burn, and I know it's time I got my engine going to get to work.

I rolled over, lifted my right knee and brought it down over my left, twisting my back as I did, and felt a satisfying crunch-click. Did the same with my left and realized I couldn't open my eyes. I reached up and touched them and felt this sticky-gluey stuff over my face.

That's when I remembered my frantic drive to Baskin-Robbins and my brutal, emotionless coupling with a litre of Gold Medal Ribbon ice-cream. I felt dirty. Depraved.

That's the last time I do something like that, I thought to myself, as I peeled myself off the covers and hobbled to the loo.

It may have been a new day, but I had the same old feeling of being the one who got left behind: the one who'd hit thirty without finding a man who wanted to end up with her.

I went down to the breakfast table dressed in camel trousers and a brown shirt. My mother stood in a patch of sunlight streaming in through a window, singing a Hindi song and making pancakes. What Indian middle-class family eats pancakes for breakfast, for God's sake? Even in America, Indians eat parathas or omelette-toast or something. My dad looked up from his boiled egg-whites and raised his eyebrows at me.

This was a bad sign. When everything is normal, my dad ignores me. I sat down and waited.

My mother swept a plate of pancakes high into the air, and brought it down in front of me with a flourish and a big smile on her face.

'Mo-orninnnnng, *bete-jaan!*'

On my right was a glass of fresh orange juice. Orange is the caviar of my mother's dispensary of juices. Apple, watermelon and strawberry are my mother's specialty, but nothing says 'I am now going to call in the thirty hours of labour you put me through' like a glass of OJ squeezed fresh and served in a frosted glass.

I looked at Sia in panic. But she was in exactly the same position we had left her in nineteen years ago: hunched over her breakfast so the ends of her hair touched the plate. The only indication that Sia is actually alive is that sometimes her nail polish is blood red instead of black. I started to text Pia.

Dude. Parents acting strange. Mother made pancakes and juice. You know anything?

She replied.

Marriage on the cards. Fattening you for the kill. Hint: shaadi.com.

My chest suddenly felt really tight. My stomach imploded.

My ears were starting to burn, and I couldn't breathe. I wanted to get up from the table and run, but my eyes remained fixed on my phone and my fingers wouldn't move to type out a response. My parents thought I was so without hope that they needed to *arrange* a marriage for me. They were going to send me out into the circuit with a label pasted to my forehead: LIMITED SHELF LIFE. ALREADY CLOSE TO EXPIRY DATE.

I wanted to say something, like how I needed them to believe in me. I needed them to tell me that it didn't matter that I wasn't married, that I was more than that . . . that even if I never became someone's wife or mother, it didn't make me any less of a person, because I was their daughter, and I was a good person who earned a good salary and bought them gifts and saved too. I needed . . .

My phone rang. Tish.

'Ya.'

'Oh, good morning, Miss Sunshine. Why so cheery?'

I sighed as loudly and expressively as I could. 'Same old. The marriage bus.'

'Please, dude! Bans is teething and he bit my nipple. So frickin' painful! You're so lucky you're single, dude!'

Suddenly, I wanted to kill her, her banker husband and their two cherubic children. Everything went blinding white and I couldn't see. I hung up, grabbed my oversized yellow handbag and left the house without a word.

Behind me I could hear my mother. 'Betooo! Pancakes I made in Lite butter and low-fat milk. You can eat it!'

I got into my car and slammed the door. I dug my nails into the steering wheel. And then I couldn't stop digging until I had gouged deep grooves into it. 'If I Die Young' by The Band Perry played loudly in my head. Tears squeezed out from the sides of my eyes, burning because I wouldn't let them flow.

3

SMS FROM MY DAD:

Please be at home by 8.00 p.m. today. We are proceeding to the club for dinner with friends. On completion, we will proceed for late-night dessert to Oberoi hotel. I expect you to be punctual and presentable, as always. Love, your father, Vir Kanwar.

He must have been in a hurry. His message was half its usual length. I replied:

K.

And then flung my BlackBerry to a corner of my desk. I had a team meeting in fifteen minutes and needed to update my project chart before that. We had found bugs in the application, and it needed to be rolled back—our third rollback this cycle. One more, and my entire team would be benched. I managed to get my stuff together in time for the team stand-up, and after that was so immersed that I forgot dinner, my dad, shaadi.com and everything else.

'Dude, are we going to get lunch, or are you still pissed off?'

I looked up and there was Tish, wearing a transparent top

with flowers on it and a huge silver pendant with a painting of a naked man where a stone would normally be.

'*Chal,* yaar! We can fight over ganache tart.'

She was dying to get out of there and I didn't blame her. How she had managed to enter my IT office with its million rules and restrictions is beyond me. How she managed to navigate herself to my characterless desk through a sea of about two hundred others is a bigger mystery. But now, all the geeks with their jeans halfway up their chests and their white keds were staring at large Tish with her flowers, jewellery, and magenta handbag that could transport Jon & Kate Plus Eight anywhere they wanted to go.

It was IT inquisition versus one hour of Tishisms. I chose lunch.

'OK, so I don't get it. I said you're lucky you aren't married. How is that a bad thing, ya?'

'Tish, you're married. I'm not. Stop patronizing me by telling me what you think I want to hear.'

'OK, yaar. I'm sorry. Here, have this kokum thing. It's good.'

'You don't get it! Pia says my parents are looking for a guy for me. Even they've given up on me being able to get someone for myself. I'm so sick of this marriage tamasha, man! Why can't people see me as the successful working woman that I am? The first thing they see is "single woman".'

'Babe. That's how it is, yaar. The first thing they think when they see me is "fat woman"— Indians are narrow-minded. But you know that's how it is. You live with your choices.'

'What's wrong with me, Tish? Why won't anyone marry me? Why do I meet such jerks? Why is it so hard?'

Tish looked at me long and hard. Her electric-blue-lined eyes held mine in a look of pure empathy.

'Here. Have the last piece of ganache tart.'

~

By seven fifteen I was rushing home to be on time for dinner. I was still pretty gutted about everything that had happened that day, but ditching the programme was not an option. Even at thirty, I was afraid of my taciturn dad, and, besides, there was a tiny part of me that really was curious about this person my mother had lined up to meet her ageing, virginal, 'fattish' daughter.

I went directly to my room, did an armpit-face-hairline rinse, and slipped on a simple sleeveless dress in a red-and-olive print. I pulled my hair back into a high ponytail, so Pia wouldn't point out it needed a wash, slipped into red ballet-flats and started down the stairs again. Thirty-year-old Cinderella—whose carriage has wheelchair access, and it's either midnight or menopause.

Pia and her husband, Anant, were already downstairs. Pia, in a skirt and a drapey emerald maternity-top, and Ant in his trademark kurta with brightly coloured scarf flung over it—today's combination was brown and green. Sia, as she had done since she was born, was trying to blend in with my mother's knick-knacks. She was dressed in a black serial-killer-type outfit and was standing motionlessly next to a five-foot-tall statue of a fat Buddha with 300 teeth. I don't know which was scarier.

'*Chalo*, girls!' My mother crackled past in a silk sari, and we piled into the cars and drove in abject silence to the club. Pia and Ant were the first to get out of the car. The heat had begun to get to Pia ever since she had entered the third trimester of her pregnancy and started spending her life going from an AC-to-AC environment. The last time we had dared take her to the open-air restaurant she had loved for the past five years, she had stomped off and insisted on being served in the car, and we had to drive home in a car that smelt of garlic chicken-tikkas.

My mother catapulted herself from the passenger seat before the car had completely stopped and almost bumped into Pia. She was the only one who had seen the boy's family and was keen to ensure that some other family with an unmarried daughter didn't try and snap him before we had had a fair chance. Of course, Mummy, raised in a family of seven brothers and sisters, didn't stop to think that potential grooms were not like the last two lychees in the bowl. Sia, Dad and I walked up to the reception last, just as the receptionist informed her, 'Your guests have arrived,' and Sia whispered, 'Oh my God.'

4

VYASH WAS AROUND 5'10", dark (Madrasi as Mummy would say), with curly hair and sparkling eyes. When Sia was a baby, she had this transparent crazy-ball with some shiny liquid stuff and a plastic fish inside it, and a silver button-type thing that lit up every time she bounced it. Vyash's eyes were like Sia's crazy-ball. They lit up every time he smiled.

He wore a blue shirt the colour of Chelpark ink, with the top two buttons open and the sleeves rolled up to just under his elbows. His trousers were pale beige with a tan belt that matched his shoes. As I glanced sideways, Sia had her phone out and was furiously texting—probably with her best friend, procuring Vyash's butt-rating, overall cuteness score and probable richness monitor.

Vyash made eye contact with each of us individually. He began with Papa, shaking his hand and smiling, and then he sparkled at Mummy, telling her she was the most ravishing woman he had seen. He then pulled out a chair for Pia, waited till she had sat down comfortably and then inquired if she'd like a footstool, while Ant stood by, thoroughly confused and helpless. He stood until both Sia and I had sat down, then turned to Ant and murmured something to him. Ant laughed and slapped him on the back and then beamed at Pia.

Pia had never looked happier. She hadn't even realized that she was sitting on the lawn and not in the AC. She looked from mummy's ecstatic face to Ant's and back again, rubbing her belly in joy. It was almost as if she was taking full responsibility for Vyash's sparkly eyes, his charm and his very existence too.

Vyash took the chair opposite mine while Ant stood behind Pia's chair. Suddenly, I was very aware of my paunch and my posture. There was a telltale prickling sensation in my boobs— and I knew they were standing at attention. Fortunately, my mother had decided to take matters into her own hands.

'Beta, you drink?' she asked, as if the sudden marriage of her middle, thirty-year-old daughter was terrifying enough to throw the world's men off drink and back to drinking their mothers' milk and eating sterilized glucose biscuits.

Vyash sparkled and said, 'Only in the company of beautiful women, Auntieji.' He took a sip from his glass of water and, as I watched him, his eyelids lazily lifted and his crazy-ball eyes met mine and sparkled. I gasped, while Pia's toes visibly curled and my mother's sari crackled loudly, set off by her coy squirming. Sia, I think, had her first orgasm since she watched *Edward Scissorhands* for the first time.

Why would he be interested in me? He looks like he should be with one of those throaty-voiced nasal girls who always ended up sitting in men's laps, hanging off their arms because they were too overcome to look after themselves. I've always been the type of girl who cleaned up puke and hauled other drunk girls home, the type who never let herself get drunk because she wasn't sure who'd scrape her off the footpath and get her home.

I had tucked myself in between my sisters. They were the only vaguely safe things I could find in that space full of my parents—my mother puffing up more every moment—Vyash, untrustworthy, charming, with hands that covered his glass completely, and finally, the Mummyji. Salwar kameez, ponytail, Kolhapuri chappals with diamante detail, and leather bag. She was any mummy on any day buying fresh peas and snapping the tails off hapless bhindis. She felt me sizing her up, looked at me, and smiled a warm, lips-shut type of smile. She wasn't about to hold me to her chest and ask that we go shopping the next day, but she wouldn't be asking me to walk so she could check whether I had a limp, either. I think I liked her.

'Vyash's Daddyji is travelling,' she said. 'He would have been here otherwise.'

Vyash looked at me (40 per cent sparkle) and said, 'He really missed something.'

I quickly looked down at my lap. The patterns on my dress blended into a red Rorschach-test blot. It looked like two kittens ripping each other to shreds. Or two pink bunnies rubbing their fuzzy noses together . . . or two diamond rings . . . ?

'Fuck, man. She's fuckin' fallen.' Sia inhaled a bottle of Coke, and began to look around desperately for a waiter like a drunk guy stuck in an AC car, needing to throw up. Pia gave her a stop-fuckin'-abusing glare and rubbed her belly beatifically.

Just as I was about to kill my sisters, Vyash asked if he could get me a drink at the bar. My parents and Pia nodded vigorously, and I got up, praying my dress hadn't got stuck in my butt.

'Crazy evening, huh?' Vyash asked as we walked to the bar. 'Your first time too?'

He laughed, and his laugh was 100 per cent sparkle, one million lamps lighting up India, Dairy Milk pouring into a perfect creamy bar, five hundred babies giggling, a warm bucket of honey and milk that I promptly jumped into and let soak into my skin.

'Yup. I'm used to meeting women on my own.' He slowed and looked at me, 'But maybe you need help meeting the exceptional ones.'

It was like someone had reached in through my stomach, grabbed my heart and squeezed till I couldn't breathe. I suddenly needed my cell phone, preferably a call with Tish hanging from the other end. I mumbled something into my handbag, hoping he wouldn't notice that I had just named our three children—two boys and a girl: Aidan, Adam (with his father's chocolate skin) and Freja (his height, my smile).

'Beer for me; and the lady?' He smiled down at me, eyebrows raised in question.

'Mmm . . . juice,' I said.

Juice? Frickin' juice?? I sounded like I was going to reach into my bag and pull out a half-complete 'Home Sweet Home' cross-stitched wall-hanging. He ordered my juice solemnly and sexily and then pulled out a bar stool for me.

The bar stool and I are not good friends. We get along when there are no men around, or when there's just Arf (Aftab. Best friend. No sexy feelings). But we don't like to hang out on dates when I'm in a skirt or a dress and lots of worst-case scenarios can happen.

'I'll stand,' I said, putting my bag on it and leaning against it.

'So, what gives?' he said, hundred-watt-smiling at me, while I suddenly realized that my anti-bar-stool stance had given me a very clear view of his crotch.

'Er . . . huh?'

'You know, pretty girl like you, place like this . . .'

'I thought the club was a family joint,' I said, trying the brassy repartee I usually used on men I was interested in.

He laughed. 'I meant the "arranged meeting" place.'

'Actually, I didn't know . . . my sister put . . .' I trailed off, realizing how stupid and clichéd that sounded.

He didn't say anything, just raised an eyebrow as he watched me die a slow and painful death.

'You're in the meeting place too!' I said defensively, my face and neck burning.

He leaned forward and suddenly I was eye to sparkly eye with him. So close that I could see a distorted version of myself in his eyeballs.

'Rhea,' he whispered. 'You may be the one to heal me.'

5

'FUCKABLE OR NOT?'

Tish was lying on my bed with her legs swung over the headboard.

'For a mother of two, you are really sick.'

'I didn't become a mother by checking if he wants to feed the poor, na!'

I threw a handful of (low-fat) popcorn at her.

'He is.'

'Good, then get as much as you can before you marry him and he gets the Madonna—whore complex and doesn't want to do you any more.'

I sighed. I had been hearing this ever since Tish had had Kahani, her daughter. According to her, she had had to take advantage of her husband one drunken night to produce Bans. ('Kahani needs a sibling, yaar. She spends too much time talking to the dog.')

'So . . . kissed?'

'Tish. Two dates. We're still talking. Besides, maybe he wants to be friends. We haven't spoken about marriage.'

'Rhea. Three more dates. If he hasn't at least got to first base by then, move on.'

'Yes, Miss PhD in Husband-Finding.'

'You're such a bitch. Pass the popcorn bowl.'

Vyash had been married before. I hadn't told Tish because it would spark off another lecture about used goods and desperate men, blah-blah, asking me if his ex was hot, and soon I would be googling his ex and comparing myself to her. OK, I had already found her on Facebook. She was a thin-tall-popular variety, who listed *To Kill a Mockingbird* and Sartre in her reading preferences, and cooking as her hobby. She was like an SUV with super mileage. You just can't beat it. She had slept with his best friend and he had found out because she had left her chat window open. He was so deeply hurt; I could see it in his eyes whenever he spoke about her.

'I'm a one-woman guy, Rhea,' he told me at our last coffee date that lasted three hours and then flowed into a two-hour walk under the stars. 'Once I fall in love, she never stops looking beautiful to me.'

I couldn't imagine any woman being unfaithful to such a devoted guy. Vyash was perfect. He was kind, strong, and he made me feel about 4 feet tall, all of 50 kilos and thoroughly helpless. Well, her loss was my gain. And, maybe, just maybe, Vyash didn't need an SUV. Maybe he just needed a Maruti 800—safe, reliable and practical.

Tish left early to pick up her kids from art class, which gave me time to put together an outfit that was sure to tell Vyash that I was ready to go to the next level with him. I wanted to be his woman in every way, and I wanted him to know it.

I wore blue jeans and an off-shoulder white top that clung

in all the right places, and created some other right places too. I washed my hair, finger-combed it and left it loose. Minimal, peachy make-up, white heels and a narrow belt, and Sunita Rao's 'Pari Hoon Main' began to play in my head, my dangling earrings making little jhing-jhing noises to the beat. If Tish could have seen me she would have gyrated her hips till her necklaces jangled and said, 'Ooooh, booty call!' But of course it wasn't a booty call. It was an invitation to 'get to know each other better'. I was going to an art exhibition with him—not a club where sweaty bodies would jostle me till I was in his arms, which is exactly the way Tish 'pinned the lizard' as she put it.

I left through the back door so my mother wouldn't see and tell me that the children were peeking out of the window or that my mummy was taller than my daddy or something. I got round to the front of the house and arranged myself next to the pansy patch. Vyash drove in and leaned over to open the door. He was wearing an open-necked white shirt, jeans and a blazer. I moulded my back into the seat and breathed in deep. I could taste him. He was raw and earthy and salty, and I felt completely in love. I wanted to be Mrs Vyash Mehta. I wanted to take away all the pain anyone had ever made him feel. I wanted to be the one who let no harm come to him, because he was my prince.

My parents hadn't asked me once about him, and I took that as a sign that they would marry me off to him with the least fuss, wearing my grandmother's jewellery as a sign of their support. It couldn't be more perfect.

'Hey, hottie!' he smiled at me and then leaned over me, his arm pressed against my thigh. He pulled at the seat belt till it came free and then fastened it near my right thigh, his hand burning a raw patch through my jeans, into my thigh. 'You've got to be careful with precious things,' he said, his eyes on the road, and started the car.

I looked out the window hoping he wouldn't notice me visualizing our wedding. (Me in peach, him in grey, white flowers, Italian food.) By the time we arrived at the gallery, our dog, Bruce, had spent a few evenings draped across our laps as we watched TV and we had felt the baby kick twice. Vyash, of course, had continued chatting to me about what he had gone through after his divorce and how he had come out of the whole thing with the help of his friends and his work. Gina had seemed to be the perfect person—until she got really close to his best friend. She even shared jewellery with his mother and took his little sister to the gynac.

The art gallery turned out to be this really swank venue that was more cocktail lounge than art gallery. People were walking around in silk dresses and designer labels. Suddenly, my white top from Bangkok felt silly and too girly. I shrank back and came up against Vyash's chest. He leaned down and whispered, 'You're the prettiest girl in the room.'

I blushed.

He placed his hand on my back and led me to the centre of the room as if I was the most precious thing in the world.

'Vee-Man!' a tall guy in jeans and a navy-blue Puma jacket came up to us. He thumped Vyash on the back affectionately. 'You doing OK, man?'

Vyash turned to me. 'Rhea, Sean. My former brother-in-law. Sean, this is Rhea.'

'Hello, lovely Rhea.' His eyes crinkled when he smiled.

His phone rang before I could reply and he excused himself, walking away while he answered.

I turned to Vyash. His eyes were lowered, his face had tightened.

'I won't let our evening be ruined, Vee,' I whispered, taking his hand.

His huge hand closed over mine, his firm grip swallowing mine almost completely. He bent his head until his mouth was in my hair. 'Nothing can ruin anything when you're around, Rhea. When you're here, I'm invincible.'

6

THE GYMMING HAD BEGUN to take effect. I was 5 kilos lighter on the scale, my skin was glowing and my breasts had developed a backbone of their own. Vyash and I now met twice a week, and he had kissed me—gently, deeply.

But mostly, we talked. He was still recovering from heartbreak. Gina had been his wife for five years and his girlfriend for six before that. He had thought they were happy. When she told his best friend that she had made a mistake when she married him, he never saw it coming.

'Rhea, she's the most beautiful woman I've ever seen.'

I cringed, feeling every one of the million shards of steel that had ripped into my heart. Gina was formidable in her hold over Vyash, and I hoped I was woman enough to take her on. What I had to my advantage was that I was nothing like Gina. I wasn't extra beautiful or high-maintenance. And most of all, I knew when I had a good man. And I knew how to keep him happy. At least, I hoped I did. I thought back to that meeting with Sean, Gina's brother. He was seriously hot. A big-shot ad executive, he had been really close to Vyash until he and

Gina broke up. Apparently he had advised them to have an open marriage—carry on with whoever he wanted to and let Gina 'have her fun' as long as she came back to him at night.

But Vee was old-fashioned that way. He believed in marriage and kids and growing old together, and finally dying together like the two old people did in *The Notebook*. The more time I spent with him, the more I was convinced that Vee and I would be very happy together. The Gina thing didn't bother me much. He'd forget her in time.

I hadn't seen Tish in a long while. There was too much I couldn't tell her about Vee and me and, frankly, just because Tish had managed to get married didn't mean she had written the Bible on men. I really didn't need my best friend predicting doom for my relationship.

I did hang out with Arf a lot. Arf is the only thing I didn't return after Slime and I broke up. He used to hang with us back when we were together, and he likely never said more than five words to me in the whole nine years. This is probably because he was stoned for all of them. After Slime left me, Arf called one day and asked if I wanted to watch a movie. We went for a three-hour-long one, all through which he stared at the screen in silence, while I held his sleeve and cried till the credits rolled. To this day, I don't know which movie it was. And Arf prefers not to talk about it. He says crying women make him turn to drugs. Serious drugs, not just weed. Apparently, weed is not drugs. Weed is natural—like drinking aloe vera juice.

Today, we were sitting in the coffee shop in the recreation area of the IT park. We had chosen my favourite umbrella, the one with a picture of a dog eating an ice-cream cone on it that could look positively pornographic if you caught it in the right light from your office window.

I was badly in need of a best friend. The last time Vee and I had gone out, things had gotten a bit steamy. He had leaned across to fasten my seat belt. His breath had licked at my ear, gently lifting a few strands of hair away from my neck. He paused, then leaned forward and sucked my ear lobe into his mouth, his teeth grazing the edges, his tongue circling it. When he leaned back, he was breathless, his eyes hooded, his mouth half open.

'Come with me to Goa, Rhea.'

Would I go? Of course I would go! We had kissed a few times and it had been really hard to stop there, but he had moved back in with his parents after his divorce and we never really had a chance to go further. I mean, I was thirty, right? I'd had the birds-and-bees talk, I'd had the 'God is watching' lecture, and I had seen all the 'always use *kundum*' ads on TV. I was doing this. And, I thought to myself defiantly, I was going to marry him, anyway. So what was wrong? I just couldn't tell anyone the truth. Except for Arf—who was behaving obscenely with a chicken sandwich and milkshake, as I made perfectly acceptable conversation with my cup of green tea. He looked up from his food fornication, 'Ree-diculous. Eat something. Have an animal. Stop drinking Lodhi Gardens.'

'Arf, five more kilos. End of conversation.'

He put his sandwich down, took a long pull at his straw and leaned back in his chair. In sunglasses, a fitted tee and bed-head, he didn't look a day older than the first time I saw him.

'Auntie. You're hot, man. Eat.'

I couldn't see his eyes behind his sunglasses. But I had none on to hide my blazing cheeks.

I changed the subject. 'So, Vee asked me to go to Goa with him. It's Level Two, Arf. What do you think?'

Arf leaned forward and said, really gently, 'Someday you'll get it, Pretty Ree…' and then he broke into this really annoying falsetto and started singing, 'If you like it then you'd better put a ring on it. Uh-uh-uh-O-oh.'

I got really annoyed and opened my purse to pay. Arf grabbed my wrist and slid some money on the table. He stood up, still holding my wrist, and then pulled me up and against him, putting his arm around me.

Without another word, he walked me back to my office.

～

That evening, Vee and I got to spend some time together, driving back after dropping his mother at her friend's place. The friend was sick, and Auntie wanted to spend the night so she could help out. Vee asked me to come along and, since I liked his mom so much, it wasn't much of a favour, anyway.

'Arf's grown up so cute! You know it's like last year he was Arf—stoner and guitar player—and now, suddenly, he's this soulful man who writes music.'

Vee took my hand and kissed my fingers. 'Ree, you're my woman.' I felt sixteen cheerleaders perform a routine to 'Walking on Sunshine' inside my chest. 'I really wish you wouldn't talk about other guys. It makes me feel like I'm not good enough for you.'

Vyash felt like he was not good enough for me?? The sixteen women were now in pyramid formation with a girl turning somersaults at the top. My totally hot, utterly sexy, sensitive man feels like he's not good enough for me! I felt like a million bucks. Like 40,000 fresh cupcakes with cream-cheese frosting. I smiled all the way home.

So, Goa . . . Yes, why not . . . I was 'his woman'. We were obviously going to get married. And I was so ready for the next level. I texted him later that night, my heart making like a basketball and my throat, a ring.

You n me and sunny sands! Can't wait ☺

He replied in seconds.

Careful. You're making me fall. Don't hurt me.

Making him fall! Making *him* fall! I stood on my bed and jumped up and down. Hurt him? He thought I could hurt *him*! It was the nicest thing anyone had thought about me. And hullo! Was he bloody kidding?? I would let him know every day how much he meant to me. How lucky I felt every morning. I was going to show him how special he was—beginning with investing in some 'racy-lacies'. Lingerie for lingering memories. I smiled at my creativity. Should've been in advertising! I thought to myself.

The best racy-lacies are never found in a fancy showroom with AC. They're found in a shop with two levels, and no name, just a number, with men to advise you on the most comfortable fit. So off I went to the nearest street of 'Bangkok shops' to find just the potion for my potent intent.

'Madam, *aapko yeh chhota hoga.*' The guy in the shop hadn't even asked my size. He just saw what I was looking at and his expertise—developed by staring at women's chests and getting paid for it—had picked up that I was too ample a sample for the pink virginal set I had picked out.

Here, in 53, Lovely Street, I was surrounded by everything

from virginal to infallible to inappropriate to downright wrong. There were lingerie sets with three strategically placed furry pom-poms in every conceivable colour. I've been seeing these in shop windows since I was three, and have always wondered who actually wore them. They were still around, so obviously it was the Indian man's seduction-wear of choice.

Anyway, the daunting range of pom-poms, strawberries, tiger prints and lip outlines had to be avoided this time. It would be my first time with Vyash, and I couldn't have him undoing my buttons to find some sort of dead animal draped across my tantalizing bits.

After the salesman had showed me around twenty choices, which he assured me were comfortable—'*phool* support'—and would look nice on me, I settled on pale-pink lace set with a white trim. It bordered on the virginal, yes, but it's not like I had written the book on sex, anyway. And Vyash had once told me Gina was into red and purple and wild-coloured underwear, and the last thing I wanted to do was remind him of her.

~

And, then, it was finally just one more night of sleep before the day I would be leaving on a dream vacation, with the dream man to make my dream life come true! I spent most of the day in the parlour de-fuzzing. I had planned a Brazilian wax, but after they had taken off about 80 per cent of my body hair, I decided that I would save the Brazilian wax for my wedding night. It made sense, I thought, to keep something to look forward to, for later.

Tish had been calling and texting asking me what was up,

but I just told her I was really busy at work. It had been three months since I'd seen her and, frankly, life was much easier without the *Tish's-Life-is-the-Way-to-Live-Your-Life Show* on repeat. I missed her when I was packing though. I needed her to prepare me for my first time. But I had to do it without her.

I surveyed the result of the frenzied hours I had just spent.

Pink unmentionables: Packed

Sunblock: Packed

Sunglasses: Perched on head

Swimsuit: Dusted off and packed

Sundresses: Packed

Massage oil: Packed (What?! I'm a virgin, not an ice sculpture.)

Shania Twain was performing 'Man! I Feel like a Woman!' just for me, in my head. I told my parents I was going to a weekend conference in Goa, told Tish that I would be too busy to be in touch for a bit, and told my sisters nothing. Normally, this would have called for all hands on deck: shopping, advice, scented bubble-bath, sex tips, and my entire support system on WhatsApp. But this time, there was no one I could tell without inviting judgement or advice and, frankly, I wanted neither. I just wanted to come back with a ring on my finger and a wedding date. And it was pretty obvious that Vee had the same thing on his mind. Arf had once told me that no matter how much a man likes a girl, if she can't turn him on, he would never take it to the next level. Sex is the final test.

7

Vᴇᴇ ʜᴀᴅ ʙᴏᴏᴋᴇᴅ ᴜs into a beautiful Portuguese-style resort in a room that overlooked the pool. The place was new, and had just one other couple staying there, or so the guy at the reception told us while dancing to the cheesy '80s music on the loudspeaker.

We entered our room and sat on the bed, and it suddenly hit me.

I had never, ever shared a room with another man in my life before. Where would I change? What were we supposed to do when we were just hanging out? Tish and I, or Arf and I, would lounge on the bed, but did couples do that? Would I give him the 'wrong idea'? What happened if I wanted to poop? He would know what I was doing if I spent a long time in the loo, right? I sent up a silent prayer that there would be a scented candle and a covered dustbin in the loo. I looked over at Vee, and he looked equally uncomfortable, just sort of standing around near the dressing table while I sat on two inches of bed.

Oh God, he was going to see my underwear!

This was turning out to be extremely unlike what I had first envisioned. In the movies, they always skipped this part. Or something really stupid and funny usually happens to break the ice. Unfortunately, my life didn't have a team of writers working on it.

Vee looked at me and then smiled gently. He came over and sat next to me and slid his hand up my back. He leaned over and kissed my neck and then smiled so I could feel his lips move on my skin and then the smooth wetness of his teeth.

'Care to get out of these clothes and into a wet . . . swimming pool?' he murmured huskily as my skin rippled into goosebumps and my nipples hardened. He then stood up and pulled off his T-shirt in one swift move. I thought I would die of a heart attack. The tension was killing me. I hadn't thought this through. I had body-image issues, for crying out loud! And here I was, with a bag of clothes that would barely cover my face, let alone my ass, stomach and thighs. I was a stupid, horny thirty-year-old with a penis for a brain. A lunatic who would die with cobwebs between her thighs.

He leaned close to me and said, 'I can't wait to see that beautiful body in a swimsuit.' And I catapulted myself straight into the car with the 'Just Married' sign hanging from it—he thinks my body is beautiful!

By the time I had changed into my swimsuit and examined myself from every angle, Vee was waiting in the pool, his dark skin even darker in the sun, his hair wet and clinging to his forehead. He turned to me and held his arms out, smiling, and I leapt right in. It was perhaps the first purely happy moment I had had since I was ten.

Vee held me close, his hand splayed against the small of my

back, our legs touching and separating under the water. His skin felt rough, sexily abrasive, making my skin feel extra smooth and feminine. The water pushed and pulled me away from and against him. As my breasts pushed up against his chest, the waves suddenly began to feel warm and my breath began to come in short bursts. Vyash moved his hand up between my shoulder blades and pushed me up against him, his forehead resting on mine, his eyes closed. He drew in a ragged breath and his body shivered.

'I want to make love to you, baby.'

His voice was tortured, as if he was fighting the desire he felt. He moved us to the edge of the pool, still holding me against him. Then he turned around, placed his hands on the ledge and pulled himself up in a glimmering arc of shiny skin, water droplets and back muscle. Before I could navigate to the ladder, he had leaned forward, grabbed my forearms and pulled me up and out of the water, and I landed, flush against his wet skin, heaving chest, and a hardness below his waist that both frightened me and made me want to rip his clothes off.

Without waiting for me to pick up a towel, Vyash had led me back to our room. He placed the 'Do Not Disturb' sign on the door and shut it behind us, then drew the curtains till we were ensconced in the pale-pink glow of the sun shining through the peach curtains. He wrapped a towel around his waist, then reached below it and pulled off his swim trunks. He took another towel and brought it to me, but pulled it away when I reached for it.

'Shh,' he said, wrapping it around my chest.

He untied the strings of my halter top, letting them flop over the seam of the towel, then reached his hands through the opening in front of the towel, very slowly easing it through and down till it rested on my waist. He let his hands rest on my waist as my wet skin dried off, warmed by the intense heat of his palms. He then pulled it down farther under the towel until my swimsuit was off completely and I was naked underneath. He looked into my eyes, his gaze intense, and took in another uneven breath and then his hands were on my breasts, holding them, squeezing lightly.

He groaned 'Oh baby!' and squeezed harder; then he was kissing me, his lips sucking on mine urgently, his hands squeezing my breasts. One hand moved between my legs and then slid over my hip, gripping me hard. He pushed me down on the bed, leaning on one hand, while the other ran all over my body. 'You OK, baby? You're doing good?'

I nodded, unable to meet his gaze. I was doing more than good. I was doing a jig on cloud nine!

He kissed my cheek, then my neck and then rolled over on me, his legs between mine. Suddenly, he was inside me, sliding in more easily than I had expected, the pain-pleasure of it all too overwhelming to think about other things. It seemed only natural to move my hips back and forth, and the more I did it, the more he moaned and moved in response. With his eyes closed, his expression rapturous, I moved faster, more vigorously and, suddenly, I was taken over by some other rhythm that steered me towards my own pleasure. I had a fleeting thought—when does the condom happen? And then it didn't matter as he reached behind my bottom, grabbing each cheek and ground me against him, his hips circling and bucking into mine. Suddenly, I was screaming with him, my nails digging into his back, some inexplicable feeling racing through me. I wrapped my legs around Vee and held him, collapsed against my body. After we got our breath back, we leaned against each other—I was still covering up with the sheets, in case he peeked. We spent the day chatting lightly about nothing in particular, calling room service so we could eat stuff off each other.

Then, the next morning, I woke up to a sweet soreness that reminded me that I was now officially Vyash's woman. I raised my right arm and stretched over to him. He was sprawled over three quarters of the bed, his back big and broad, his eyelashes thick—he was edible. I smiled and ran my nails up and down his spine. He moaned and turned over. My man, I thought.

After a delicious breakfast of warm, buttered poi, scrambled eggs, fresh juice, and each other, we meandered down to the beach, him in blue shorts, and me in specially-bought-for-the-occasion purple full-coverage swimsuit-and-matching-sarong that covered all body-image issues and also made me feel very *firang*.

We were lying on the wooden deckchairs, watching the sea, sun-drugged into that sort of half-consciousness between sleep and waking. Now was as good a time as any.

'Vee?' I said, playing with his fingers.

'Hmm?'

'I was just wondering, shouldn't we have used a condom?'

His head snapped around, and he looked at me with horrified eyes.

'Condom??'

'Yeah, I mean, I don't . . . I didn't . . . um . . .'

He sat up and ran his hands through his hair repeatedly.

'Don't you take pills?'

My expression answered him.

'Gina did. We never used condoms. I hate them.'

Little rose-coloured rocks and bricks that had made up my perfect life began to rain down around me. Who was this man? Who was this person telling me that he didn't use a condom because his ex-wife was on the pill?

'Really, Rhea! You are such a kid!'

Vee got up and walked away, his shoulders stiff in anger.

I stared after him. I felt so confused. I shouldn't have assumed that he'd take care of birth control. I should have talked to a gynac.

I looked for Vee, but he must have returned to the resort. I didn't know where to go. I waited at the beach till sundown. He still hadn't come looking for me. There was no option. I didn't have my phone, my money or my bag. And it was obvious that he wasn't going to come back to get me. It looked like Vee was never going to talk to me again, and I couldn't call home, so I lay my head down on my knees and closed my eyes, hoping I would figure out what to do next.

8

'HE WHAT??'

Pia was on all fours in front of the TV doing her Lamaze exercises. Normally, Ant would have to do the exercises with her, but he was travelling, and my mother had suggested Sia and I go over and stay for 'sister-bonding'. I hadn't told a soul about Goa, but after a few hours of being slowly beaten down by Pia's incessant questions and Sia's unflinching gaze, I broke, and told them everything. Leaving out the part where we hadn't used a condom.

I nodded sadly.

'Has he called?'

'Nope.'

'Creep. I never liked him.'

Pia sat down heavily and raised both legs in the air, her hands supporting each thigh. She peered at me over her bump. 'So listen, there's another guy, I . . .'

'ANOTHER GUY?? Pee, another guy?? What the hell?! Am I supposed to keep meeting men like I'm an apartment on sale? If I had said no the first time you psychos set me up,

I wouldn't be in this position! I wouldn't be dumped!'

All I could see were Pia's eyes—round like those sago balls you get in falooda glasses—staring at me anxiously from behind her stomach. My head and shoulders were aching. My chest was a slowly shrinking dark room of claustrophobia and anxiety. Another guy?

We sat in silence listening to Pia breathe: a loud, forced inhalation, her exhalation like a soft snore. Sia was making small noises as she tried to eat her entire fingernail. I looked at my sisters, both looking traumatized, and relented.

'Guys, I can't do it. I love Vee. It feels like I'm being unfaithful. And . . . what if it gets messed up again?'

'Ree, this is it. This is what meeting people is like. And it won't be the first mess-up either. But what if the next guy was supposed to be "It", and you never met him, because, you know, you didn't have the guts to face the possibility that he wasn't. What if he's two more guys away, and he's wondering what's taking you so long?' Sia looked around her as if she hadn't just dropped a bomb that had annihilated ten countries, done thirty orbits of the moon and then blown up the neighbour's adorable French poodle.

Pia wobbled over to Sia like a screaming, swollen dove, her ponytail working up and down in agitation. 'My poppet! My angel! I always knew you had a brain—it was just getting suffocated by all those black outfits! I'm so proud!'

As the heavens opened and the cherubim began to chorus in time to the heart-warming scene of a skinny Goth girl being mauled by a very pregnant woman in a white nightshirt with lipstick print, a small realization was beginning to snake-dance in my head.

There was beginning to be a chance I would remain unmarried for the rest of my life, which would make *me*—and not Sia herself, with her unhealthy obsession with plucking out her own eyebrows—responsible for her remaining unmarried.

I thought about my options. I was no longer 'hymenated' (as Tish would have said), so that ruled out the possibility of developing some magical power that could grant women instant babies, cure thrush or remove body hair permanently, thus enabling me to die a saint with a big hoarding decorated with marigolds dedicated to me. Things like that only happened to blemish-free, Full Virgins, as my mother called them.

I was officially 'once-rejected', so unless I mounted some desperate-to-marry horse again, people would be saying that the Kanwars' middle-daughter was frigid or unable to have babies or was asking for too much money or, worse, had some body hair where 'the public' could not see. These were consequences that could affect my entire family, not just me.

I was thirty—which pretty much ruled out my right to live at all. At thirty-one, I would become invisible, and at thirty-two, I would become Bubbles Auntie. Bubbles Auntie is my mom's 'college friend', who works in film production. She was tiny and loud and always wearing animal prints. She comes over for all festivals and some family meals because she was, say it with me, 'UNMARRIED!', and was always saying things like, 'Fuck, yaar! I'm a recycled virgin. My heyman has grown back,' or 'Girls, there's was this cute-cute-sa model at the shoot yesterday. I asked him *ki* are you into tigers. But he looked confused. He's the no-talk-let's-fuck types.'

Sia claims she overheard our mother telling her it was cougar and not tiger and that was probably why Bubbles Auntie's model had rejected her. The thing about Bubbles Auntie is that she is always angry. She is angry because the auto driver called her 'Behenji', she is upset because the fruit-wallah winks at her, and she is livid because people in their twenties think they own the world. Bubbles Auntie is 'Unfulfil'—that thing that happens to a woman when she gets everything in the world, except marriage.

The future is not exactly rosy for an unmarried girl in a middle-class Punjabi family. In an upper-class one, it's worse, because your four-foot-ten-inch grand-aunt has already learnt the word 'menopaujj', and is convinced that that's what has happened to you, and has phoned your mother at least three times to tell her that 'Surgery-*vurgery, v'jlazzin kara de iska, p'rhaps poss'biltees aa jayenge.*' This is marginally better than having to hear my grand-cousin-uncle Binnoo say he needed some time to do 'manscape-vanscape' before the next party.

So shaadi.com it was going to have to be. With bells on.

But, first, there was some crying I needed to do. I called Tish.

'Yeah?' she sounded cautious.

'Tish?' my voice was wobbling.

'That bastard!' The phone went dead, and I knew she was driving over in her bright-yellow car with its pink seat-covers—after a quick stopover at Paradise Pastries. I texted her to come over to Pia's, who took out her prized bottle of Pimm's and set about making the Ultimate Breakup and New Woman Cocktail.

Pimm's is the family drug of choice. It really helps that it comes from our motherland: Dhi UK. When we were kids and my dad trudged home after a hard day, my mother would materialize with a glass of Pimm's and soda, onion bhajia and her sadsmile. My father would accept her offering and collapse on the sofa. By the time he had poured his fourth glass, he was calling everyone a sisterfucker and excreta and waving his bhajia around in rage. He would then pass out. My mother would tell us to serve ourselves from the kitchen and then get to bed, and the next morning my father would be at the breakfast table, ignoring all of us again. From this we learned that communication is crap in front of Pimm's.

We were all lying around feeling the goodness, a jug of Pimm's, cut fruit and Sprite melting into an almost colourless glinty mixture. Pia was sitting in her prayer room, apologizing loudly to her stomach for the one glass she had had, promising that this would be the last time 'Mommy fucked up'.

Sia was sprawled on the floor, staring up at the lights. Tish suddenly came over to me and held me. When I started shaking, I realized she was sobbing. 'Rhea, I'm so sorry, babe. I'm so sorry.' She looked up from my chest and deep into my eyes, her green eyeliner melting on to her cheeks. 'It's like . . . it's like . . . you'd be such an awesome mooommmyyyyyy!' She turned away from me and looked into the prayer room, 'Why, God? Whyyy? Why couldn't you get her some man—*any* man! And now, she's so olddd! If you had made me a man, then at least I could have married her.'

Then, she passed out.

9

SMS FROM MY MOTHER:

Rh bta, lts g 2 gkhna @ 8 k bcoz tis tmbla nite plsk thnx lve mmy.

I replied:

Mother. You're 55 years old. Please use complete sentences.

She replied:

Fne duz nt hve cmplte sntc optn. 8j z 56 yrs.

Great. I still didn't know what tonight's plan was, and my mother was dyslexic. I SMSed Sia:

What plan tonight?

She replied:

Tambola nite @ club. Wear push-up bra.

Maybe it was a three-SMS clue. I SMSed Pia:

FGS what is happening tonight?

She replied:

Rhea I do not think you should swear on SMS. Plus you will give my baby bad habits.

I had no choice. I SMSed my dad:

Papa, could you please let me know what we have planned for tonight, so I can organize accordingly? Thanks. Love, Rhee.

He replied:

We have received gracious invitation to join esteemed families of Mrs Kapoor for dinner at Chor Bizarre, tandoor and lounge this evening. We will return the honour by return-invite for a short but enjoyable game of tambola at our Gymkhana club, rooftop, after which both families will proceed for dinner, on completion of which we will return to our respective residences and retire for the night. As is customary, please present in neat and ironed clothes, we will depart from our residence at 7.15 p.m. sharp . Your loving father, Vir Kanwar.

I looked at the time. 4.00 p.m. Four hours to meeting a new guy and pretending that I really cared if he liked me or not. I still hadn't heard from Vyash. He hadn't blocked me on Facebook, though, but his profile was this impassive, anonymous wall of nothing-happenedness. I couldn't make out from the rows of 'Hey, nice to hear frm u', 'Thnks man, same 2 U', 'Happy birthday dude', 'Lookin' cute'—whether he missed me as badly as I missed him, whether he was seeing someone new, or whether I had been a rebound, a quick fuck to forget a lost marriage. If I thought the word 'fuck' one more time, I would be seriously channelling my inner Bubbles Auntie and soon I would be wearing leopard-print miniskirts and purple bras. I raced out of the office in the direction of the salon, determined to avoid any shade of red, purple or fuchsia nail-polish.

One day, when I'm eighty and finally have my bikini body and will have got rid of all my boyfriend problems, I will still be trying to understand why my parents would want to meet strangers over a game of tambola. Nobody should see my parents at a game of tambola. God shouldn't see my parents at a game of tambola.

My mother buys fifty tickets to increase her chances of winning, and insists on choosing the table closest to the guy who calls out the numbers, so she can hear every little ducky, fat lady, and fishy he calls out. She will then guffaw loudly at the same jokes, looking around her to see who else got it, and raise her eyebrows expectantly at anyone who makes eye contact. She also hovers two inches above her chair so she can shoot off it and reach the judges' table first in case she gets a '*jaldi* five', full house or full row. My most embarrassing memory is when I was fifteen and my mother won a game of tambola. She held the chair-cushion above her head in joy and danced around in her sneakers and silk salwar-kameez and cardigan, shouting, '*Wahji wah* oh *wahji wah!*' She slipped, fell, flung the cushion into the air, shouting, 'Oh yo! Yo! Yo!' and then jumped up and went to collect her prize: 500 rupees.

My father whacked the table loudly and yelled, 'Drat!' when his own wife won. Arranging to meet a new would-be over tambola was, I was sure, a failproof way of ensuring that I would become Bubbles Auntie.

I left the salon looking suitably buffed and shined, and got home in time to change into a grey shirtwaister with a black belt and black boots. Predictably, my mother was in a peach-silk salwar-kameez, white cardigan, her wedding jewellery, a pair of immaculate white sneakers, and white socks with a peach border. Sia was going through an existential phase, and wore an outfit that expressed her current belief that one should appear as one is, without artifice and show. This was expressed with a tight black top with a skeleton drawn on it in white, with satin camouflage pants. Pia, a week away from delivery, was dressed in a deep ruby kaftan with armholes so big, I could see her boobs, and Ant was in blue and yellow, looking apologetic about my sister's display.

Well, it took the pressure off me at least. This was sure to be a rejection, but who cared. Certainly not me, I thought, as I checked my make-up and examined my pits for sweat patches for the eighteenth time in the last hour.

We arrived with ten minutes to spare. Enough time to choose a table close enough for my mother, far away enough to be able to talk, decide seating, do a quick pit-stain check and share a bottle of cough syrup with Sia—Sia needed the courage to be without artifice. And I needed the courage to be with. By the time we came back, my father had bought tambola tickets for everyone and had put them in the middle of the table. Ant was convincing Pia to keep her elbows on the arms of her chair so the sight of her about-to-deliver-a-baby-size boobs would not send the Kapoors racing over the terrace of the nearest building in the unlikely case my mother's victory dance didn't.

Sia was standing near the bonfire, her skeleton glowing neon-orange in the flames, Pia was sitting in her chair with her arms spreading out on either side of her, refusing to put them down, while Ant knelt in front of her, his hands folded, begging her to be decent. My mother's outfit looked as if it were on fire. And just as we realized how ridiculous we must have looked, the Kapoors arrived.

In a confusion of orange bones, boobs on display and lots of rustling silk as the Kanwars and Kapoors raced around trying to make an impression, I registered a lazy, amused smile, hazel eyes and a physique right out of *Gladrags* magazine. I blinked twice to get my mother's peach glow out of my eyes. And then, as if Moses had made a quick appearance, the sea of colours,

tinted orange, parted, in time to the three-part harmony of
'I finally found someone', Jay Kapoor was revealed, every
glorious, 'Made in Delhi' inch of him: his fair skin glowing
orange, his brownish hair outlined by orange smoke, his
undulating throat and chest framed by a beige V-neck sweater,
his brown corduroys fashionably loose, but lovingly clinging to
what looked like a promising butt. As my sisters and I made
breathless eye-contact, our thoughts were unified: Why did
this God have to be the one to see my mother play tambola??

'What say, girls, shall we get a table to ourselves, in case my
mother gets violent and pokes our eyes out during the game?'
he said as the lead singer in my head went into ecstatic whoops
and loops on 'Found'.

We fell into groups as we walked. Pia, with her arms
interlocked with mine and Ant's, Sia with Jay. He turned to
her, looked down at her top and said, 'It's like seeing the real
you.' As Sia's face lit up, Pia mumbled, 'Now all he needs is a
borderline psychotic younger sister and it's a match made in a
teenager's collection of psycho dolls.'

We found a nice table far away from the tambola players
and, as we settled in, this girl around Sia's age joined us. She
was dressed entirely in black, had thick lines of kohl drawn
around her eyes and her hair was combed straight down from
a centre-parting to hang loose around her face.

'Hi, I'm Sunny, Jay's sister.'

My eyes were being pulled as if by magnets by Pia's, but I
resisted.

Jay had us all in splits that night. By the end of the evening
he was doing impressions for Sia and Pia and had them giggling
and simpering every time he said something. He did this

German puppet thing with his napkin that was too adorable and had me cracking up every time he even picked up the napkin. We were in the middle of a tissue-paper fight—him and me against the others—when our parents came to pick us up to leave for dinner, their faces as flushed as ours, their voices as hoarse. It was obvious that the Kanwars and Kapoors would not be welcome at the club for a long, long time.

Dinner was boring. Although the bloodshed over tambola had broken the ice and Jay had done the same for us, it wasn't working with all of us sitting at the same table, answering the endless 'And, beta, what do you dos'? Jay had excused himself, I assumed for a cigarette or loo break, Pia was chatting with his mother about her impending delivery, and Sia and Sunny were looking in different directions. I decided to wander off to the loo and check my make-up.

I didn't bother to excuse myself—no one was even looking. I navigated the crowded restaurant and turned a corner, and suddenly an arm grabbed me around the waist so tight, I couldn't breathe. I got an overwhelming whiff of something lemony and vetiver-y, and then I was slammed up against a wall and pinned to it by the two, very manly hands gripping my wrists. It was Jay. And him being so close and so overpowering was doing something to my insides.

'So?'

'So, what?' I asked.

'Do you like me?'

'Why should I tell you?'

''Cause I need to know, lady.'

His stubble was grazing my cheek, his breath fanning the tiny hairs near my ear. His perfect face was very close, his eyes, intense and hazel, locked into mine. I drew a shaky breath.

'Well, that's for me to know and you to find out,' I said, trying to be cheeky, but just sounding shaky.

'How 'bout I find out like this . . .' he whispered, his knee pushing between my thighs, his lips closing over mine as I parted them to speak.

His mouth was soft and warm, and I was sort of semi-turned on and, before I knew it, I was lost, straining up to him, my leg curled around his knee, drawing him closer. As we pulled apart, he looked as shaken as I felt. His once-spiky hair was now bent in all directions. We looked at each other and, in unison, said, 'LOO!'

Resting my head against the cool mirror, I finally got my only chance to think all evening—and realized that Vyash hadn't been anywhere in the vicinity of my mind at all. Jay was hot— 'panty-twisting hot', as Tish would say. He was charming. My sisters loved him. Our parents could never embarrass us, because his parents were as prone to killing a silver-haired tambola champion as mine were. Did I like him? Hell yeah, I liked him.

He was fun and unpredictable. And I never thought how enjoyable it would be to actually spend an entire evening with a man and not hear one word about his ex.

10

I WAS EXHAUSTED.

And supremely happy.

I was having the time of my life. For once, I wasn't living from office to home, with the occasional night-out. I had A LIFE. For once, I had stopped checking email at seven in the morning and again at midnight. I shrugged off mess-ups at work with a 'Shit happens'. Because I had something—someone—better to do.

Jay was this supercool, super-popular guy who lived from party to party. And he wanted me—ME—to go with him. We hadn't had 'The Conversation' yet, but since we were pretty busy communicating in other ways, I figured talk could wait.

It had already been a month since Jay and I had first met, and I was a wreck of dark circles, aching feet and throbbing head. We were out partying all night, three or four nights a week, Sia, Sunny, Arf, and Tish, with her husband, Karan—K—in tow. We'd set out at eight, the eight of us, and along the way we'd lose Sia and Sunny, pick up some friends, add on some white people, lose Arf to one of the white girls, pick up some people from Jay's work, lose Tish and K, pick up Sia, lose the white people, pick up Sunny, lose the work friends, and finally crawl into bed at five in the morning, only to wake up again at eight.

And not know who these new numbers on WhatsApp belonged to. It didn't matter, anyway, because there would soon be a new group and we'd be hanging out at someone's terrace, smoking up, or making out in a corner with a person we hated ten minutes ago. Not me, of course. I would only make out with Jay—in as respectable a manner as I could manage with so many people around.

Of course, I had begun to screw up at work. 'Screw up' as in small things like leaving work for the next day, bunking meetings—things every manager I've ever had has done and got away with! Life was calling, and I was so on the pink phone, baby!

The cool thing about all that partying was that when Pia welcomed her baby girl, Zara, into the world at 2 a.m., we were all there to see her, propping each other up and shushing the whole group, trying not to look as drunk as we were, saluting the ugly wrinkled little peanut and calling her Pant—the logical combination of 'Pia' and 'Anant'.

We got into the habit of WhatsApping in the morning and, by four, we'd sort of have an idea about what we'd be doing that night and who with. Tish and K were all excited about getting to party again like they used to, and I'd drag along Saroj, my friend from college, to Khan Market for something designer and sexy, and then we'd have coffee and sometimes she'd come along and need to be dropped back by midnight, and so Arf and I would drive her back, then hang in his mom's garden chatting till it was time for me to get home. It was like my dating days with Slime—everyone was a best friend. And the biggest thing we had to worry about was not waking anyone up when we crept back into our bedrooms. Work? It was something I did to pay for the pretty clothes and the shiny shoes.

One Monday morning, my boss called me in. 'What's going on, Rhea?' both of him said, trying to make eye contact through my squint.

'Huh?'

'Rhea, are you all right?' he said very slowly.

'Oh yeah. Yup. Yeah. Fine.' Why did he have to be so loud?

'Rhea, you've missed every stand-up this month. You look like hell and you're making mistakes. Is everything all right with you? Because if you don't straighten out, I'm going to have to issue a formal warning . . .'

'Oh!' I was shocked. Yes, there were a few mornings that had passed in a blur, and last week my colleague had taken me aside for a 'chat'. But I didn't take it seriously. I mean, I never take leave, I've never had a sick child or husband to look after or to go home early to, and I work pretty hard.

And, OK, so, for the last month, I'd been flaking out here and there. Surely I was allowed that much! It was nothing I hadn't seen other people do. In fact, they did worse . . . Unless any more eff-ups were happening. Who knew? I was barely checking my mail.

'Rhea? Rhea?'

'Ya! Er . . . yes.'

'Buckle down, OK?'

'OK!' I sang, giggling a bit. Who says buckle down, man? Who did he think he was? The headmaster?

Assholes, I thought to myself as I left his cabin. Screw it. I was off to a farmhouse party tonight, and I was going to wear my black shorts, boots and a silk shirt. And I had only four hours before the party cart took off!

This time it was Arf, Sia and Sunny who joined us along with Sunny's 'current', and some of Jay's friends. We helped ourselves to some bright-red stuff everyone was drinking out of paper cups and sort of bounced to the music, randomly smiling at people. Then Sia and Sunny took off, and Arf joined a bunch of potheads in the garden.

Jay seemed to know everyone and he pulled me into a group that was dancing in a circle. The music was pumping, the air was smoky, and soon we were part of a heaving, thrusting, panting body of people held to each other by the beat. One of Jay's friends was behind me, his hands on my hips as we ground together to the music. I looked over at Jay, just as the smoke machine blew a new cloud, and saw him looking greyish and blurry. The girl he was dancing with turned around and pulled his head down to hers. I squeezed my eyes shut and then opened them again, but all I could see was Jay dancing with her, his arm loosely around her waist.

My head was beginning to throb, and I couldn't get a handle on how much time had passed. I tried to call out to Jay, but he couldn't hear me. Sia had left long ago with some friends of hers, and I couldn't see Sunny. The thump-thump of the music felt like the pounding of my heart. And I was feeling pukey. I couldn't remember how many drinks I'd had, but I'd had many sips of the drink Jay's friend was holding. As the lights began to swoop and swing and chime loudly, I felt like running for the open air.

I stumbled through the swarm that now looked like one big, animal-like fornicating mass. This is Sodom, I thought to myself. I have to get away, or I'll turn into a pillar of salt, and they'll break me down and sell me to . . . sell me to . . . the Tata Salt company!

I broke through a clump of people on to the main road and cold air. I had outrun the Tata Salt company, but now people were looking at me strangely. I tugged discreetly at my shorts, hoping I could get them to at least cover my knees. There was a stale-dal taste in my mouth and my fingers were freezing. I tucked them into my elbows, rubbing them against my skin to warm them up. Everyone who could help me was inside that farmhouse somewhere, and I didn't know whom to call. The corners of my eyes began to sting. Suddenly, I wanted my Nike-shod, salwar-kameez-wearing Mummy to walk in, propelled by her violently pumping left arm, shouting, 'Hullo! Can you please turn this *dhik-chik, dhik-chik* down, so I can collect my beti?'

Just then, a pair of strong, warm hands came up under my elbows and held me against a solid, male chest. I heard Arf's voice through the woman screaming in my head.

'OK, I got you.'

He steered me to a car—I don't know whose—opened the door for me and settled me in, fastening my seat belt and brushing my hair back from my face. He kept murmuring, 'OK, it's OK. Everything's going to be just OK now.'

He drove me home in complete silence, his hands sure and steady on the wheel. In the glare of the oncoming headlights, I noticed that his eyes were brown, and his hair was actually really shiny and soft-looking. And he always had this little frown when he drove; and that both his hands were always on the wheel, not just one, like most men. I leaned my head back against the seat and snuggled into the jacket that he had draped across me and closed my eyes. I was home.

A loud bashing of cymbals woke me. As my eyelids fought to open against the light in my window, I realized the full-on Punjabi *baraat* was the one marching through my head. And it was accompanied by a loud woman singing wedding songs.

As I took in the blue smears on my pillowcase, the heels with the ankle strap on one shoe broken, and the smell of smoke clinging to my hair and clothes, I began to piece together what had happened. I had some memory of a phone call from Jay, his voice obscured by music and people screaming, and another, strange one of Arf kissing my forehead and saying, 'Sleep now, baby', and switching off the lights. I stumbled to my bag and took out my phone. Eight missed calls. Four from Jay, one from Sia, one from Tish and another from some unknown number. I called in sick at work and then SMSed Tish to see if she could feed me and help me make sense of yesterday's pool of sick.

11

'TAKE THE CALL FOR the sake of my sanity.'

We were at Tish's. In the last two days, the memory of Jay kissing a girl on the dance floor had turned into full-fledged sex with positions, eye contact and dirty talk. And a public declaration of love.

The truth is that I still couldn't remember what had really happened that night. But by the time Tish and I had got through two 3 a.m. calls and one decadent sangria-and-pizza lunch, the 'truth' was just a symptom. What mattered was that he had screwed around. And I had been right there. Pia was too busy with Pant, and Sia had met someone at the farmhouse that night. I hadn't seen her or spoken to her all weekend, although both Sunny and Jay had been calling me and I hadn't answered.

'Rhee, if I have to listen to "Baby, you're my firefly" one more time . . .'

'Tish, it's "firework"! "Baby, you're my firework"!'

'If I can't remember it, it shouldn't be your ring tone. For anybody. Pick. Up. The. Phone.'

'FINE!'

'Er . . . Rhea, baby?'

Oh fuck, I thought.

'Hey, um, so, what's up?'

'Baby, I've been worried sick about you! Where did you disappear that night? What happened?'

'Jay, I . . . I, um . . .'

I sighed. What was I supposed to say? Tish had said 'play it cool'. Let him come out with it. But I heard his voice all sad and soft and worried and a bit like he hadn't slept, because he was so distraught, and I pictured his lips all bruised because he had bitten them in that way he does when he's worried, and his sexy square jaw all covered with stubble, and I felt like a total bitch for cutting him out this way and not giving him a second chance.

'Babe, I need to see you. Right now. Where are you? I'll come get you. Rhee? Babe, please, I need you.'

His voice cracked as he pleaded, and I imagined his baby brown eyes getting all misty and sad.

'Tish's place,' I said, and hung up.

'WHAT DID YOU JUST DO?'

'Tish . . . er . . . I . . . er . . . What?'

'Do you not realize you look like shit?'

Fuck. I did. It was Tish's place. It was a wonder I wore clothes at all when I came here. I looked down. Trackpants, T-shirt and greasy hair. Hardly an outfit that said: 'Bet you're sorry you kissed a hot girl.' I couldn't borrow anything from Tish, and there wasn't time to go home and change.

'Wait! Dupatta!'

'What?'

Tish rummaged through her closet and surfaced waving

two dupattas in the air. 'One for the titties, one for the arse!'
she yelled triumphantly.

'NO. Tish, I am not meeting him wearing just those.'

'Honey, it's this or your stinky chudds. WEAR IT!'

~

'Wow! Um . . . I didn't expect *this*!'

Jay looked fantastic, as men have the bad habit of doing
when they've done something really unforgivable. I, on the
other hand, had considered looking like Mandakini without
the blue eyes but with the fleshy thighs, and decided on staying
in my sweatpants. Jay had the good grace to not turn and run
screaming from the room. And he had the good grace to have
stubble and bloodshot eyes too. He looked like he had been
through hell and like he felt even worse than I looked.

He had arrived just as I'd managed to rub talcum powder
on my scalp to take off some of the grease and soak in Tish's
212 Sexy. He froze for a second when he saw me—probably
for the first time without make-up, and hair styled to the
point of break down. He rushed over and grabbed me by the
shoulders, looking me up and down searchingly, 'You're OK?
Did anything happen to you?'

Tish appeared in the doorway, brandishing the carrot she
was munching on.

'Dude. She came back from a farmhouse. Not Iraq.'

He gave her a dirty look before she went back into her
bedroom.

'What happened, baby? Why did you leave me like that?'

My hand was tightly wrapped in his, making it hard

to call him an asshole or slap his face. But given that he had asked nicely, I said, 'Jay, I saw you! I saw you and that girl and . . .' And as the tears came, I wailed out, 'juvekshinghyaaarunaivasssomishaaable!'

He stared at me through narrowed eyes as he tried to understand. And then, to my shock, the tears began to roll from his eyes! What had I said? Had I insulted his manhood or something?

He took my hand and pressed it to his chest and inhaled deeply. He lifted my chin with his other hand until he was looking at me and my teary eyes made it seem like I was looking at him through butter paper.

'Babe. I'm a bad guy. I'm shit. I'm an asshole, and I wish I was dead.'

Had I sent him an SMS about the way I felt about him and forgotten? Or had Tish told him what I'd said? Because he was doing some serious quoting here.

'But when I met you, babe, I realized you were the only good thing about me. That you could make me good again. I need your pure, innocent love to stop me doing this shit. I need you to make me good. And only you can do it.'

OK, it was corny. But he was my sporty, funny, outgoing guy. He wasn't Gulzar. So what if he sounded like he was doing bad Bollywood translations. He made me feel happy and fun. He ducked his head, giving me a naughty below-the-eyelash glance.

'Now, smile?'

And I had to. He was so goofy and stupid and adorable when he was wrong. So I did.

12

I CHECKED EMAIL ON Monday.

There was one from HR about some loss-of-pay crap. I had missed ten days of work. I flagged the mail; I would deal with it later.

The next one was from a lady named Pammi Anand from Panchkula. The subject read: *Lovely wife and mother is around the corner. No more lonely you.*

When I opened the email, there was a picture of a lady wearing a pink-flowered salwar kameez with a cream-coloured cardigan and white sneakers, sitting astride a scooter. On the seat behind her was a pot of flowers and, in front, with its paws on the handlebar, stood a white Pomeranian. It included some text about north India's premier matchmaker, high success rate, 99 per cent happy marriage with multiple, fair children, and some testimonials from couples: *Ever grateful to Pammi Auntieji for finding my loving mate forever; Thanks Pammi Auntieji, you are toh best!* Another one made me pause for a minute. It was a picture of a couple who looked pretty normal—she was in a dress and knee-high boots, he in a cable-knit sweater. Its caption simply read *You found my soulmate!* They looked so happy.

But marital happiness has no place in a daily scrum, and I left my desk to join it, so I didn't have to contribute to the latecomers' ice-cream (beer) fund. Plus, I had my soulmate. And he was hot.

Speaking of whom, he was invited to dinner tonight with my family. Pia, Ant and Pant were coming over. Pant was now six weeks old and officially allowed to leave the house. No one had any news of Sia, but apparently she had texted my mother that she would be there. Sunny wasn't invited and neither were her parents. Jay and I were still officially in our 'deciding' phase and, until we gave our answers, there would be no more family-*shamilies*, my mother said. It was allOKnoproblem to be goodfriendsandall until we were sure. Nowadays, even gaygiri was accepted. It's not like there were no lesbos in her college, it's just that they didn't come on TV and all the way they do now, but you could look at some girls and just sense that it was a matter of two negative electrons going against nature. It was a time of same-same love. So the boy, Jay, would be welcomed for rajma and chicken tikka masala.

Jay had begun to bring up the topic of sex with me. We were officially at second base and had strayed a little bit south once at his place when his parents were at tambola, but had been stopped when his Alsatian, Ninja, heard him moaning and thought he was under attack and decided to rescue him. I was topless and had to run around the room until Jay managed to grab his collar. After that, every time I thought of sex with Jay, I pictured myself running from a dog, half naked, and decided it might be best to get to know each other better first.

I was totally ready for sex. I mean, once you lose the Big

V, there's no big deal any more, is there? It's not like anyone's going to know the count. Hell, I'd give sex easier than I'd give my home address. But we couldn't do it at mine. Evidently, we couldn't do it at his, either. Tish said I 'shouldn't give the milk for free'. Pia started yelling at me the moment I brought up the topic, and one can't talk about sex with a younger sister; it's a bad influence. So I focused on praying that my father wouldn't ask him whom he voted for, and that my mother wouldn't take off on 'this AmmTV-ShamTV waste channel showing all lesbo dancing'.

~

Dinner was weird.

Jay walked in all 'Hullo Auntieji, here are some flowers, your house is beautiful.' And my mother was all *'Theek-sheek*, but when are you proposing, *hain?'* Nudge-nudge, wink-wink, poke-poke. Pia had taken my attempts at the sex conversation as evidence that Jay had tried to rape me, so every time he got up to bring me a drink or pass me a bowl of snacks she would go right up to him and stand by his arm staring at every movement of his hand in case he tried to slip in a roofie. Ant had been put in charge of watching the baby so Pia could protect me, and all he did all night was walk her baby up and down, because every time he sat down, she would wake up and scream. This was because, Pia said, eyeballing Jay, there were unsavoury characters around and babies can sense everything.

I wanted to sneak around the back and drown myself in my mother's prized Japanese-style pond. It had been built the year before when she got into her Ikebana phase and we kept finding her in the garden staring at the flowers and listening to them tell her how they wanted to be arranged. Then she decided we must have koi carp in a pond to make us more ambitious. The first few months, I had nightmares of the fish staring at me, one-eyed, keeping me rooted to my position with that dead-but-strangely-all-seeing gaze. If I jumped in that pond, there was a good chance those fish would finish me off in minutes.

But, then, Sia walked in, or, rather, a person who looked a lot like Sia—but she wasn't. Sia had stringy black hair and two kilos of black eyeshadow on her lids and a whole wardrobe full of black clothes. The girl in our living room had shiny, blow-dried hair, clear brown eyes with tasteful, minimal blue eyeshadow, and was dressed in a white Hakoba top and blue jeans. The room was silent, all eyes on Sia. Until Ant called out from the back of the room, 'Congratulations, Vir Daddyji! It's a girl!'

Everyone cracked up at that, pausing only so Sia could announce that she was going through a 'minimalistic' phase. She would no longer be hiding behind layers of artifice and paint. 'Good,' said Pia. 'Then can I have my MAC make-up you flicked back, please?'

13

I WOKE UP THE next day to the raucous tones of my mother yelling in Punjabi. She must have been really upset because she called my father a 'husband-eater', and the cook a curse on humanity. I ran downstairs in my pyjamas to find out what was wrong.

My mother's diamond earrings and a small jade Pichu had gone missing from the house. The earrings had been on her dresser at nine the previous night, but no one could remember when they last noticed the Pichu amid my mother's menagerie of dragons, owls, Pichus, Buddhas and Ganeshas.

Sia walked in and my mother ran over to her and clutched her hands, looking imploringly into her eyes. 'You're not into drugs, na, beta? All this cleanliness and new clothes and talking nicely. It's made me so nervous! Did you take my earrings to sell for Mary-Joanna??'

I was tempted to facepalm, but I felt bad for my mom. Those were her favourite earrings. But no one had been in the house apart from the family. Saro Didi, the cook, lives around the back, not attached to the main house, and she had left by eight thirty. They were sure to turn up in a pair of socks or something.

But I was late for work and Pia was best at this kind of stuff, anyway. I rushed to work.

Phone call from Pia at lunch break.

'Weird, no?'

'Still not found them?'

'Nope. Neither the earrings nor the cat . . .'

'Pichu.'

'Same thing. You think Sia's on drugs and stole it for money?'

'Don't be stupid, Pee, she's not on drugs.'

'But we haven't seen her in really long. She's always home late. And this is a total personality change, ya.'

'Yes, Pia, but druggie personality change is torn clothes, weight loss and being smelly. Sia's looking great. Maybe, she grew up. She's blooming.'

'Why are you sounding like you just produced six children and married five of them off? What is this "blooming" business? You know when people tell you you're blooming? After you've had sex . . . Sia's had SEX??? I told her to wait at least five years, the slut!'

'Pia, she's twenty! You can't possibly expect her to wait till she's twenty-five!'

'Oh, come on! She's not going to die a virgin! Not unless she's like . . .'

It hung in the air for a minute, vibrating with threat and menace.

'Me,' I said.

'Rhee! Rhee? Rhee, listen . . .'

'I got to go, Pia,' I said, and hung up.

I stared at my phone for a few minutes. I would have said I was thinking, but, honestly, there was nothing to be thought. Can people really live together for so long and never really know the people they are living with? Is it so easy to become blind? I called Jay.

'*Oh meri johrazabeen!*' he sang terribly, but it was cute.

'Jay, er … I was wondering … do you want to get together … tonight?

'Who's Together? Is she cute?'

'Jay! I mean, like, *together*.'

'Oh. Oh.' I could hear his breathing on the other side. 'Are you sure, babe?'

'Jay! Don't make this harder for me!'

'Oh! Right. Right. OK, yeah … Lemme figure. I'll pick you up after work, OK?'

I still had half an hour of lunch break left and there was a parlour in the tech park. I punched out to see what I could salvage in time for tonight. Inexplicably, 'Rok Sako To Rok Lo' played loudly in my head for the rest of the evening.

14

JAY HAD BOOKED US into a hotel for the night. It was a small, clean place called Lovely Stay. He had gone ahead and booked us in the name of 'Mr and Mrs Kapoor'—of which, I'm sure, there were at least 5 million in Delhi. He held my elbow and rushed me upstairs to our second-floor room. No matter how 'I-give-a-shit' you are, in Delhi, you can't just walk into a hotel for a one-night booking. There are only so many sleazy smiles and 'Welcome, Madams' you can deal with.

It was a nice room. Clean, non-smelly, and an unyielding reminder that I, Rhea Kanwar, yesteryear's virgin, would be 'doing it' with Jay Kapoor. A boy with a shaven chest. Not that there was anything wrong with Jay. It was just that we had been hanging out for two months now and he hadn't said anything about commitment or marriage or even love. Then I looked over at him and he had taken off his jacket; his T-shirt stretched thin over his chest, and his jeans slipped lower over his hips, exposing that little dip right above his crotch, and I thought: Who was I kidding? He could have said 'Open sesame' and I would have undressed and jumped right into bed with him.

He held his hand out towards me.

'Come.'

I arched an eyebrow, channelling my inner diva.

'You're going to have to work a lot harder than that.'

He laughed, running his fingers through his hair. Then he grabbed my wrist and pulled me towards him. 'You have no idea how long I've been waiting for this.' Holding me against him, he used his other hand to pull off his thick gold chain with a tiger-claw pendant.

Yes. *I know.* But his biceps were 16 inches, and by the feel of it against my thigh, it was likely the other things he had to offer were around the same size.

His other hand slid between my shoulder blades, pressing me completely up against his chest, holding me there with his forearm, while the tips of his fingers pushed my head towards him. In seconds, we were kissing, sucking hungrily at each other's lips, biting each other, as if we had just minutes to get out of there. It's only when I felt the mild rasp of his chest stubble against my skin that I realized he had somehow taken off all my clothes and I was standing in just a pair of (freshly bought) panties, while he still had his jeans on.

Smooth. But it was time for some equality.

I ran my hands down his chest and then unbuckled his belt and pulled off his jeans along with his underwear. I heard his shocked gasp as he pulled back a little from our kiss. But I hooked my hand around his neck and pulled him back in. He moaned, his hands on my breasts, pulling, tweaking, kneading, squeezing. Then he placed his hand on my chest, fingers spread, and pushed me backwards on to the bed, landing neatly between my thighs. He ran his mouth down my neck and farther down to my chest, sucking in some places, licking in others. He moved lower and fastened his mouth on one nipple, gripping it firmly between his lips, while his tongue worked on it intently. His other hand pushed between my legs, his fingers warm and gentle while they explored me, working me to my absolute edge. Before I knew what I was doing, I had rolled him over and got on top. I needed to do this my way and I couldn't possibly shout instructions at him. He looked a little shocked. Like this had never happened before. I arched my back, feeling myself rub along his lower torso. I held his palms and then slid slickly on to him, and then suddenly remembered: Oh fuck! Condom!

'Er . . . Jay?'

'Raincoat?' he gasped.

(*Raincoat?!* Who says 'raincoat'?)

'One sec,' he said, pushing me off him and groping for his jeans.

While he got our birth control organized, I suddenly realized I was naked and tried to pull a sheet around me. We hadn't even turned off the lights. Hell, we hadn't even paused for small talk. This is why the Mills and Boon people never used condoms. As it is, your average M&B woman would barely know the guy. Or he'd be her boss or something and she'd have to sleep with him or she'd lose her job or her grandmother would die. Then she would be seduced in a way very similar to this, except it would be in his mansion and she would have got there in his private jet. But then, after all that, if she were to stop while he rolled on a condom, that was sure to get her thinking about how he had practically jumped her without even asking her surname and how he was pretty attractive now because he was all broody and serious, but when they were forty, he'd be really boring and she would rather be with someone with whom she had something in common. And by the time he turned back to her, she would have rethought things entirely and said, 'OK, we'll have sex, but please drop me back home afterwards and don't put any kind of pressure on me to go for dinner with you in Paris or something, because I don't think we'll work out in the long run.'

Just when I was thinking about all of this, Jay turned back to me and grabbed my ankle and slowly started kissing up my foot. Which pretty much quashed my M&B theory, because I hadn't anticipated *this*. It pretty much quelled everything, because, very soon, I was on top of him again, slowly rocking against him, enjoying the feel of his skin against my most intimate parts. He suddenly bucked upwards holding my elbows and I began to move faster, till I was mewling and screaming alternately as the release came in waves, until I flopped back down against him, my breathing out of control, my entire body on fire, but cooling so quickly it felt like ice too.

He stroked my hair and then my face, gently tipping me over until I was lying next to him. We didn't speak for a while. Actually, I realized, I had never really had a conversation with Jay. We had always partied, or hung out in a group, or made out. Was he into books? Then I saw the tattoo on his back.

KEWL

Well, that ruled out books and all movies without songs in them, for sure. OK. Bikes. But what was I going to add to the conversation? 'Umm . . . so . . . bikes. Kewl, huh?' Nope. OK, family. Family was a good place to start.

'Jay?' I said tracing the little baby-soft blond hairs on his back.

'Hmm?'

'Tell me about your family?'

'Hmm, mom-dad and Sun. *Bas.*'

OK. Topic One ticked off the list. Which led me to . . .

'Babe, come here.' And then his lips were cutting off my train of thought.

15

I<small>T WAS FIVE IN</small> the morning. Jay switched off the engine and rolled to a silent stop outside my house. I had stuffed my underwear in my pocket and hooked my fingers through my slingbacks. I gave him a quick kiss goodbye, then tried this awkward run-without-landing-on-a-pebble to the backdoor. If I could wake up Saro Didi, she might let me in and not tell my parents if I promised to buy her 'liffstick and scent'.

Wonder of wonders, the back door was open, and just the screen door was closed, but not latched. I did a little victory dance outside the door and then sauntered in and came face to face with Vir Kanwar, loving father, dressed in ironed white shorts and striped navy-blue polo shirt with his socks pulled up to his knees and the morning newspaper rolled up and placed in his hip pocket to read over tea after his morning walk.

His morning walk.

How could I have been so stupid?? I knew he left at five fifteen every morning! I just had to wait a few minutes more and he would never have known that I'd spent the night outside. But, no, I had to come home now. And here I was face to face with my toothpaste-and-coffee-smelling father while I smelt of cheap wine, sweat and Jay Kapoor. And *his* sweat.

Papa spent a few minutes absorbing my partially washed face, bare feet, shoes in one hand, office clothes rumpled and the big stain on my blouse from post-coital chicken tikka last night. And then said, 'Tell your mother to invite the Kapoors for dinner tonight.'

It was official. Now I had slept with him. Spent the entire night out with him. I was spoilt by Jay Kapoor. So now he had to buy the cow A.K.A me. The man with the KEWL tattoo on his back was going to marry me whether he liked it or not.

~

'Well, at least he's good in bed,' said Tish on the phone, giggling like it was her sex life we were discussing. 'By the way, have you spoken to Arf?' Her tone sobered and my mood flipped over and landed in the deep, dark pit it had been avoiding since that night.

'Umm . . . why?'

'Don't know . . . just asking . . .'

Tish was trying to sound mysterious, which she sucked at. But I didn't want to probe. I was seeing Jay, and Arf was an old friend who had never said anything about anything. So things were better left that way.

'OK, so listen. No more sex until he pops the question, OK? You have to appear *susheel*, or he'll think you're a slut.'

'What?? Tish, I've been seeing him for two months now. Exclusively.'

'Yeah, but they all want to marry virgins. On our wedding

night, I just did a little ooh-ouch, and Mutt thought I was a virgin. He still doesn't know about Ron and Kishore. Men are idiots that way. I look at Bans and I think: Honey, if you're stupid enough to believe everything women tell you, then you deserve to be a man.'

'Tish, he's not even two.'

'This is the time they learn maximum. Anyway, tonight be extra nice to your sister's baby, OK? Be all loving and mother-type. They have to look at you and think . . . Madonna.'

'Conical bra?'

'Jesus's mother.'

~

I tried to look as Madonna-like as possible, doing my best to erase all resemblance to the crazed seductress of the night before. I had my hair ironed, dressed in a salwar kameez, and used minimal make-up. My naked-body count was two, and more than two in six months would make me Tish. More than four, and I would be those girls in college who sat on car bonnets outside the gate while we were at lectures, and went off with guys in canary-yellow cars with disco lights that lit up every time they braked.

As I visualized myself sitting on those red-velvet thrones at our wedding reception, as Vyash and Slime swung from their suicide nooses from nearby trees, I had the uncomfortable feeling that I had never stopped to think why Jay—sexy as hell, earning a good living, charming—was looking at a girl of thirty. He was just thirty-three; he could easily marry someone younger. Why me?

I suppose I would get the answer tonight. Rhea Kapoor. Sounded pretty cool to me.

Jay, his parents and Sunny arrived.

My mother said, 'Why don't you children talk in the room; Tonyji and Linnyji and we have to discuss some matters.'

Children. That was Jay, Sunny, Sia and me. And Pant. Pia and Ant got to sit with the big people. We went up to my parents' room to sit around and watch TV. Sia was still in her sunshine-girl avatar and, I have to say, was beginning to seem really strange to me with all that shiny, blow-dried hair, rouged cheeks and those big smiles. It was like my sister had been abducted by cokehead animators and replaced with a Disney princess. Sunny and she pretty much just sat around giggling and whispering to each other over their phones. Jay and I were sitting on the bed with Pant between us. He kept looking at me strangely in my straight-to-the-altar outfit, but I hadn't worn it for him, anyway. I just focused on looking maternal and Madonna-like.

Then we heard yelling. Sia and I looked at each other in panic and ran down the stairs, Sunny behind us. We ran into the living room where my mother was standing, yelling at the Kapoors. '*Lau ji lau!* Dhi joker *toh raha mera*, OK? It's mine, yaar! Linnyji, yeh *buri baat!*'

That's when I took in the rest of the scene. It was Tony Uncle and Mummy teamed against Linny Auntie and Papa. They were playing cards. Cards?? Weren't they supposed to be discussing our future instead of gambling it away?

'Mummy, what are you doing?'

'Huh?' My mom stopped mid-abuse. 'Erm . . . actually, beta, we were just indulging in some friendly competition . . .'

All four adults had the grace to look embarrassed and uncomfortable. But they were saved from explaining by Pia's long scream, who realized that her three-month-old baby had been left alone in our parents' bedroom. She and Ant ran towards the stairs, but Jay was already coming down, carrying Zara with him, a tender expression on his face. Looking more susheel and Madonna-like than I had managed to look all evening.

While Pia examined Pant for any injuries or emotional trauma, the families moved to the dining table. There was still no mention of marriage or dates or congratulations offered, and Pia was too busy apologizing to her three-month-old for being a bad mother to give me any sign of what had happened.

We ate in silence, punctuated by an occasional, 'And how is studies, beta?' or an '*Achha*, and when is the promotion?' They finally left without saying anything in particular. Jay waved cheerily at me, and his parents just threw a casual 'OK, Beta!' in my direction. Weird. Anyway, I figured I'd ask my parents for details, but a few minutes after the Kapoors left, chaos struck.

A small brass pot had gone missing from the display outside my parents' room and, inexplicably, Papa had lost his underwear. He had laid it out to change into at night, but it was gone. Saro Didi had gone to her quarters at seven and, anyway, she had been with us for years and nothing had gone missing, and, *anyway*, what on earth would she do with Papa's underwear?

16

JAY'S PARENTS LIKED ME. They had said as much to my parents. And they were pretty sure that Jay liked me too. They were just waiting for him to say something. But they knew their son. He was shy. So they had asked for another month for us to 'get to know each other' before any decisions were made. My parents weren't too happy about that. But when you're trying to marry off a thirty-year-old, you have to take what you get. And it was pretty obvious that Jay was going to ask me. We were exclusive. And he had 'ruined' me, which was as good as a marriage proposal.

In fact, he was taking me out to dinner tonight—our first date, one-on-one. No party. No group. Just us.

Fuck. What on earth were we going to talk about?

He said we were going to a 'nice place', so I wore a navy-blue suit with a white-lace top inside, and minimal gold jewellery. If he proposed, I didn't want anything to clash with the diamond, and if he got down on one knee, then people's gazes would be directed to my legs and I didn't want the other diners to be all like 'Oh, she has chubby thighs' or something.

It was a nice place. But it was Chinese. Somehow, I had never imagined being proposed to in a Chinese restaurant. For one, being handed a ring when a noodle just slapped your forehead as you tried to suck it up, is not ideal-case scenario. Second, where is he going to hide the ring? In the American chop suey?

He ordered sweet-corn chicken soup, chicken fried-rice and sweet-sour chicken. Now that I was going to marry Jay, I felt a sudden pang for Vyash. Vyash would have never brought me to a Chinese place. And if he had, he would have ordered something besides three varieties of chicken. Jay would have ordered chicken for dessert too if they had it. He once told me that he could eat nothing but chicken his entire life. Even when the whole country was not eating it because of bird flu, Jay was eating it at twenty rupees a kilo. Vyash was different. Vyash would order lobster. Or at least prawns. Oh well, Vyash wasn't fun and cool and *Vogue*-magazine handsome. Plus, we would have dark children and my mother would be rubbing them down with gram flour till their skin peeled off or they turned albino.

The food arrived pretty fast, which was a relief, because Jay and I were running out of topics to talk about. We had talked about the people we partied with, the parties we had been to, and chicken. There was one more topic left—our sisters—and after that, he would have to propose, or we would have to skip dessert. Or green tea.

I was about to start the sister topic when this girl came up to us. She was all-Delhi girl, fair, leggy, designer boots, ironed hair and nail art.

'Jayee-Poo!' she squealed and put her arms around him

from behind. 'Are we still on for tomorrow? Don't back out, OK? *Meri toh* FB status *bhi ban gayi hain!*'

Hello? Jayee-Poo? FB status? TOMORROW? I tried giving this chick the stink-eye, but she was too busy flicking her hair and undulating around Jay to notice. I could have made a scene, but then, my proposal?

She pulled out an iPhone, stuck her cheek to Jay's, took a selfie and then waggled her fingers at me. 'Ta-ta!' she simpered, then wiggled away, her walk a neat, non-jiggling combination of back-to-back papaya diets and three-hour gym routines.

I looked at Jay.

'Jay . . . I . . . er . . .'

Before I could shape what I wanted to say, he stood up abruptly.

'Babe, let's go, I want to spend time with you with no one around.'

He looked so charming, with his hazel eyes twinkling at me, his head cocked to the side, a half smile on his face. Plus, this was beginning to sound like he had something special planned for me. I happily pushed back my chair, abandoned the birds on our table and picked up my bag to go and be proposed to.

Jay had a special evening planned for us. He had the keys to his friend's flat and had bought us a bottle of wine to share. The flat was pretty basic, but it had a little balcony tucked away from the road that overlooked a garden. He drew up two plastic chairs and switched off the lights so no one could see us. He handed me a plastic cup of wine and settled down next to me. I felt a bit overdressed for this date, but who wants to remember Proposal Night as the one she wore jeans to? So,

I focused on the prettiness outside, and threw back my head and let the wine work its sweet magic.

Jay reached out to me, his hand grabbing my wrist. I let him pull me on to his lap and melted against his body, all warm and solid behind me. His hands slipped up to my neck, pressing deep and long and then peeled my jacket off. He reached under my top, hands against skin, and popped open my bra, glided around to the front and rested his palms on my breasts. I arched, pushing my breasts into his hands. He began to roll my nipples in his fingers. I twisted and moaned, raising my arms and wrapping them around his neck, pulling his face down to my neck so he could nibble and nip me there. I felt something wet trickle down my shoulder, followed by his mouth sucking up the liquid as he lowered his hands, slipping my pants off. He pulled my knees apart and pressed his hands against me, his fingers rubbing, encircling and dipping in and out as I writhed, trying not to make a sound, in case someone was enjoying an evening smoke on their balcony. But he teased and pulled and brought me to orgasm, and I couldn't help myself and sucked in my breath to scream as it hit me. But he grabbed my chin, twisting my face around to his, thrusting his tongue into my mouth as my thighs squeezed over his hand and shuddered at the intensity of feeling. His fingers dug deep into my flesh, the pain adding to the intense sensation. He stood, with me still leaning against him, and led me to the bed. As I lay there still liquid and hazy, he undressed, put on a condom and then entered me, leaning over me while my legs still hung over the side of the bed.

Another explosion and Jay then lifted off me, kissed my forehead, gently brushed my hair off my face and then pulled me into a seated position. I grabbed a sheet and pulled it across my body to hide my anticipation and increase the sexiness quotient. He stayed my hand, and pulled the sheet off, shaking his head.

'I want to see you,' he said quietly. 'Rhea.' He was still holding my hand, sitting next to me on the bed. 'Babe, it's getting damn serious.'

He looked out over the balcony into the distance and then looked at me, his face twisted. 'I'm a bad guy. The purity of your love is not for me. I'm a guy who can't give love. You should be with someone . . . *gharelu* . . . you know. Some guy who will give you babies.'

That's all I heard before the buzzing in my ears got too loud. I was too shocked to speak. I couldn't even cry. Was this really happening to me, or was I hearing of it happening to a really close friend? I stood, picked up my clothes and went to the loo to get dressed. I pulled on my pants and then the white-lace top and saw the wine stain that the piece of shit had gotten on it. He ruined my white-lace top. He fucking ruined it, that piece-of-shit-crap-chicken-eating PENIS who even had a fucking spelling mistake in his tattoo! He ruined my top, and he didn't even apologize! I grabbed my blazer and stormed out of the bathroom with a hairbrush in my hand, raised it high, and beat him as hard as I could about the arms and shoulders and anywhere I could access. His arms were up, trying to protect his face. For some reason, this made me angrier. I grabbed his blonde hair and pulled, trying to yank his fake-ass foreigner hair out by the roots. 'You shit!' I yelled. 'You dick! You ruined my top, and I can't even get it cleaned! ASSHOLE!' I grabbed my bag, kicked in the direction of his now bright-red, shocked face, and walked out, calling Tish on the way down.

I couldn't wait on the road. This was Delhi. And I didn't want to go back up there and see that asshole outfit-ruiner again. So I hid in the building car-park, concealing myself behind a pillar till he had pulled out of the slot and driven off. Ten minutes later, I heard the thrum of an SUV, and my phone began to ring. It was Arf. Arf? What was he doing calling me? I answered.

'Tish sent me. I'm outside the gate in the jeep.'

I felt my spine uncurl at his voice and ran out of the building and into the car.

Arf didn't look at me once the whole way home. He waited till I got my key in the front door and then drove away. When I got to my bedroom, I opened my handbag to get my eye-make-up remover, and noticed that a small bottle of perfume and my Police sunglasses were missing.

17

I RANG PIA AND asked her to tell my parents that Jay had dumped me. I didn't give her the details, although she was dying to know. I just needed someone to handle my parents. Especially my mother. Then I went over to Tish's and told her everything. She lost it.

'Rhee, are you fucking mad?! He slept with you, knowing full well he was going to dump you after that! Someone should do something to that creep! It should be illegal. Plus he's been unfaithful. He's used you, Rhee! Can't you see? Woman, how could you be so stupid?'

As I watched Tish's face change colour as her mouth formed the words, my mind wasn't listening to her. It was on another track. Thinking that Jay had never intended to marry me. He slept with me knowing that he was doing to dump me later that night. And, yeah, he had a date tonight with that other chick we met at the restaurant. He didn't even deny or try to explain it. It really felt . . . it felt as if he used me. How could I have been so stupid?

I snapped out of my reverie. Why was Tish repeating stuff that I had already figured out for myself? I put my head in my hands. What was I going to do this time? I didn't want to go home and face my parents. I didn't want to answer any calls from my sisters who had both rung me at least three times each. My best friend, Arf, hated me, my white-lace top was ruined, and the only person who was talking to me was Tish. And she just kept repeating what I already knew.

I picked up my stuff and went to work. Nothing like a late night at work to face one's problems. I made sure I got back home when it was dark and everyone was asleep. Tomorrow was another day, and I would deal with it when it slapped me in the face.

I awoke the next morning to this crazy noise downstairs and, reluctant as I was to face my family, it got so loud that I couldn't ignore it any more. I washed my face and tied my hair off of my face and went downstairs to see two cops talking to my parents. *Cops?* What on earth?

'Ma? Sia? Pia?'

My mother flapped her hand at me, so I shut up. My parents were reporting the earrings, the Pichu and the brass figurine as stolen, and they had named Jay as the suspect. *What?* But it was beginning to come together. Jay had been the only one over when the disappearances had happened. This was a lot to take in. Jay was sick. I mean, *he took my father's underwear?* What in the world did he want with that?

The cops wanted to interview me. I agreed, but only as long as my mother was in the room.

'Didiji, what is your relation with this man?'

'Family friend,' my mother said before I could answer.

He looked at me knowingly. 'Where were you at the time of stealings?'

'Downstairs, in the family room,' said my mother sternly.

'Auntieji,' said the man, who was at least five years older than my mother. 'We are asking Didiji. Please.'

My mother looked at him darkly before standing with her arms crossed, staring at him, while he asked me how well I knew Jay, how often I had met him, if I had been alone with him, did I love him? When the questions got really lascivious, my mother interrupted.

'Enough, Bhai-sahib! What is the connection?'

The inspector grunted, put away his notebook and said he'd be in touch. I left for work. My product was releasing today, and release days were always suicidal. I didn't wear eyeliner. Just in case.

Fortunately, it was the craziest day in the history of crazy days. A product meant to enable collaboration across large organizations of over 500 employees was released. But every time more than fifteen people tried to update their profiles at the same time, their names would get interchanged, so a woman who had put up a picture of herself in her wedding dress had the name Ranganathan Subramaniyam Jagganathan next to it, 'her' weight clearly mentioned: 112 kilos. We had to roll back in a hurry, find the bug and patch it up as quickly as possible. I didn't have a chance to think about Father-underwear-stealing-turd-face-Kapoor.

When I got home, I saw five missed calls from Linny Auntie. I didn't know what to do. Should I call back? Was the Bas-turd trying to ring from his mother's phone? Although I wasn't particularly fond of Linny Auntie, I was really curious. Why had she called? What did she want? Should I call Tish and ask what she thought?

'Linnyji called.'

I screamed. It was my mother sitting in the living room in the dark. And apparently reading my mind.

'She is very sad, beta. She said to tell you to take him back. He has had this problem for many years and that is why he is not getting married.'

'What problem, Ma?'

'Robbing.'

'Excuse me?'

'Yes. He robs. All the time. She said to forgive him. Marriage will change him.'

'Ma, I . . . I didn't leave him. He said he didn't want to marry me.'

My mother froze, her eyes widened like Kali, her chin lifted and she stood up.

'He said no to you? *Behenchod chor!*'

'Ma, what did you just say?'

'Never you mind what I just said, *uski penn di phuddi*! I will ring up that Linnyji and the entire ladies' circle and tell them. *Aag lage!* Rejected my daughter when actually he is robbing us blind.'

Mummy had never looked so beautiful—in her blue-flowered flannel pyjamas and a navy-blue cardigan and fluffy slippers, with a monkey cap on her head—as she stood there, back to the TV, its blue light peeping from behind her in miniature rays, her skin grey from the dark, and her eyes glinting in anger. I went up to her and put my arms around her, laid my head on her shoulder and cried.

'Don't worry, *puttar*,' she said, patting my back. 'He too shall get gas.'

'Ma, don't you mean "This too shall pass"?' I said into her cardigan.

'No, Jesus meant that. I am cursing him.'

She was quiet for a while and then she looked up and said, 'Enough of this friend recommendation, net-shet. We need a professional. Someone who does it with her heart. Someone who will line up ten-ten men for my daughter. And after she rejects him, laughs and says, this was nothing, here, take twenty more!' She nodded firmly and started up the stairs, calling, 'Virji! Oh Virji!'

I trudged up to bed. It was all too much to take in. But it felt good to cry. And what about my mother getting all warrior-princess and stuff? What was that all about? I fell asleep with a smile on my face and the *Deewar* dialogue playing in my mind.

18

THE NEXT DAY I got another email at work. It had a picture of a Pomeranian wearing sunglasses, proffering a ring with his paw. There was a speech bubble over his head that said: 'Don't dipress. Meet me immediately for happy life.'

Where had I seen this dog before? Pammi Auntieji's matchmaking service! I was about to click delete, when I remembered the soulmate couple and the way he looked at her. Pammi Auntieji had a 90 per cent success rate or something, if I remembered right. Maybe she had a soulmate for me, too? I forwarded the email to my mother and got back to work.

Sure enough, an hour later, I got a call from my mother. 'I called the Pomerrian lady. We will go meet her at six o'clock, OK? I've told your Papa also. He is not angry.' Her voice softened for a moment. '*Koi nahin*, beta. God sends us down in pairs. *Darte nahin, sher ke bacche.*'

Pammi Auntie lived in a colony full of children and parks and naked-lady fountains. No wonder she had such a high success-rate, she was probably just introducing neighbours to each other and then taking all the credit. Her apartment wall was painted bright green in an uneven patch that covered only the area that surrounded her front door. Every other apartment in the complex was off-white like the rest of the buildings in the colony. She had a parrot in a cage hanging outside her front door, and a photo on the door of her dog with a knocker hanging from his nose. I rapped hard on the Pomeranian's nose and, in a minute, the door opened an inch.

It was Pammi Auntie, in a bright-pink kurta with a green pyjama and green dupatta. Her hair was dyed jet black and shaped into an unyielding pudding that framed her head and then stuck out perfectly symmetrically behind her ears.

'Er . . . Auntie?'

'No, no, no, no, beta,' she said, smiling widely and shaking her head. 'No formality. No formality at all. Just call me Pammi Auntieji!'

She pulled me into her house and then reached out and pulled my mother in, so we bumped into each other at the threshold.

'Come, come,' she said, ushering us to a flowered sofa with white-lace doilies. There was a low, black coffee-table with a huge bunch of artificial flowers on it, next to what looked like wedding albums with flowery covers. In fact, the whole house was covered in flowers. The walls were decorated with flowers cut out from greeting cards; every table had a vase of artificial flowers, and the carpet was flowered. The Pomeranian from the email was sitting on a single-seater sofa, staring at us gravely.

'This is Dev Anand—you may recognize him from my communications.' Pammi Auntieji sat down on the three-seater sofa, gesturing to me to sit next to her. 'You sit there, Behenji,' she told my mother, indicating that she should sit on the other one-seater. 'Bride, next to me.'

Pammi Auntieji listened patiently to my mother's story, her eyes appraising me every now and then. When mom had finished, she took a deep breath, dipped her chin on to her chest and breathed out forcefully, her nostrils flaring. Then she looked up and said, 'You'll take juice?'

Without waiting for a reply, she stood up and went into the kitchen, while Dev Anand continued to gaze at us sombrely. She came back with two glasses of orange Rasna—over-concentrated by the looks of it—and placed a glass in front of each of us.

'Look-see, Behenji, I have understood everything. Of course, we can get our daughter married—after all, she is my daughter, too, and I, too, feel depress that at thirty she is still a virgin. Anyways, let me tell you the prollems. One prollem is: she is fat. She will have to lose weight, OK, beta?' She looked at me and I nodded obediently. 'See, the older they are, the slimmer they have to be, hain na?'

'Number two prollem is that she is old. Now that she can't become young!'—her belly shook in silent laughter as she looked from mom to me, waiting for us to get the joke—'So you have to compromise.'

'Compromise??' my mother said. 'Look, Pammiji, we don't want some college dropout, drunkard or *langda-loola*.'

'No, no, no, no, no, no ji!' Pammi Autieji said, her hands up in defence. 'You are my sister, this is my daughter—would I give you a cripple as my son-in-law? Never! However, maybe we have to try out of caste.'

'Untouchable? Bathroom-washer?' said my mother, while I stared at her open-mouthed. How could she be so politically incorrect? 'See, Behenji, Madrasi is OK with me; my husband is also wheatish,' she said of my practically dark-brown father.

'*Chee!* Never, Behenji, no black ones! What I mean to say is that the boy is,'—she looked around in fear and then lowered her voice to a whisper—'Muslim.'

Oh. I could deal with *that*. I thought she was going to say impotent or something. What was all the drama about? One look at my mother's face and I got my answer. She looked dismayed.

'Pammiji, couldn't you do better?'

Pammi Auntieji took my mother's hands in hers. 'Behenji, just try it. It's a very nice, modern family, no burka-shurka, namaz type. He is a doctor, and really handsome like these Muslim boys are. If you don't like, *bas* throw him like some garbage on the road; but, try.'

Ma looked at me and then back at Pammi Auntieji. 'OK,' she said. 'We'll try.'

19

Pᴀᴍᴍɪ ᴀᴜɴᴛɪᴇᴊɪ'ꜱ ʀᴜʟᴇꜱ ꜱᴛᴀᴛᴇᴅ clearly that the first meeting had to happen at her house. So the meeting with Monty Shah was to happen under the all-seeing glare of Dev Anand in the plastic-and-nylon garden that was Pammi Auntieji's Eden, where 90 per cent success-rate had happened.

Although it was expected to take the entire family along for a visit, we decided to take only Pia and Ant along for respectability, while Sia stayed home with the baby. Sia, in her new avatar, was reasonably OK to take along, but space would be an issue in Pammi's garden and, plus, Sia, in her new yogic phase, might show up in a leotard and a shaven head—you never knew how she was going to interpret things.

Did I want a Muslim guy? Hell, I didn't care. It's not like I scored ten on ten in the Finding-a-Good-Man Exam. I just wanted someone kind and sweet and willing to marry me. But I had decided on one thing: No more sex. If sex was what they wanted, they'd have to marry me to get it. Tish told me that Muslim penises were more aesthetic though. According to her, they 'looked better without the polo neck'. So at least that was something to look forward to.

I dressed with care. I didn't want to look like I was trying too hard, but I didn't want to put his family off either. A white salwar-kameez and silver jewellery seemed the right option, and I teamed it with minimal make-up and hair blow-dried and left loose. We all squeezed into Pia's car, Ant and my dad in the front. In the whole two weeks since Jay the Turd's and my break-up, no one had said a word about it. Except my mother, of course. Sia still hung out with Sunny, but didn't mention when they met or what they talked about. Tish was dying to slice, dice and dissect, but I didn't give her a chance, and Pia and Ant just pretended like nothing had happened. Pia did let it slip once though, that my parents had decided to drop the charges against Jay. They didn't want to be excommunicated from all the parties and weddings in Delhi, as Linny Auntie was quite well-liked in their social circles.

Arf had called in the interim period, during which I wailed, wrote letters I never sent and sleepwalked through workdays. He came and picked me up at work and then took me for a long drive.

'So, why?' he said.

'Why what, Arf?' I leaned my head back against the seat and closed my eyes.

'Why do you need to marry a man to feel like you achieved something? Why can't you see how beautiful you are?'

He asked so matter-of-factly, without looking away from the road, that it took me a minute to register what he was saying. A few months ago I would have swatted his arm and said, 'OK. What do you want, Arf? You earned yourself something big!'

But, suddenly, the sight of his profile in the lights from the road reminded me of that night he had brought me home, without judgement or excess drama. I looked at his strong, capable hands and wondered why he wasn't married. He was a year older than me. And he'd had a girlfriend once, Pooja—a tall, poker-straight-hair variety who loved classic rock like him, and was totally crazy about him. They had dated for four years and then she went abroad to study and never came back. I never asked Arf the details, but I knew he was single, because since then, he had dated here and there.

But why didn't he have a steady girlfriend or a wife or a live-in?

'Arf?'

'Hmm?'

'How come you don't have a girlfriend?'

'Because I don't have an agenda. I have no reason to be exclusively tied to one person.'

'But what if you meet the right person? What if she wants to be tied to you? Would you change?'

There was a pause. Then he said, 'What if I have met the right person? And what if I wanted her to be "untied" with me, but she wanted to be "tied"? Why couldn't she change for me?'

I felt a little flutter in my chest. I looked straight ahead, not daring to check whether he was looking at me. Then he laughed and reached out and tweaked my nose. 'OK, Danielle Steele. Let's get you some ice-cream. I want my five kilos back!'

It was nice to have him back in my life. However elusive he was, he was my comfort zone.

We reached Pammi Auntieji's place an hour late—perfect etiquette by Delhi standards.

'Come, come, come, come in!' she yelled, holding my
mother's hand with one hand, and my sister's with the other.
She yanked them into the house and then came out of the
door. 'Quickly, go in from the kitchen-side and fix yourself.'
She pushed me around the back and then pulled Ant and my
father in. The Shahs were already inside, and I could hear her
make the introductions from the kitchen. From what I could
make out, there was a brother, a sister-in-law and a mother.

Pammi Auntieji was truly professional. She had created a
small dress-up area in the kitchen, complete with full-length
mirror, tissues, wet wipes, safety pins—even basic make-up.
I'm sure she could have produced a new outfit had I needed
one. I refreshed my make-up and hair and was adjusting my
kurta when I heard her say loudly, 'Pia beti, why don't you go
and bring your *behena*?'

Pia rushed in, refusing to make eye contact, and led me
out into the flowery living-room. Dev Anand was sitting at
the dining table today, and extra chairs had been drawn up
around the coffee table. There was a lady in a salwar kameez,
with her head covered; a beautiful young couple, both tall, fair
and slim, with delicate, etched-in-a-fine-brush features—he,
with grey eyes, and, she, hazel. And, then, as he stood at my
entry, my eyes rested on the most beautiful man I had ever
seen. He was tall and broad-shouldered—suddenly making
the room look tiny in his presence. He had a perfectly carved
square jaw, a straight, narrow nose, full, sensual lips, grey eyes
fringed with thick black lashes, and black curls falling over his
forehead. He smiled tentatively, hinting at the incredibly shy,
incredibly sexy personality underneath.

'Hi,' he said, holding out his hand. I took it; it was large and perfect. I smiled up at him, only because if I opened my mouth, it would only be to stick two fingers in and whistle loudly with appreciation. I could sense my family's silent wolf-whistle in harmony with mine. This man could be forgiven murder, let alone his God.

Pammi Auntieji waved me over to sit next to his mother, who looked appraisingly at me, checking out first my feet, then my hands and face. His brother had already gone out on the balcony with Ant, and his sister-in-law smiled widely at me and then started chatting with Pia.

'Any questions, please ask,' Pammi Auntieji told Monty's mother, encouragingly flapping her hand in our direction.

'You're working?'

'Yes, Auntie, in IT.'

'Achha, then, like cooking?'

'Umm . . . a little . . . I . . .'

'Arré! She will learn! All your kebab-koftas, mutton-shutton, she will do!' Pammi Auntieji said while offering us a plate of samosas.

'Children?'

This was getting a bit awkward. I hadn't given all this any thought. So far, the meetings had been casual. This whole centre-of-attention Spanish Inquisition had me completely out of my depth. *Children?* What was the right answer? *At least five? No, I'm barren? Not sure after the last abortion?* Shouldn't this be something a couple discussed after marriage? I mean, I hadn't even had a cup of tea with this woman yet!

'Oh, Rhea beti, why don't you show Monty beta the nice balcony?'

'Sure, Auntieji, where is it?'

Pammi Auntieji pointed us in the direction of another door which opened out into a beautiful little balcony with an ornate swing made for two, and no other seating area—obviously, another one of her little innovations to facilitate matchmaking. Honestly, this woman's entrepreneurial skills were amazing. I pulled my shawl securely around me as we walked out into the night air. The balcony overlooked a small garden round the back of the building. I sat on the swing, looking out at the flowers, breathing in the heavy smell of night-blooming jasmine and frangipani, the foggy Delhi night thick and cloying and cold, like a too-sweet dessert you can't stop eating. Monty followed me out and almost sat next to me, then walked over to the balcony railing and leaned against the wall, his arms crossed, his home-knitted red sweater and collared shirt making an adorably nerdy combination juxtaposed with his glorious movie-star looks. He smiled shyly at me.

OK. I was supposed to make the conversation.

'So, what sort of doctor are you?'

'A paediatrician.'

What?! And did he also save baby dolphins on weekends and read to old ladies on his day off, too? This guy was the male version of a Stepford wife. He was the male Martha Stewart, or the non-porn Nigella Lawson! All I needed was for him to go and fix my car or something!

I looked at him and smiled. 'Soo . . . you have a private practice?'

'Not right now. I work with a hospital. You can do more for children there than through a private practice, which is more about making money.'

Come on!

He suddenly looked at me and smiled. 'This is awkward, isn't it? We know everything about each other, so it's hard to start a conversation.'

And with that the dam burst. When Pia came to get us forty-five minutes later, we were sitting side by side on the swing, in deep conversation about Ireland and its landscapes. He had studied there and hoped to go back there someday—with his wife. He stood as I got off the swing, and stepped aside to let me go back into the living room where everyone was standing and saying goodbyes.

As we walked towards the car, Monty's sister-in-law turned around and gave me a huge wink. Did this mean he . . .? Obviously, we would know only tomorrow. But first . . . the Kanwars had to swap some notes!

'Did you see her diamonds?' Pia asked.

'Whose?'

'Naaz.'

'Who's that?'

'His brother's wife! She had solitaires on all fingers!'

'Oooh! Cool!'

'If they were truly cultured, she would have on her neck-sheck also. These Muslims only show money, no taste,' grumbled my mother—she of the suede walking-shoes and shiny silk salwar-suits. 'Chalo, at least they are *tameezi*. Tasneem-behenji has invited us to her house for food. It's only proper and respectful, na? I toh say, all religions are the same. And we are open-minded. We'll toh eat in anyone's house. Virji, you had that friend, na—Afeem . . . Hashish . . . or something?'

As Ant tried to disguise his snorts of laughter behind a

coughing fit, my father said, 'Hafeez, Cocoji, Hafeez.'

'Haan, Hafeez! We used to eat in his house all the time. So clean and nice it was. And his wife was also no burka-shurka type. I believe they don't kill their goats inside their house. So it's OK to eat there.'

'His brother's a good guy,' Ant spoke up, now over his laughing fit, anxious to stem the flow of inappropriateness coming from my mother. 'He's a lawyer. Went to Cambridge. Old Doon School boy. Plays golf with my brother.'

'Ooooh!' said my mother in delight. 'He plays golf! See, I told you they were cultured! They have a bungalow in Sunder Nagar, did you know? The only thing is, they eat all those cows and pigs, but that's OK, Rhea can put a stop to that after marriage. For now, we'll have to tolerate. This Sunday, when we go for dinner, everyone only eat the chicken, OK? God knows what-all animals these people cook, otherwise! If you don't know what it is, don't eat it. Only plain rice and sweet dish.'

Ant sighed. 'Achha, Mummyji, what gift shall we take on Saturday?'

That did the trick. My mother loved the topic of gifting. She firmly believed that one should never go to someone's home empty-handed—except, of course, in the case of Pammi Auntieji, who was merely a business associate—and she had an entire cupboard full of opened and unopened gifts she didn't want, that she dipped into when a gift was required.

'Beta, I have this mini grandfather-clock, but *kehte hain* that you should never gift clocks—it's a bad omen. What about a perfume? I smelt it little bit, but it's not *jhoota*, and I can easily reseal it; she will never know. That we can give to the *bahu*. And, for older son, we can give that shirt I bought for you last year. Yes, yes, don't deny, Pia, you told me you never wear it because you don't like it. Koi nahin! We'll give it to Bunty!'

'Who's Bunty, Ma?'

'Arré, if he's Monty, his brother must be Bunty, na?'

'Actually, Mummyji, it's Amaan,' said Ant quietly from the driver's seat.

20

THAT NIGHT I LAY awake thinking about Monty. Not Monty, Mazher. That was his real name. And I was determined to call him that. I didn't know what his family thought of me, but wasn't it important what he thought of me? And we had gotten along pretty well for a first meeting. Plus, his mother had invited us over, which was a good sign. Pammi Auntieji had told my mother that the fees we paid her would entitle us to as many boys as we wanted to see for me, depending on availability. But after one year of aggressively looking, if I still remained unmarried or unattached, we would not be eligible for a refund, and Pammi Auntieji would keep me in her file. Meaning, if a fluke happened and I was a match, she would introduce us. But if it didn't, it was my bad luck. If there was a marriage, then, of course, Pammi Auntieji could rightfully expect some silk saris, small jewellery or a silver coin, sweets, and an invitation. But only if we wanted to.

It seemed fair. But one year of meeting guys?? There was another thing. I would turn thirty-one in eight months, and I wanted to be at least engaged before that. Would Monty—no,

Mazher—reject me, too? I couldn't sleep. I got out of bed and turned on the light and looked at myself for the first time in years. I had lost quite a bit of weight over the last five months. I wasn't size zero, but I was no longer chubby. My skin was clear, quite luminous actually, my eyes were a nice shade of brown, and I was really proud of my hair, which was shiny and wavy. I was no translucent-skinned Muslim beauty, but Mazher could do a lot worse. I turned on my laptop and waited for it to connect to the Wi-Fi.

In a moment, a dialogue box popped up from my Google Talk icon. It was Vyash: 'Hi' he said. My stomach twisted. Had something happened?

I stared at the monitor for a few moments. Should I or shouldn't I? I felt like I was over it and really didn't want to restart the whole hearing about Gina, being his shoulder to cry on about his broken marriage again. But we had had a good time together. He had treated me well. And what if he didn't want to start things up again? What if it was just a 'Hi' mail? What if it literally ended there and he didn't say anything else apart from Hi? What if it was a virus? That did it. I logged in.

Sub: Hi

Dear Rhea,

I should have written this email to you a lot earlier. I miss you. Can we meet?

Can I call you sometime?

Vyash

I minimized it as soon as I saw it. Why was he mailing me now? It had been five months. What did he mean he missed me? Should I call him? Did I want to call him? Suddenly, I didn't know. What about Jay? I had been pretty into him. And I really, really liked Mazher. Maybe if I met Vyash, saw him in person, I would know how I felt. I mean, he was my first. And I had missed him from time to time. And at least we could be friends.

I looked at the time. 11.30 p.m. Vyash would be awake. But if I called him at this time, he would think I was desperate. I replied with just one word: Cool. I looked at it for a minute. Should I write Dear?

Dear Vee (no, *Vyash*)

 Cool.

Rhea

No.

Dear Vyash,

How nice to hear from you? Of course I would like to hear from you. Do call when you have time.

Love (No, *Regards.* No, *Sincerely.* No, *Thanks.* Aargh! NO!)

I pressed Control-Alt-Delete, and replied: *Cool.*

Sent.

My phone rang. Vyash. I quickly checked the mirror to see if I looked all right. Yes, he wouldn't know. But I would. And I needed all the courage I could get.

'Hello?' I whispered, as if I had deleted his number and didn't know who was calling.

'Rhea?' His voice was cracked, like he had been crying. I had a vision of his amazing, shiny eyes, now dull and not so shiny, like how they got when he talked about his divorce.

'Yeah.'

'It's me, baby. I've come back.' His voice shook, and he sniffed.

'Oh.' What was I supposed to do with this information? 'Vee . . . what are you saying?'

'I'm saying I'm sorry. I'm saying I messed up and I want another chance, Rhea. Won't you give it to me? I'm broken without you.'

'I don't . . . I don't know, Vee. I . . .'

'Just meet me, Rhea. Now? I'll pick you up in half an hour . . .'

'Vee! Vyash!' I panicked. 'Vyash, no! No! Wait. Just give me some time, OK? Let's talk tomorrow. I'm tired.'

We said goodbye and hung up, and I lay in bed staring at the ceiling. Too much was happening at the same time. Jay had used me and made me the target of his own sickness. Vyash was everything I wanted in a man, and it had taken me too long, and disgusting Jay, to get over him. And now there was Monty, and he showed every sign of being sweet and uncomplicated and easy to be around, if my mother could get around the fact that he was 'out-of-caste', and that his ancestors were toilet-sweepers which is why they probably converted. And now Vee was back and I really wanted to give Monty a chance, but I didn't want to lose Vee.

Five months ago, I would have been happy to be one of a thousand girls in an Axe commercial. Today, I had two men that I could actually choose between, and I didn't know what to do. My thoughts turned to Arf. He would have taken me out for a beer and dropped me back safe. Five months ago. Now, he would do something incredibly sweet and sexy like carry me out of the car, or go searching for a bottle of Pimm's for me and pay some ridiculous amount for it, or stand guard in a parking space till I arrived, so I wouldn't have to walk too far back—and then disappear from my life again. Or maybe he had always done stuff like that and I just hadn't noticed, because he was Arf. He was sexless. Plus, he had never made a move on me, never even said anything to Tish, whom he adored, and we had known each other for ever. That asshole. Adding to my confusion.

I needed a drink. My dad kept the bar locked, but I knew how to open it with a credit card. Actually, the whole family did, and Dad never looked surprised when he asked for a drink and we brought it to him without asking for the key. I tipped the vodka bottle into my glass till it was about half full, mixed in some orange Tang with ice and settled down in the armchair that looked out into the garden. I lay my head back and tried to make sense of this man-fill my life had become. The instrumental track of 'This used to be my playground' played softly in the background of my thoughts.

21

IT WAS LADIES' NIGHT. I was going to forget about work, not take calls from anyone, and not worry about the fact that I was thirty-and-a-half. I would only focus on the fact that I now had a hot body, wear me some nice clothes and make-up and forget my cares tonight. There were a couple of Tish's friends joining us as well as some girls we had hung out with in college and occasionally caught up with. One of them was a girl about my age. Freesia.

Freesia was cute in a fair, dimpled sort of way. She had light-brown hair that she had had cut so it curled around her face, and this cutesy way of talking which wasn't entirely annoying if you visualized her being eaten by a crocodile while she spoke. I had met Freesia a couple of times before. She was a dancer and gave dance classes to girls from 'good families'. She didn't want to teach at a school or an institute, because she couldn't be sure that her students would be 'her type', which meant rich. So she taught Group Bollywood, Sangeet Performance Special, and Modern Dance (a euphemism for pole dancing), which was apparently becoming very popular among girls prepping for their honeymoons. Freesia was also not married, but the first time we had a conversation about it, she said she wasn't because she hadn't time from her career to meet the right person. I wasn't married, according to her, because I was fat. Sometimes, when Freesia was talking, I visualized her being run over by a car over and over again.

She arrived 'dressed to kill'—if she lived in the jungle that is. She was in a leopard-print catsuit, and the only thing missing was a fake tail and plastic fangs. We had managed to elbow our way through the crowd and get to our table, which we had, thanks to Tish. There were eight of us, all dressed better than we would have if we'd been there with men, and we all stood to do our first—free—shot of the evening together. We held our glasses up, all touching, over the table, then Tish yelled, 'To girlfriends!' We all yelled 'To girlfriends!' loudly and then shot our watermelon tequilas. Someone ordered for pitchers of something, someone else ordered carrot sticks with yogurt dip, and we were well on our way to having some good girlie-type fun.

As the music turned to 'I will survive', Tish screamed and then got up to dance, yelling out the lyrics to the song. Chinky and Saroj were sitting with me, chilling, downing daiquiris and looking around. The seating was comfortable—wide sofas, low tables—with a good view of the dance floor and the bar. I was feeling good.

As I looked around, I saw Freesia standing at the bar, chatting with some guy. I pointed it out to Chinky and Saroj. 'Oh yeah,' said Chinky, 'looks like the plan's working.'

'What plan?' I had missed a few of these nights over the last five months so was a bit out of touch.

'Her plan, yaar.'

'To catch a man.'

'Freesia's been trying to meet someone for ages,' said Chinky. 'She thinks she'll meet someone here.' *Phoooooosssss*—she made an explosion with her fingers. '*Kismat se!*'

'Don't make fun, bitch,' said Saroj, spraying warmed-up daiquiri in my face. 'Looks like she's caught one, na. And he's cute-shoot, yaar. See cute-sa bum, cute-sa . . . bum!' She collapsed back into her chair and snapped her head back on the headrest. 'Bas!'

Chinky looked at her, took the glass from Saroj's hand and put it on the table. 'Expired.'

We hung around till about one in the morning and then everyone started to get worried about getting home and going to work the next day, etc. So we hauled Saroj to her feet, rounded up the rest of the girls in their various stages of drunkenness, and started preparing them to go home. Three of them called their husbands to come pick them up and then ran to the restroom to stick their fingers down their throats so they could be done throwing up and clean up by the time they arrived. Chinky, Tish and Saroj would be taken home by Tish's driver. There was no way Saroj could go home the way she was, even though she lived with her brother and not her parents. Her sister-in-law would be 'publically embarrassed' by twenty-eight-year-old Saroj coming home drunk when it was bad enough she had broken one engagement which had come from her (the sister-in-law's) side. So, she would stay at Tish's and get cleaned up, changed, fed and sent back first thing in the morning, when she could tell the neighbours that she had gone to help look after Tish's kids.

Chinky didn't give a shit what anyone thought. Everyone knew she was gay, although she didn't talk about it openly. Her 'roommate' had recently moved out, and Chinky had put on weight, shaved her head and started drinking every night. But she still hadn't got a new roommate even though she was borrowing from her parents to make rent. She didn't want to drive home that night and would get herself back on K's Enfield whenever she woke up. K was used to Chinky using his Enfield and didn't mind so much because he never rode it. It was just important to him that everyone knew he had one.

That left me and Freesia. We always got stuck in the pool together, but she lived the closest to me and, honestly, it wasn't fun driving back home alone, late at night, in Delhi. While the others started getting their stuff together, I went to get her. She was standing in between the guy's legs and simpering at him while he sat on the bar stool.

'Erm ... Freesia? Everyone's leaving and ... er ... I thought we should, too.'

'Oohh, hey, Ri-Ri!' she said all fluttery eyelashes and fake smile. 'So, erm . . .'—she looked at the guy she was with—'I really don't want to go home, but she's my ride ... so ...'

To my amazement, he fell right for it.

'Don't go, baby,' he said, looking cross-eyed into her eyes. They were standing so close, the only way he could look at her was if he got both eyeballs that close together. I tried to hide a smile. 'I'll take you home.'

Great! So it was me. Driving home alone. Well, it had its benefits. I rolled the windows right up, locked myself in, dialled 100 on my phone and kept it within reach, then put the music on full blast, singing along loudly while I raced home. I felt good. Sometimes you just need a night with the girls to make you feel like life is worthwhile.

That night, when I got home, I lay awake for some time thinking about Freesia and the guy she met at the club. Should I have tried that route instead of this arranged marriage-Pammi-Auntieji-band-baja-turtle-doves-kissing-babies one? Every time a match didn't work out, my whole family—and therefore my parents' tambola group—also knew. Could I have met someone at a club, though? I sighed. It would have been easier if I was gay. Chinky was good fun. And she had been pretty cute before she gained heartbreak weight.

Whatever.

I rolled over and went to sleep.

22

IT WAS THE NIGHT of the Monty (Mazher) dinner. Mummy had allocated gifts for every member of the family with Pia's help, and she was pleased to see the immaculate white house overlooking the park, with two cars parked in the driveway and another two right outside the gate. The family was cultured, she said. Just like us.

The Shahs were really hospitable. They had a gift for Pia's baby all packed and ready, and welcomed us with a refreshing rose drink. Then we were led into their sitting area, where they had placed a wooden cradle for Zara to lie in so Pia and Ant wouldn't have to keep carrying her.

We all settled down, me in one corner of the sofa, Mazher strategically in an armchair next to me. The couples had grouped together automatically, and my mother had already gotten Mazher's mother to take her on a tour of the house. My father wandered around aimlessly for a while. There was no alcohol and no smoking. Then he spotted a TV in a corner of the living room. He went over, looked around surreptitiously, and turned it on, with the volume on really low, and began to watch the news. When I turned back from my father, I caught Mazher looking at me. We exchanged an indulgent smile and then he asked me how things had been.

I found myself telling him everything about work, my boss, my team and how one budding romance in the team was really beginning to bug me because I was tired of making allowances for them. He listened patiently, his eyes locked on mine, nodding occasionally.

'Want to go for a walk?' he asked, tilting his head towards the outside.

'It's freezing . . . but, sure!'

We walked over to the park in front of his house and began a slow stroll around it.

Mainly, we talked about work and movies and a little bit of travel. He was so easy to be around. Not complicated or overly intense or particularly heartbroken. It was just nice. Nice and easy. By the time we got back, I had his jacket wrapped around me. We entered to an exchange of warm and approving looks from everyone in the room—except my dad, whose team was losing.

Naaz sat next to me at dinner. I noticed that her plate had just some vegetables on it, with a chapatti, when the table was practically squatting under the weight of all the trays piled with koftas, kebabs, tureens of mutton curry and one large swimming-pool of bright-red chicken curry, which was delicious. She saw me looking, and grinned.

'Can't do any more meat!' I smiled back and we began an animated conversation about Naaz's life.

Naaz had married Amaan when she was just twenty.

'Why?'

She shrugged.

'We got the proposal; it was a nice family. My dad said I wouldn't get such a nice guy again if I refused. Plus, who wanted to study?! If I didn't get married I would have had to finish my graduation. After marriage also Amaan tried to force me to go back and finish. But I hate studies! Marriage is easier.'

I glanced up at Amaan, who was still talking about golf with Ant. The Cambridge-educated Doon boy, married to this admittedly lovely girl who married him to avoid going back to college. I wondered what they had in common. There were lots of girls like her in the pre-university college that I went to. They'd hang out in huge groups, sit at the back of the class doing their nails, and spend most of their time outside the college gates chatting with each other, flirting with boys or going off on short drives with them. And she was so happy! I was beginning to wonder if all this crap they tell us about identity and personality and actualization is all part of some conspiracy to make you unhappy. My mother used to say, 'All this self-esteem is a Western concept! White people crying that they don't love themselves. Arré, love some poor children, no? What is the need to love yourself. Cracks!'

Naaz was happy being married to Amaan. She enjoyed looking after him and looked forward to his return home every day so she could be with him. I was tired of being an individual. You know what I would be happy being? A wife. Preferably with no first name—just Mrs Handsome-Kind-Rich-Man-Who-Loves-His-Wife. Yup. That sounded good.

I looked around the room. I wouldn't mind being the daughter-in-law of this house. They were good people. His mother laughed easily, the brothers seemed to get along, and

Naaz would be good company. Mazher came over to me with a dessert bowl full of creamy phirni with rose petals and slivered almonds on it. He smiled.

'Calorie overload?'

I giggled. He was so cute when he was trying to get all girlfriend-y.

'Movie on Friday night?'

I nodded eagerly. Finally, a night alone with Mazher. I had a date! I had a date! All I needed was a dance troupe to come out from behind the curtains and join me in a victorious, ecstatic dance. But, first, I had to meet Vyash tomorrow. And my date with the toe-curling Mazher would make it oh-so-easy to put out Vee's rekindled heart under my stiletto!

23

I TOOK THE DAY off. Vyash and I were meeting at six in the evening, and I had to look eat-your-heart-out good. He was going to twist and writhe with pain and regret at letting me go. He was going to feel the stabs of a million swords when I walked in. And, then, when I told him I was going to marry Mazher, the gorgeous doctor whose picture I had on my phone, he would crumple up into a little ball and hate himself forever. And that would maybe, perhaps, just about take away 10 per cent of the pain I had felt when he left me crying and broken in Goa. Honestly, forgiveness was overrated.

I went to get myself The Outfit. The Outfit had to have superpowers. It would have to be able to reduce Vyash to a quivering mass of regret and, later, when I wore it for my date with Mazher, it had to whisper 'Propose to her' in his ears until he was no match for its persuasive voice. The Outfit could not be bound by mundane limitations such as budget or inappropriateness for the occasion. If I had to land up for *The Amazing Spider-Man* in an evening dress, so be it. I once saw a man in a black patent-leather trench-coat and wrap-around sunglasses at a *Matrix* movie.

It took me about four hours to find The Outfit. But when I did, I swear I heard choirs of angels sing. It was a floaty, sheer, asymmetrical, spaghetti-strapped tunic the colour of champagne, with the subtlest smattering of silver sequins, and matching tights. It made me look slim and tall and hinted at a small waist. And I had the perfect pair of silver sandals and a silver bag to go with it. I smiled at The Outfit and whispered, 'Hello, lover.' I wanted it to know how much I loved it.

Then I took off to the salon to get my hair spa-ed, ironed and made love to until it shone like a diamond.

We were to meet at the coffee shop at the Taj Palace—which was just as well because The Outfit didn't like to go to cheap places. I reached—fashionably late—handed my keys to the valet, and walked into the glittering reception-area of the hotel, with my new theme song playing in my head: 'Radha Teri Chunari'.

Vyash was sitting at a corner table, in indigo jeans and a black shirt. He was thinner, which suited him somehow, the dark shirt against his chocolate skin giving him a dangerously sexy air. I swallowed. Maybe this was out of The Outfit's league. Maybe I should have bought the other one. The one that was cut really low in front and cost twice as much as this one did. Then, all of a sudden, he turned and saw me, and his mouth fell open. He slowly began to rise from his seat, his mouth still hanging open.

He ran around to the other side and held out a chair for me. Then we had this awkward moment when he came forward to hug me while I held out a hand. Then he saw that and offered me a hand, but I had already leaned forward for a hug, so he ended up with a hand squished against my boob. I pulled away, embarrassed, but he grabbed my hand and said, 'You look breathtaking, Rhea.' And then he sparkled at me with those mad, disco eyes. And I, full as I was of hurt and betrayal and let down, smiled back into them.

'We were moving too fast, Rhea,' he said before we could get into a how-are-you/your parents/your siblings.

'I felt like I was shallow, falling for you so fast, when I was hardly over Gina. I lashed out at you, my innocent girl, and I'm so sorry, baby. Can you forgive me?'

Damn that bloody asshole eyeliner! I wanted to cry and I was going to look like Dracula. I shook my head, breathing deeply so I wouldn't cry. 'I . . . I . . . Vee . . .'

He reached across and held my hand. 'Don't cry, baby. I know. I know I was a bastard. Please don't cry, baby.'

This was not how I had envisioned it. He was supposed to cry. He was supposed to be out of control. He was supposed to look like crap. And I was supposed to walk away—after showing him Mazher's picture.

Mazher. Suddenly I was pissed off. I had moved on. What was he doing bhangra-dancing back into my life like it was open house or something? And he hadn't even asked if I was seeing someone before he started touching me. In public that too. What if someone saw? I drew myself up and pulled out my phone, accessed my picture of Mazher and slid it across the table so hard that it fell off. Vyash looked confused. 'What's this?'

'Pick it up, Vyash.' It was a tone I had never used with him before, my voice sounding strange and wobbly with rage.

He picked it up and looked at it and then looked up at me.

'I'm getting married. To him,' I said, pointing at the phone. And then, because I couldn't say anything more without crying, I got up, grabbed my phone and walked off, hoping he wouldn't follow me and make it complicated. I was walking as fast as I could and I couldn't hear any footsteps, but I didn't want to turn around and make sure, because he'd think I was having second thoughts.

Yes! I did it! I told Vyash to eff off! I now had 'Rubaru' from *Rang De Basanti* playing loudly in my head. I was an activist. A broken-heart activist.

As the song trailed off, I realized there was just one problem.

I needed Mazher to propose.

24

It's amazing how much advice you get when you decide to get proposed to. It was also a huge surprise to me how many of my friends and family have decided to be proposed to in the past.

Tish met K at work. They had stayed back one night because an ad was going to print and, while they both pored over an 8-by-10 layout, his elbow had bumped her boob and they had ended up making out in the passage between the creative department and the studio. The trick, Tish always said, was to not give the milk out for free. Well, she gave him a taste of it. And, then, she made him beg till he proposed.

Pia and Ant met in college. Ant got no milk. According to Pia, he got nothing more than a peck on the cheek. But I'm sure that was the impressionable-younger-sister version of the story. All married people claim that there's some impeccable way in which they behaved that got them married. Either it was denying sex, being nice to his parents or, in the case of my college friend Rinku, it was being gharelu. Gharelu means cooking-cleaning-loving-babies types.

Apparently, every time Rinku went out with Santy and they happened to see a baby, Rinku would go coochie-coo at it. Then, she said, she would position her face slightly sideways, chin tilted downward, like all the Mother Mary pictures, and stand where the light was dim. She also never worked late, never drank or smoked in public, but did elaborate pujas and went to the temple every Friday. Santy proposed to her six months after they started going out. Now they've been married eight years, even though Rinku told him on their wedding night that she hates cooking and was not sure if she wanted children. Maybe it's the fact that she still goes to temples. Men like women who pray for them.

I was desperately thinking over this proposal thing. I had Tish's, Pia's and Rinku's stories. I needed another perspective—someone who'd been doing this a long time; someone professional; someone with a 'Pomerrian' named Dev Anand. Pammi Auntieji!—who was only too glad to meet me and help me get proposed to and close herself a deal. She invited me over for tea and chutney sandwich (without 'battir' to 'figure-maintainofy'). I was there at the dot of four, scrubbed clean and looking as marriageable as possible.

'*Dekho*, beta,' she said, rubbing my thigh suggestively. 'He has to think ki you will love his mummy, cook his food and have some babies.'

What?? I had come here to hear something that was preferably from this century! I mean, yes, she was a matchmaker, but she was also making matches for Generation Y. I knew this cooking, cleaning, leg-pressing shit, but, *hullo*, we were in a time when same-sex kissing was happening on daytime television and in Hindi movies! I was hoping to get advice that was more pole-dance and less puri-paratha!

'But Pammi Auntieji, that's all old-fashioned, no? Haven't things changed?'

'Hainh!!' she sniffed. 'When things change, men will be having babies and removing them from their private parts. Until then, things are same-same only! Big-big they're coming, things change!' She looked at me intently and, perhaps sensing my distress, said, 'OK, look-see, beta. You are as it is old, fat and little bit dark; chalo, if your neck was long, it would be OK, but you know you are like this. We have to do you the speed-track. What I am telling you, I will tell no one else. But you are like my daughter, so I tell you. You do sex with him.'

I blinked. This was going into another tangent altogether.

'Pammi Auntieji . . .' I spluttered.

'Shh, shh now,' she murmured soothingly. 'It's a universal truth. You catch him by the down-unders.' She winked suggestively. 'You will have a bond for life!'

How was I to tell Pammi Auntieji that it hadn't exactly worked out for me the first two times? Well, it kind of had with Vyash, he had come back; but what if it didn't work out with Mazher.

'Haan, haan, I get it. Monty is a . . .' She made a cutting motion with her hand. 'Chalo, OK, he may not want to do with you because religion-viligion, at least then give him one small taste, do some little romance, and then say, "Want more? OK, then, marry me." Just like in restaurants they give you Horr-Doos, then main course, like that you do same-same. OK?' She grinned broadly and then ate an entire samosa, shaking a finger to indicate that I had eaten enough chutney sandwich without battir.

I had a lot to think about now. Which was not great, considering I was meeting Arf for coffee straight after this. I wondered whether I should ask him what he thought. Given our most recent conversation, it seemed pretty obvious. I had to find myself and be all Oprah Winfrey.

But then Arf had always been pretty great about giving advice when it didn't concern him. Plus, he was the only guy I could really ask. I mean, I was pretty close to Ant, but it's not like he was going to spill the beans on my sister, who, for all I know, was swinging from the chandeliers in a leather catsuit or something to hook him. Shaking my head to tip out that visual, I quickly said bye and thanks to Pammi Auntieji, who waggled her fingers in farewell and said, 'Remember-Horr-Doos!' I left to drive down to Bengali Market for chaat and juice with Arf. It had been our group's favourite hang-out when we were in college, so we had decided to go there for old time's sake.

I found us a table and waited for him to order, fiddling with the tissues and looking at the mix of people who came to Nathu's to eat. A few minutes later, Arf arrived, in a white shirt, with his trademark brown beads on his wrist. He looked good. And his eyes lit up when they met mine.

'Rheesputin!' he grinned and pinched my cheek. 'What's up, Bum-Face?'

I swatted at him, trying to hide my grin. 'Shut your face, Keeda King!'

'Heh,' he snorted.' You keeda-makaudi! The usual?'

'Yas!'

'OK, two minutes.'

I watched him as he walked over to the counter to get our stuff. Worn jeans, brown leather shoes, white, slim-fit shirt with two buttons open, three rows of brown beads on his left wrist. The man had style—and a nice butt! I thought to myself with surprise. Why hadn't I ever noticed the small, round number? Because, I suppose, it was like checking out my brother . . .

He came back with one channa bhatura for sharing, and a sev puri which I just know would be perfectly spiced: *teekha-meetha barabar*. There was something to be said for a friend who had known you forever. We settled down to eat and I began to ask him about Mazher. A look of irritation distorted his face for a second and then he sighed and said, 'Rhee, why do I get the feeling that this is all we talk about nowadays? You used to be cool, babe.'

'Arf, I'm thirty. I don't have time. I wasted whatever of it I had. And besides, I don't want to be Bubbles Auntie.'

'Bubbles Auntie?'

I sighed. 'Forget it.'

'OK, auntie, don't sulk,' he said, tucking a strand of hair behind my ear. 'But just one word of advice . . .'

I perked up. This should be good.

'Please count your dad's underwear before you say yes.'

~

After we were done at Nathu's, we parked near Sunder Nagar and walked into the lanes between the houses. It was dangerously close to Mazher's place, but we steered clear of his block and just walked, arm in arm, chatting about stuff.

Finally, I asked him, 'Arf, if you were a guy—' I ignored his smirk, 'you know what I mean—what would it take for you to propose to a girl?'

'For me to love her,' he replied. 'To feel like I can say anything to her. To feel that I have to marry her, because I can trust only myself to protect her.'

He looked down at me and smiled. I tried to smile back, but I felt like crying. I wanted those words to be said about me, by someone who'd treat me as if I should be wrapped in cotton wool. I got that headache you get when your head fills up with tears, but nothing comes out of your eyes.

Arf put his arm around me and drew me close.

'Why do you want an arranged marriage, Rhee-Bee? Why don't you want to wait it out?' he whispered into my hair.

I couldn't hold back any longer. I burst into tears and choked out, 'Because I just want a guy who's serious! I want someone who wants to go the distance. Not someone who's checking out the scene!'

He rested his chin on my head, while I soaked his clean white shirt with the tears that finally exploded from my head and then wouldn't stop.

25

It was the night of my date with Mazher, and The Outfit stood at attention, all clean and spruced up for *The Amazing Spider-Man*. I had taken extra care with my hair, ironing it till it was silky-soft to touch and looked like something out of a shampoo commercial. I was going for the head-on-shoulder move tonight, come what may. Mazher and I had been talking on the phone; we could talk for hours on end, and it really looked like he liked me enough to marry me. I had tried everything—the cooking talk, the baby talk, the never-working-late talk. If I got any more gharelu, I would be making pickle from mangoes plucked in my own garden. I needed to get a little *Cosmopolitan* magazine on him. So, I decided, tonight, he was going to get his Horr-Doos.

He picked me up, looking glorious in black jeans and a leather jacket, his grey eyes as sexy as I remembered, his hair curling on his forehead. I was hearing 'Ek Ladki Ko Dekha' in my head, and I hoped he was hearing it too. He smiled at me.

'Woman, you are a sight to behold!'

'I hope that's a compliment,' I said, giggling flirtatiously.

He looked a bit surprised when I bent one shoulder forward and flipped my hair, but didn't say anything.

The Amazing Spider-Man was nice and cute, even though Emma Stone's teeth really put me off, but, really, my head was everywhere but on some teenage superhero! At exactly thirty-five minutes into the movie, I sighed, yawned and flopped my head on to Mazher's shoulder, letting it rest there for a few minutes. When he didn't show any signs of resisting or stiffening, I snuggled closer, allowing some boob—arm contact as well. He slipped down in his seat, so I could get more comfortable. This is a good sign, I thought. I just have to make sure my make-up doesn't smudge on his shirt.

He took my hand in his and rubbed his thumb over the back. I smiled to myself. How sweet was this! I grinned up at him and found him looking down at me, smiling. It was my own romcom-heroine moment. All I needed now was to be zapped with a spiderweb and twirled into a kiss, just like Emma Stone. And some flying around the city wouldn't be too bad either.

He held my hand all the way to the car, and over dinner too—when we weren't eating, anyway. People kept giving us those indulgent smiles they give couples who are in-love-but-not-in-an-irritating-way. And at the end of dinner, the restaurant gave us a little box with a heart-shaped chocolate in it that we were supposed to share. Mazher put his arm around me, keeping it there until the valet drove up in the car. When we reached my house, he didn't immediately get out to open the door, like he normally did. Instead, he switched off the engine and turned to look at me.

'Rhea, I . . .'

I smiled at him and took his hand. And then leaned over and

kissed him. Not full-on tongue and all. Just a kiss on the cheek.

Suddenly, he turned his face and was kissing me—tongue, teeth and all. I think he even put his tonsils into it. I should have enjoyed it, but I kept thinking about how I wouldn't have any lips left by morning, and how would I look then, with this big nose and no mouth to balance it? Should I push him off and say something Mae West-ish to save my mouth, or just let him be and hope for a proposal? I decided to opt for the ring and my name on the gate of the house in Sunder Nagar.

Mazher suddenly shifted into fifth. He surged towards me, his fingers dragging urgently over the skin on the top of my breasts, his other hand digging into my butt. This man obviously hadn't been around women a whole lot and, as sweet as he was, and as well as we got along, I really didn't know how to tell him that he and I would probably enjoy this more if he didn't act like he was deboning a cow. His breathing got really urgent and he moaned, getting in a little deeper and then suddenly he pulled back, looking at me, his expression shocked and disgusted, still breathing heavily.

It's hard to look confused yet sexy when you've just been mauled by an over-eager thirty-three-year-old virgin, but I did my best, looking down coyly, adjusting my neckline, frantically feeling the fabric for any tears or missing sequins. There was one silver sequin strategically positioned on his crotch, but now was not the time to try and pick it off of him and transfer it to my bag so I could stitch it back on later.

He looked at me all puzzled, and said, 'I'm sorry.'

Hullo? This was not exactly what I was expecting.

'This is wrong, Rhea. It's wrong.' He looked really distressed. 'I'd better get you home.'

'But . . . but . . .'

One look at his face and I realized I should just go home and figure out whether he was referring to his making-out style (in which case he was right), or the fact that he'd kissed me (in which case, *WTF?!*).

He practically trundled me to the front door and then slammed it shut before I could even say anything. This was weird. Was it some religion thing or something?

I changed out of The Outfit, whispered to it that I was beginning to think it was unlucky for me and then went down to the kitchen to see what I could eat. Obviously, I hadn't *really* eaten in front of Mazher. Who does that on a date? And who should be sitting at the counter but my newly spiffed-and-polished younger sister. This time in pink. *Pink?* This was getting scary. Sia hadn't worn pink since she was two and Satan began to have one-on-ones with her.

I wondered if I should talk with her. Ask her if she was OK. I sat across from her with the box of curd I had salvaged from the fridge and ate it while she made tracks into the aloo paratha I wished I could eat instead of plain curd. She looked kind of cute in her pink PJs, scrubbed face, with a dot of curd on her chin, and her hair tied up in a ponytail. Just like when she was two.

'Whaddup, Soo-Soo?' I asked, using the name Pia and I used to call her when she was a kid and we wanted to annoy her.

She looked up, smiling. 'Nothing, Fatty! Whaddup with you?'

'Shaddup, Dustbin Reject!' I yanked at her ponytail.

We grinned at each other.

'How's Monty's Python?' she asked, sending us both into a

giggling fit. Then she looked at my face closely and said, 'Dude, who killed your lip?'

Oh shit!

'Is it bruised?'

'Not badly. Just swollen. First kiss?'

'Umm . . . yeah. Sort of.'

'Reject?'

I sighed. 'I don't know. See, I just don't know. Anyway, what's with the Little Miss Sunshine look?'

'What do you mean?' she asked suspiciously.

'See,' I was serious now, 'you've changed. Are you into drugs or anything? You can tell me. I won't tell Mama–Papa.'

'No! How could you think that?'

'I don't know. You've changed so much!'

'Yeah, but drug addicts get all thin and don't have baths and things. I'm . . .'

'Ya, you're all shiny-happy, dude. It's just not the Sia I'm used to. That's all.'

She sighed.

'Rhee, you wouldn't like . . . stop talking to me, would you?'

I was about to answer when my BlackBerry chirped. I looked at it. It was another email from Vyash. I felt inexplicably happy. I opened it and began to read.

Dear Rhea,

I know you're angry with me. Let me make it up to you, baby. Just come back and these arms will never let you go.

V

I smiled. It was a nice email. *Oh shit! Sia.*

I looked up, but she was gone. And I had an email to gloat over.

26

'OH PLEASE! OH PLEASE! Do it again!'

Tish was lying on her bed with her legs in the air—screaming with laughter. I had just told her about what had happened with Mazher, and she thought it was just the funniest thing she ever heard.

'Tish, can you please be serious?'

'OK, but first can you say, "This is wrong" the way he does? Please?'

I had to smile. I did do a good post-making-out-guilted-out Mazher. 'This is wrong, Rhea. Just wrong,' I said, with the same outraged expression he'd had on his face when he said it. Tish did her rape-rocket laugh again.

'Too good it is!' she said once she had caught her breath.

'Why did he say that? What did he mean?'

'I don't know. Have you tried talking to him about it?'

'No! . . . I mean, what am I supposed to say?'

'Hmm, good point. Maybe he feels you came on to him . . .'

'I just kissed his cheek, Tish! I didn't exactly do a pole dance in leopard-print chudds.'

'That would have been difficult in his car,' she said with one eyebrow raised.

'Shut up, Bum-Face.'

'OK, Atlas, put the world down for two minutes, yaar. Maybe he feels you're too pure. It must be the Madonna–Whore complex.'

OK, that would be a bit hard to deal with. I mean, I didn't exactly want to be doing the entire Kamasutra every night, but I definitely wanted a good sex life. Plus, if I didn't make out with him a little bit, how was I going to get my proposal? And the truth of the matter was: he needed some practice! I was doing him a favour, offering him some performance-improving practical sessions.

Tish suggested that I pretend nothing had happened and ask him on another date. She said it could have just been a bad day or a triggered bad memory or something, and if I talked to him about it, then I would remind him that I would be a nagging wife and that is something no man should know about a woman till he's married her.

I rang Mazher, and we fixed up to meet on Friday.

I hadn't told Tish about Vyash's email. I didn't want to analyse it to death with anyone. But I did write back to him that night. I needed to tell Vyash how badly he had treated me. How hard it had been for me to get back from Goa after he had walked out on me. And how sick I was of hearing about Gina, Gina, Gina. I mean, if she was so perfect, then what did he want from me? He should have stayed with her lying ass! I typed out a long email and sent it to him. I did write about how hurt I'd been, but I couldn't bring myself to mention Gina's ass. What if he thought I was an over-possessive, bitchy type? He hadn't responded, but I didn't care. It's not like we were getting back together, and I was going to marry Mazher, anyway. And, I told myself, Vyash probably needed a day to absorb everything and get back to me.

I hoped Mazher would propose to me soon. I had been getting in trouble at work for being distracted, and I was sick of being called into my boss's cabin every week. If he proposed, then maybe I could take some time off. Or just concentrate on work once and for all.

I had called Mazher and we'd had a nice chat. He was buying a new car and he wanted my opinion on the colour. Was this a sign? I wasn't sure, but I did suggest red, just in case I would be sharing it sometime in the future. I could hear him smiling at the other end of the phone when he said he might surprise me. I smiled and stretched out on Tish's bed. Me. A doctor's wife.

'Rhee?' Tish interrupted my fantasy, suddenly sounding really serious.

'Ya?'

'Do you think K still loves me?'

'Say more?'

'I don't know. He's been distant lately. Been coming home late. I'm beginning to wonder if he's having an affair.'

'Are you crazy, dude?! K's madly in love with you! He's got his appraisals going on, right? Maybe he's just caught up with that.'

'Ya, but that day, he got a call on his mobile from Sudha Motors, and I just began to think, what if Sudha is a chick and he saved her named like that, so I wouldn't know. I haven't heard one mention of Sudha Motors on top of it all.'

I had to laugh.

'Tish, that's pretty creative! Do you really think K is that smart?'

Tish stared at me for a second. I wasn't sure if she'd taken offence. Then she smiled sadly.

'We've been married a long time, Rhee. It gets hard.'

'You're not happy, Tish?'

She laughed.

'What is "happy", Rhea? Movies should stop selling that concept. You're happy in pockets. Just like life. When you're happy, you're happy. When you're sad, you're sad. Whether you're married or not has very little to do with it.'

Easy for Tish to say. Did she really know what it was like to be thirty and single? To have people asking invasive questions all the time? To have a Career when all you really want is a husband and two children, PTA meetings and play dates? The worst thing was, New Year's was coming up—and whom would I spend it with? Another family dinner, where we all found random things to talk about just so we could stay up till twelve and wish each other, then crash. Tish used to say it was no different when you were married. Except K and her timed it so that they were having sex when the clock struck twelve, just to ensure that they would be having plenty in the new year. Honestly, I didn't see what was so bad about that. I wasn't expecting them to be skydiving or something just because they were married. I was just expecting them to be doing something better than counting down with some guy in a velvet suit and some people dancing on some stupid TV show, which had been filmed one week earlier, anyway, while their real selves were partying or having sex at midnight.

27

I RECEIVED AN EMAIL from Vee. Just two words: *I'm sorry*. I couldn't suppress the little giggle that bubbled up and overflowed. It was going to be a good day. I just had this meeting with HR to get out of the way. I went straight to the office.

There was my boss, the head of HR, Chandni, and her sidekick, a woman just back from maternity leave, but still carrying her tummy from three months ago. They smiled at me, all friendly and would-you-like-some-tea etc. I said no, and sat down. It was probably going to be a long list of complaints about my team. Downloading movies in office, non-delivery, someone had hit up bills of over a lakh making calls to Germany, or it could be about my team member, who couldn't come up with ideas unless he cycled and so he insisted on cycling all over the office at all hours. They were good guys, my gang, but every now and then, they'd lose the plot. Like the guy who tried to teach one of the expats in HR the lyrics to a Yo Yo Honey Singh song. I'd be out of there in fifteen. I'd just say sorry-sorry-will-look-into-it, and leave.

'Erm . . . so, how are things?' said Chandni in this fake-jovial voice. 'Been enjoying, haan?'

I smiled and shrugged.

'Ahh naughty girl!' she said, her voice all high-pitched. 'So, how are you enjoying work? How are things at home, hmm?'

Suddenly, my boss cut in.

'Rhea. We're letting you go.'

I began to hear a loud drumming—stupid construction-workers. I grinned.

'On leave?'

Chandni cut in.

'So nice! You are making jokes. Raghu will give you a box. For your things.'

'What? *What?!!*'

'You understood, na, Rhea?' Chandni was looking really distressed. 'One-month severance pay . . .'

'B-but why?'

I was sounding IQ-challenged even to my own ears, but I really didn't understand.

'Rhea, I warned you. Leave-taking, coming in late, non-delivery. Missing client-calls! *Client-calls, Rhea!* Your head's been in the clouds for five months, and the team is complaining like mad about you.'

When did he warn me, the half-dead sod?

'Ya, but Vivek downloads porn! Fire him! And Lucky sings Honey Singh!'

'Rhea, I'm sorry. Clear your desk.'

My boss walked out. Chandni was looking at me sympathetically.

'He's angry,' she said, shaking her head.

What was I going to tell my parents? What was I going to do? I got my stuff and fled without looking anyone in the eye.

As I left the building, I was still hearing the construction workers bang away. I realized they were at work in my head.

I couldn't go home. This was not the best thing to tell Mazher. I couldn't deal with Tish right now. I called Arf. We went for a movie. He bought me popcorn and ice-cream and held my hand and then agreed to keep my box of office-stuff until I was ready to tell my family what had happened.

After he'd dropped me home, I sat at the kitchen window and watched him leave. His slow, strong walk, like a lion, sauntering away with purpose, but in no hurry to be anywhere; the careless way he tossed his bag in the back before he got into his jeep—a fifteen-year-old model, maintained to perfection—the way he was so careful not to run over a plant or a tree. He was like a monk in many ways. He needed so little and he had such peace about him. I wondered how much he really kept from me. Whether he would like to be in a relationship, or whether he was really all right, living in his parents' *barsati*, the red-painted door, a broken guitar turned into a lampshade. He hated talking about Mazher and Pammi Auntieji and Mummy, so I couldn't ask him whether he thought I should tell Mazher about being jobless or whether I should keep quiet for a while. But Mazher had to love me for me, right? It shouldn't matter to him if I lost a job because of internal politics or people's personal vendettas. I decided that I would tell him on our date tonight. We had decided to just walk around Hauz Khas—this time, nothing major.

I changed and got out of the house before my parents could ask me what I was doing home so early in the evening.

Mazher was so stomach-twistingly good-looking. Even his fingernails were good-looking—perfectly shaped and not yellow. We chatted easily about his work and books and the *Spider-Man* movie we had watched, and he took my hand in his and tucked it in his pocket, so I was drawn up tightly against his side, his hip bumping mine with every stride. Well, I wasn't complaining. We stopped for a soup-and-croissant dinner and then he asked if I'd like to drop in at his house. Sure, I figured. Not like I had to wake up early the next morning for anything. Besides, it would give me a chance to be susheel.

When we got there, though, the lights were suspiciously off.

'Umm . . . Mazher?'

'Yes, Woman?' he said in this faux-cocky voice.

'Are we going to be home alone?'

'Yes. Is that cool?'

'It's cool,' I said, thinking that, OK, so if he asked me to marry him tonight, I could tell everyone that I was quitting my job to arrange for my wedding. And, then, maybe I'd take some time off and we'd travel, have some babies, find ourselves . . . The possibilities were endless.

He had led me up to his 'rooms'—a bedroom and attached study.

'Want to watch a movie?' he asked.

'Sure,' I said, picking out *Dabangg* from the movie folder on his desktop. We settled down on the pull-out to watch it. The movie was some weird combination of *Mission Impossible* with Salman Khan freezing and doing fighting-twisting things in mid-air, but I wasn't concentrating, anyway. Mazher's breathing had become laboured and his fingers had begun to dig into my upper arms. The next thing I knew, he had rolled on top of me, one hand between us, fumbling with his belt. He kept making these frustrated grunts and clawing at his belt. So I gave him a few minutes and then tried to help him. In a second, he was off me, my hand was pushed to the side and he was staring at me, all red in the face and running his hands through his hair. Sexy, but also weird. He was breathing too heavily to say anything, so I asked him, 'Ummm . . . Mazher . . . Is something wrong?'

'You've done this before?' he managed to get out in between heaving breaths and gritted teeth.

Ookaay, what was the right answer? This. Was. Not. In. The. Syllabus. I mean, obviously, the right answer was NO, but there was all that Honest Marriage-Happy Marriage scene, too. But then I chose Happy Marriage over Rampaging Mazher. 'No.'

'No? No??'

He looked disbelieving. So I back-pedalled a bit.

'Umm . . . I've made out a little bit . . . My boyfriend forced me . . .'

He stood up and paced around the floor, muttering something to himself. Handsome as he was, if he turned out to be reciting his prayers, I was out of there and dialling Bubbles Auntie's number, even though my mother had called her 'Sexless', and Saro Didi had confirmed, 'Of very less sex.'

He stopped and looked at me, 'You've enjoyed it?'

'Huh?'

'As in, you encouraged it? You took it forward?'

'Mazher, please tell me what you want to know. I really don't understand . . .'

'You should have stopped me!' he cried out, his voice a bag of nails all scraping against each other.

His eyes teared up. I didn't know what to say. I just wanted for us to stop fighting; for him to stop looking at me like I took Santa Claus's virginity. I said the first thing that came to my mind.

'I thought I was going to marry him.'

He sighed heavily and turned away, still rubbing his fingers through his hair. Then he turned around. 'I'll take you home.'

Back home at my laptop, I realized that this was probably the run-up to Rejection Number Three. So I had managed to lose three men *and* a job in six months. I ran my finger aimlessly over the mouse pad for a few moments. And, then, as 'Hit Me with Your Best Shot' played in my head, I opened my inbox and hit reply—to Vyash's last email.

OK. Let's meet. You say?

And Thanks! ☺

That sounded cool yet warm, right? I added 'XO'.

Yup. That looked right. I sighed. If he hadn't left me in Goa, we wouldn't be in this position in the first place. I would have been checking out mehndi patterns. As things stood, I had no option. I'd have to tell my parents about losing my job. Or at least about not having one. I had no place to go for eight hours every day. And I had no energy to make up lies. The making out with the ex-boyfriend one had been a real fluke.

I had tried lying in school when I was a kid, but I'd end up saying really lame, hard-to-believe stuff like my mom had the TV on, watching some serial, so I couldn't concentrate on my homework. That'd blow up into the school calling my parents in and my mom coming in in her keds and cardigan and aggressive rowing-arm walk, all determined, to tell my teachers that they were good-for-nothings and they might as well 'dissipate' if they couldn't teach her daughter, and then she would be told that she shouldn't be putting on the TV during homework time and then she would get all wide-eyed and her chin would jut out really far and she would yell at me and call me 'husband-eater' and 'juvenile delinquent' all the way home. I was better off telling the truth.

28

THE OPPORTUNITY CAME THE next morning. Everyone was at the breakfast table doing normal things, and I took the plunge before I fixed my plate, because if it went very bad, then at least they would feel sorry for me later because I didn't eat.

'Mama–Papa, if I tell you something, you won't get angry with me?'

They both looked up, with that look in their eyes that said: Well, obviously we will—you've obviously done something very, very bad.

'They asked me to go . . . I mean . . . they fired me.' I looked at their horrified and worried faces and quickly added, 'They were downsizing!'

Time froze. Then it began to cool everything around it. My parents' faces began to turn blue-grey. Moisture droplets began to form and drip from everything around us. I opened my mouth to speak, but couldn't for the sudden chill around me.

Then, Papa spoke. His voice was perfectly modulated. 'I am very disappointed.' He looked old and tired. 'I will open some fixed deposits in case more funds are needed.'

My eyes filled with tears. Anything but this quiet acceptance. This feeling of responsibility my poor old Papa was going through. After all the stress I had caused with my not-happening wedding! Mummy was quietly sobbing into the kitchen towel, which she had used to wipe the counter with just a few minutes ago.

Sia stood up.

'Mummy, Papa . . .' She swallowed visibly and then squared her shoulders. 'I'm gay.'

My mother straightened up from her crying and began to twist the kitchen towel around her hands. She turned to my father and began to yell at him, 'Virji, it's all your fault. Fostering competition between my girls. Saying ambition, ambition, ambition all the time! Now, one has lost her job and is not married and has no future, and the other one goes around saying she's happy! They're not even there for each other!' she wailed loudly, clutching her chest.

Sia stared at her, her mouth wide open. She looked at me, in panic. But I honestly didn't know what to do. Rejoice because the attention was off me, or slap her upside the head for her outburst. And wait a second. *My sister is gay?!* When exactly did that happen? I looked at her closely. No manly dressing or haircut. No hot female cut-outs on her soft-board. In fact, my sister was glowing and well dressed. I had never seen her so happy either. But *Sia*? I had never seen the signs. Crap. Now, how was she going to survive? Just as I began to hope she would leave things as they were, she spoke.

'Mummy, I'm not happy. I'm a lesbian.'

In the silence, I heard my father's lowered voice on the phone, 'Harjeet, can you tell everyone I will be on leave today?'

He disconnected and we all sort of stood-sat around the dining table, staring at each other. My father kept looking at my mother, waiting for her to react. All our lives we had been our mother's 'department'. Dad was only called in when reinforcements were required. He would appear after a particularly bad argument between us and then say quietly, 'Listen to your mother.' And we would have to listen. And we did. It usually didn't go beyond that. Now, he looked lost. Obviously, dealing with lesbianism wasn't in the Punjabi father's handbook.

Papa then rang Pia. We were all still hanging around the dining table, not saying anything. Mummy had begun to wash the dishes, banging them around here and there. Papa was just looking down at his hands clasped on the table. Sia and I were looking at each other in despair. Neither of us had the courage to speak to each other in front of our parents and we didn't have it in us to leave the table either.

The kitchen door swung open and Pia walked in with Zara. She took a moment to look at all our faces and then handed Zara to Mummy and walked out. When she walked back in, she had a bottle of Pimm's with her. She put it on the table and then placed the fruit basket next to it. She handed knives to my father, Sia and me, and said, 'Peel.' As we began to peel and slice the fruit for the Pimm's cocktail in silence, Pia pulled out some potato chips and sausages and put them on to cook. No one dared question her as to why we were preparing for a cocktail party at eleven in the morning. She then turned to me and said, 'What happened, Rhea? How did you get yourself fired?'

You know those people who shield you when you're in trouble? Who stand up and take the bullet when it was you who deserves it? I am not one of those people. I snapped, 'Maybe we should take the heat off of me and my unmarried, embarrassing status, Pia! I'm not the lesbian in the room!'

'*Haye!* Lesbo!' my mother clutched Zara to her chest and looked skywards.

Pia gave me a dirty look. 'Maybe she's experimenting.'

'Experimenting lesbo! Yeh koi try *karne* ki *cheez hai*? It's not like a new flavour of ice-cream!' Mummy was now yelling. 'Trial *karni hi thi* toh you can go jeans-shopping, no, nose-cutter! What is this behaviour?! You mother-killer! Murderess! You killed your mother! You killed me! I hope you're happy!'

We had managed to pry the now-screaming-and-completely-bewildered Zara from my mother's arms before she was choked to death by her homophobic grip.

Poor Sia had tears running down her face, but what had possessed her to come clean in the first place? Couldn't she have stayed in her closet? Couldn't she have been Bubbles Auntie on the outside, Ellen DeGeneres on the inside? Honesty was overrated. Especially in our family. But now that Sia had stepped out, she was determined to come out all the way.

'I'm not experimenting, Mummy. I love her!'

'Her?? Who her?' my mother screamed, while Pia and I looked on open-mouthed.

'Sunny,' she said quietly.

I could feel the vibrations set off by all the pieces falling and locking into place. Sia's sudden change in personality, the fact that she and Sunny were still in touch, the late-night almost-conversation with me, the fact that she had stayed out of the Jay issue completely. My God. Well, there was certainly one pair of parents who were going to seriously question their own child-raising methods if Sunny was going to come out today as well. One kid, a kleptomaniac and general-user-of-people, the other, a lesbian—which I didn't really have a problem with as long as said lesbian's partner was not my little baby-sister. If Sunny had been a guy, we could have got some cousins to go beat her up. But what were we supposed to do now? Go and have a ponytail-pulling session? Bribe her tailor to sew butt-pads into her salwar?

'Her brother has stolen from us, you useless! How could you . . . How could you . . .?' Mummy shuddered. She couldn't bring herself to think what lesbos did. She knew it was bad and wrong, though, and that was enough. But what was really bothering her was the cards group. How on earth was she supposed to handle telling all her friends that her youngest daughter was a lesbo? Suddenly, my mother flew across the room and grabbed Sia by the hair. She began to hit her back and shoulders, all the while crying that she had brought shame on the family, that she had been exposed to too much MTV, that she, herself, was too modern a mother and that's why she had raised such a good-for-nothing lesbo. Sia was screaming and crying, asking for her to stop, and Zara began crying too. Pia ran to pick Zara up and I was stuck. I wanted to go help Sia, but what if my mother turned on me?

'Naina. Stop!' It was my father. Standing up to his full height, he repeated, 'Stop right now.'

My mother froze, her hand still raised.

'Virji . . .?' my mother's voice was shaking.

'Sia, go upstairs,' he said quietly. Sia left, sobbing.

'Rhea, Pia, sit down.'

We sat.

'Naina, wash your face and come back and sit down.'

While we waited for Mom to come back, Papa poured us half a glass of Pimm's cocktail each, diluted it with more Limca, and served us chips and sausages. He then took a plate and glass up for Sia. Sia's glass was 10 per cent Pimm's cocktail and 90 per cent Limca. He was gone about fifteen minutes, and by the time he had come back, my mother was at the table, twisting her dupatta between her hands.

'Children, and my wife,' he said. 'We have a crisis on our hands. But Sia is our child, and however bad she is, we have to accept her. OK?'

Silence.

'NAINA! OK?'

'*Lau* ji, ok,' my mother responded sullenly.

He looked at my mother and his face softened. 'Good girl, Cocoji.'

'As for you,' he began, turning to me.

My sister had just come out. You would think they had worse things to worry about than the fact that I had lost my job.

'I expect to see your résumé up on every job site, Rhea. No daughter of mine will while away her time at home. OK?'

'Yes, Papa,' I mumbled. Perhaps today was not the time to tell them that I had outraged the modesty of my latest—and only—marriage prospect and, so, he wouldn't be marrying the out-of-caste-rapist A.K.A me.

'Everybody, please disperse.' He took his glass and the remainder of the jug of Pimm's with him into the study.

Mummy glared at us, cursed us in Punjabi, cursed her womb for producing us and then went into the living room. Pia and I waited till she was gone, then took the remaining food and

went up to Sia. Before we entered her room, we managed
to steal some beer from the fridge in my parents' room. We
weren't drunkards. We just needed some strength to deal with
the tribulations life had put in front of us. And since there was
no Pimm's, beer it would have to be.

We knocked. No reply. We barged in to find Sia sobbing
into the phone. It was obviously Sunny. Poor Sia. She looked
exactly the way I had seen Tish or Pia or any of my friends look
in the middle of a fight with their boyfriends.

'OK, I'll call you later,' Sia hastily ended the call and then
stood, looking at us defensively, her chin thrust out, her fists
clenched—just like she used to when she was a little kid. Pia
and I looked at her, then at each other, and cracked up.

'What're you two laughing at?' Sia said angrily.

'You!' we said and dissolved into giggles again.

'Seriously. Could you have chosen a worse time to come
out? I mean, *seriously*? If you had kept quiet, we all could have
enjoyed Rhea getting bamboo-ed, no!' Pia was grinning. 'And,
why gay, ya? Couldn't you just be a drunkard or something? At
least that way we could say you got it from Dad.'

Sia began to laugh.

'Though,' Pia said, 'I have to admit, Sunny's pretty hot.'

We opened up the beers and sat around drinking and
chatting. Sia said she had known since she was eleven that she
was attracted to women. That explained a lot actually. And,
hey, it struck me as perfect that I had a gay sister. I could ask
all the questions I had ever wanted to.

'Are you going to look like a boy now?' I asked.

'Well, that depends,' Sia said, 'now that you're unemployed,
are you going to look like a cow now?'

'OK, but now you don't like any men?'

Sia shrugged.

'It's not like that. It's not like I hate men or that I want to be around only women or anything like that. It's just that when I'm with Sunny, I'm happy. And I feel really sexy and pretty and I feel like dressing up for her, even if she doesn't notice. And when I know I'm going to meet her, I feel really excited. Like I can't wait for it. You know? It's not that I hate men. It's that I love Sunny.'

This coming from a kid who used to poop on her shoes.

We raised our beer bottles, clinked, and drank till we drowned out the sounds of our parents arguing.

29

Ten days. Ten days of being holed up in our bedrooms, while war raged below. Mummy was livid with Sia. She was cool about a lot of things. When I was in college, my friends would come over and Mummy would make them pakoras and listen to their problems. Tish has even had long conversations with her on sex. She once called up a friend's ex-boyfriend pretending to be the college principal and threatened to expel him if he didn't stop bothering my friend. But to have a daughter who was a 'lesbo' was, to my mother, something heinous and unacceptable. She had even gone and researched them on the net and all she saw were bald ladies with piercings, and she was not prepared to accept a daughter who went around looking like 'those punks'. She had confiscated all scissors, hair spray and hair colour from our rooms and none of Sia's trousers had yet come back from the wash.

While surfing the net, mom had come across some lesbian porn too. That wasn't a good day for us. We had heard her alternate between praying loudly and crying. She was of the borderline-witch-doctor variety. When we were younger, she'd sprinkle us with silver water to chase out distractions from our minds, so we would study well. Sometimes, she would randomly sneak up on us and snip some hair off our heads and soak it in milk and saffron and crap. Despite all this, I should have reminded her: Pia had a girl child, I was unmarried and unemployed, and Sia was gay. But now was not the time. Now was the time to wait till she was bathing to sneak into the kitchen for chips and chocolate.

Vyash and I had been emailing. It was cute. He was busy with work and stuff, but he missed me and said he often thought of me in that 'frilly dress' I'd been wearing the last time we met. He said I was the sexiest, sweetest girl he had ever met. Sexiest. Sweetest. That meant, sweeter, sexier than Gina. We had a phone date this evening. Maybe I would be getting married after all!

Speaking of which, Mazher had called, too. Right in the middle of Mummy's speech about how society hates lesbos.

'They stone them to death.'

'No, Mummy, that's adulterers in Arabic countries.'

'You shut up, you moral-less child! You young things think everything is OK! There are no rules! You children became worse and worse with every pregnancy of mine! Pia got married. OK. Then this Rhea—no marriage, but at least she was working and doing correct things. And you! My last child didn't even inherit 5 per cent morals from us! Next, you'll be wearing suit-tie and asking to get married to the robber's sister!'

'Don't call her that, Mummy!'

'YOU HAVE CALLED ME A SINNER'S MOTHER! I WILL CALL WHOEVER, WHATEVER! GET OUT! GET OUT!'

Tringggg!

'Umm, Rhea? Can we talk?'

'Umm, no, Mazher, this is a bad time.'

'I'm sorry, Rhea . . .'

Meanwhile, Mummy hollered in the background. 'SPOILING YOUR BODY! SPOILING IT FOR SOME FAD! GET OUT, YOU BLACK SPOT!!'

'Mazher, I'll call you back.'

It was like a scene out of a 1980s farce where everyone ends up slipping around in whipped cream or throwing salami slices in each other's faces or something.

I didn't know whether I should call him back. I mean, was I really horny or something? I had no one, really, to compare to, but, I figured, if you discovered sex at thirty, it was all right to be a bit overexcited. Did he find me off-putting or desperate? I didn't want to stop him. I wanted more. And did he really expect me to be a virgin at thirty?

The answer was: Yes. He expected me to be an absolute, shocked virgin. I should have waited. I should have waited till I was married. But didn't guys want to have sex with you before they figured whether they wanted to marry you or not? I kept getting conflicting reports. Pia still hadn't opened up. Tish didn't count—she claimed to have slept with everyone, including the sociology lecturer in college, who really smelled, but whom everyone found really sexy for some reason. She said it didn't matter once you were into it and all the juices were flowing, anyway.

The last time I checked, women were supposed to enjoy sex. And he was the one who couldn't control himself. Not me. What was I supposed to do? Hit the brakes mid-orgasm and ask him to stop so we could kneel together and say a prayer? Maybe he was just scared. Things were moving too fast. I called him back.

'Hey, you!' His voice was smiling in the way it did when I called him at work. 'I'm so happy you called.'

'Yeah. Me too,' I said, feeling pretty good to be talking to him, thinking of the way his hair curled over his phone, so it looked as though his hand had disappeared into his hair.

'Can I pick you up for a movie?' he asked. *Another* movie? Movies and dinner and chatting were about all we seemed to do. He had mentioned he didn't like partying, but a road trip or a pub would have been nice. Anyway, he was asking me out, and that was a good sign. I liked hanging out with Mazher. We never ran out of conversation. Sometimes, we'd just sing Elvis songs to each other. He was really caring and gentlemanly. He'd always pay, and, last time, he had run out of the car without his sweater on to get me ice-cream, and it was eight degrees. And his sweater? It was tucked around me.

I had a sudden vision of our lives together. It involved a lot of prayer and virtuous work. Maybe weekends at an orphanage. Which was all very moralistic and good. A year ago, this would have been really appealing. I would have happily thrown in some fund-raising and Christmas parties for poor children. But then, Jay had come along. And I had really enjoyed the partying and the dancing and the eating out. I was thirty-and-a-half. If I maintained my weight and kept gymming, there was a strong possibility I'd live another forty years or so. Did I really think I could live that long or longer with a man who believed I was a virgin and whose idea of a wild night was ordering in ice-cream? It was a lot to think about. I figured I would go for the movie and then see.

Besides, I had been so low these last days. I had spent a lot of time just sleeping and reliving the hurt and embarrassment of being fired. I needed an outing. Something not too stressful, but feel-good variety.

I wore a skirt and a sweater-top and blow-dried my hair nicely. I met my mother on my way out.

'Yes?' she said, sweeping her eyes up and down my outfit.

'Movie? Mazher?' I said, assuming a swagger I did not feel.

'Hmm,' she said, turning away.

I ran outside and, when I saw him, I gasped. Mazher was leaning against his car, his arms folded, smiling that movie-star smile at me, looking breathtakingly hot as he had that way of looking. He nodded towards the car. 'We go?'

'We go,' I breathed.

30

I T LOOKED LIKE MY sister-of-lesbian ban was finally over. I was meeting Vyash today, under the pretext of going for an interview. No one knew he was back in my life yet. He had taken the afternoon off work and was taking me to The Banyan Grill. I didn't even know if I was doing the right thing by continuing to hang out with Vyash any more.

Last night, Mazher had chosen seats up front and centre of the dress circle, so we weren't tempted to 'do anything wrong'—which would have been OK provided the movie had been more exciting. But it was like being dipped in a large tub of sweetness and light, or watching a hundred fairies rise up and shower gifts on little naked urchins. Sweet. But hardly anything to set one's thighs squeezing.

And then there was the fact that I seemed to have a choice between two men. Which was a lot more man than I'd had in a long time. Of course, I would choose Vyash if he asked. Provided I could get over the fact that he had left me all alone in Goa. Mazher wouldn't do that to me. Mazher was reliable. He was safe. He was so safe, I might even 'grow a new hymen which even a cement-breaker couldn't break', as Bubbles Auntie was fond of saying. Or, end up having sex exactly twice in my life: once, to have the first baby, and then to have the second. I sat down heavily in front of the mirror, looked at my done-up face in the mirror and sighed so gustily, the photographs stuck on my mirror fluttered. I was confused again. Pammi Auntieji had sent across a small box of dried fruit with hearts on the cover, so obviously she still expected it to work out between Mazher and me. My parents hadn't said anything, but considering Sia wanted to marry a woman, I think my parents would be relieved to just see me choose a man—regardless of colour, height, nationality and religion. My mother had yelled at me during one of her rants, 'Bhai, even a Afreekan would do!'

I wonder what she would say about Vyash being back in my life. She didn't know the details my sisters did. She would probably prefer me marrying him to a 'cultured Musallman'. I glanced at the watch. It was already two hours past the time Vyash had promised to pick me up, which meant he should be here soon. I finished getting ready for our lunch at The Banyan Grill.

'So, have you met anyone yet? For an actual job, I mean,' Vyash said with a cute, tentative grin.

'Ummm . . . Not really.' I twirled my hair around my finger, quickly checking if I was showing cleavage in the alluring-not-slutty range. 'I thought, I'd, you know, take a break, do some cooking classes.'

I laughed nervously. Vyash's face seemed to have fallen a bit.

'Baby-making time, I guess?'

What was I feeling so self-conscious about for God's sake? I had met him because we both wanted to get married. Was I supposed to pretend I was a hard-nosed career woman, now? What was it with men wanting women to not seem interested in marriage? He sparkled his sparkly eyes at me, restoring my sense of well-being.

'So baby-making means no money-making?'

'Uh . . . I mean . . .'

Now, what? Admit that, yes, I expected to be taken care of for the next five years at least? That I was so done working? That deep down, I felt that I had wasted so much time working that I hadn't had the time to meet the right man? And what if Vyash wanted a working wife? Man! Men were so hard to read!

'I . . . er . . .'

He laughed.

'Easy, Kanwar,' he said, his voice low and husky. 'Blush a little more and I won't be able to keep my hands off of you.'

I choked on my rice wine a little bit. The shit tasted like neat vodka and I don't know why I was drinking it. I much preferred the sweet, cinnamon tea they gave at the end of the meal. But Vyash had called it by its full name—something sexy and Korean-sounding—and I couldn't appear gauche. After all, I had lived a lot of life in the five months since we had been broken up. I watched him sneakily over the rim of my glass. Vyash was sophisticated, mature and sexy. I shivered a little at the one-second reel of our night in Goa that played at that thought. Could I see myself married to him? Yes, if I could get past his constant brooding over Gina, and the suspicion I had of this other side to him that there obviously was. He had left me all alone in Goa to fend for myself. What if we had a really big fight? Did he have severe anger-management issues?

OK, so meeting these guys was obviously not helping.

Maybe I would find my answer if I didn't meet them for a while. Like, maybe, a week.

The solution came when I spoke to Tish. Arf was going to vipassana—a ten-day meditation programme, during which we would be expected to take a vow of silence. Tish wanted to go, too, and said she'd go if I did. Hell, of course I'd go. Right now, I'd go to bloody Mumbai and hang around the suburbs with my gross cousins if I had to. I said I'd go if she'd go and then we both told Arf that we were going, and he tried to dissuade us from coming along, telling us that we'd have to give up our phones, books, everything. And we wouldn't be allowed to talk to each other, either.

'So, what?' Tish said, throwing a bottle of perfume and a tube of lipstick into her bag. 'We'll hide, na? Stick-in-the-bum Arf doesn't need to know what you and I are up to for ten days. Plus, as if he's getting nirvana tomorrow, the dead fish!'

Dead fish?

'What are you on about, Tish? Why you insulting Arf so much?'

'Never you mind, Miss Lights Off!' she said darkly. 'If you had half a brain, we wouldn't be in this damn situation, anyway!'

'What situation, dude? Do you not realize what I'm going through?'

'Oh, big deal, your sister's gay! My kid looks like Groucho Marx. Shit happens. Go and pack. We have to be there by bloody one o' clock tomorrow. Some crappy silence vow needs to be taken also. Hurrry!'

31

THE DHAMMA SOTA WAS gorgeous.

Arf had been strangely silent all the way to the centre. Tish had said he was introspecting and preparing for the course. And, she had added, the dead duck never spoke when he was supposed to anyway. That had broken through Arf's facade for a moment, and he unglued his eyes from the view to give us both a dirty look. Then he looked at Tish and asked her to take off her silver necklaces. 'Couldn't you at least try and be a little more in touch with yourself, Tish?'

Tish stuck out her tongue at him. 'If I do, then no one will want to get in touch with me.'

I cracked up, but Arf looked stunned for a moment. Then his lips twitched and he went back to looking out of the window. Tish had spent the rest of the train journey bitching about K, and telling me how relaxed she felt now that she didn't have two babies yanking at her top all the time.

But when we arrived, even Tish had to shut up for a moment. A glorious white pagoda stood in front of us, surrounded by thick green grass and a well-tended driveway. Although people were milling about filling forms and looking for their rooms, it felt as if, for a few moments, life was completely still, completely centred around me. For the first time since that horrible SMS from Pia about my parents putting my profile on shaadi.com, I began to feel that all my worries were really far away. My friends were with me. Arf had already picked up our bags, my medium-sized one and Tish's huge magenta suitcase with stickers on it, and begun to walk towards the pagoda, his back straight, his strides long and strong. I smiled at him looking so purposeful. The man-child—more man than child nowadays—had sides to him I never knew.

'Come on, my love!' Tish put her arm through mine and began to walk me jauntily up to the desk, all the while outlining the plan. We were to tell the authorities we didn't know each other, so they'd put us in the same room. If we weren't in the same room, Tish explained, either she would find a way to exchange with someone, or fake extreme illness and go home. 'I'm not bloody meditating for nine hours!' she whispered furiously.

'Then why have we come, Tish? We could have easily done Goa!' I hissed.

'Shhh, idiot-fool!' she snapped. 'I had a reason . . . er . . . you need to heal!'

Before I could answer she had steered me to the registration desk and started convincing the woman in white with the shaven head why we should be given a room together in a centre that, for one, didn't have a double-room in the entire campus and, also, as a rule, didn't allow people to share.

'Do you promise you don't know each other?' she asked me.

'Promise, promise!' Tish said before I could answer.

'Promise you won't talk to each other?' she said, looking directly at me.

'Absolutely!' yelled Tish exuberantly. 'I'm so serious about Upasana!'

The woman cleared her throat. 'Vipassana, you mean?'

'Of course. Dr Gupta's bhakta, you see.' Tish triumphantly held aloft the book she had borrowed from Arf on the train.

'Dr Goenka,' the lady said sternly. 'I'll be doing *seva* on this *shivir*,' she told me. 'Please talk to me if you need anything—not to each other.'

'OK, OK, see you!' Tish yelled and then turned towards Arf. 'Oye! Arf! Room ten, OK?'

As she pulled me behind her towards our room, she told me, 'I brought biscuits, chocolates and . . .' she stopped to whisper, 'grass.'

'What?'

'Arré, for munchies,' she said as if she was talking to a three-year-old.

'Tish! I wasn't asking about the food—which, anyway, you're not supposed to bring. I'm talking about the weed. Drugs! You're not supposed to bring drugs here. If they find out, they'll . . .'

'What? Tell our parents? Call the cops? Chill, dude. Maximum, they'll send us home, then I'll say OK pay for our tickets. OK? Don't be so arse-tight.'

Tish didn't seem to be able to comprehend that we weren't here on holiday. She had insisted that I pack nice clothes, even buying me a pair of designer yoga pants and a small, travel-sized bottle of perfume. I had given up trying to convince her otherwise. Honestly, I didn't even know what I wanted from this trip. At the moment, it had seemed like exactly what I needed—time to get away from everything at home, from Mazher and Vyash, and to think about which of them I wanted to be with. Now, it seemed like the scariest thing I had ever decided to do in my life.

That evening, we took our vows in Pali—to not kill, lie or speak. I felt a bit guilty knowing that while I had no intention of killing anyone, I knew that Tish and I had plans to stay up chatting every night. And I already knew that her first topic of conversation was going to be a take-off on the recordings of Dr Goenka's voice.

Orientation ended by nine. I had seen Arf in the audiovisual hall, his back straight, his face quiet and contemplative. I thought of his sparse room in Delhi: a gorgeous red bedspread, a stained-glass lamp, an immaculately maintained antique desk and chair. Everything so tastefully chosen, yet so simple and basic. He was a strange fish, that man—that sweet, safe friend of mine. I caught myself staring at the contours of his chest through his thin sweater, the planes of his throat, his mouth. I really hoped this course would knock the frustrated sex-maniac out of me. I was now attracted to my best friend, someone I had mostly thought of as a really quiet woman, until recently.

After orientation, there was another hour of meditation, and finally Tish and I were lying in our beds, side by side. There was a lot we could have said. But somehow we didn't speak. After a while, I turned to look at her and saw that she was deeply asleep, her round cheeks flushed like a child's, one hand under her head. I smiled. She was one of a kind, Tish. I don't think hearts come in that big a size any more.

I woke up to Tish cursing. It was four o' clock in the

morning and we were expected to show up at meditation at five. 'Fucking useless fucks!' Tish muttered. 'Came here so that I could get fucking two proper nights' sleep—but, no! Bloody shits!' she kept swearing as she puttered around matching her clothes for today, choosing which perfume she was going to use and coordinating her jewellery. I ran in to use the loo before she set up camp there.

Vipassana was hard work. Anyone who thought they could get away with a free holiday was mistaken. The Dhamma Sevikas came around checking the rooms to see if anyone was bunking, and the assistant teachers kept a constant watch for anyone who didn't have their eyes closed. We got an hour every afternoon to exercise or wash clothes or sleep or whatever. That first day, I used it to walk down to the tiny wooden pagoda tucked off the walking path. I sat there on a wooden bench for about ten minutes, enjoying the still-cool weather, listening to the birds call. Then, I sensed a presence. I turned slightly and was surprised to see Tish on another bench, looking off into the mini-forest. Then Arf joined us, not making eye contact, but smiling very slightly. We could have spoken, but we didn't. We just sat there together, really quiet, till the hour was up and we heard the bell go, and then walked back to the hall. It became our ritual for all of the ten days we were there and, strangely, we never broke our silence, not even once.

I began to search for Arf in the audiovisual hall in the evenings. I would feel frantic, until suddenly, I would know he was in the room, wearing a grey sweater or a dull-green one, black trackpants or navy-blue, his earring glinting with the reflection of the TV, his eyes looking hazel in the strange light. I don't know why I felt like slipping my hand under his during the sessions. It was weird to feel so close to someone, even though we hadn't spoken, or couldn't.

Arf had been to vipassana before, so he wasn't allowed dinner. New students like Tish and me got a plate of puffed rice and a glass of lime juice in the evening. We were having a really hard time with that. Tish and I couldn't sleep without dinner and we had run through her stock of snacks in two days. We were really trying to be good. We hadn't smoked the grass—Tish had decided not to, in case we got crazy munchies and had to eat cockroaches or something, and I was trying to speak to her as little as possible. But going to bed at nine, when the last we had eaten something substantial had been at noon, was proving to be a challenge neither of us was up for.

After the last session on the fourth day, we walked up to our room, steeling ourselves for more hunger-related headaches and a sleepless night. But when we reached our room, we saw four bananas lying by the door. OK, it wasn't a cloche protecting a steaming bowl of pasta or a burger or a steak, but in this sanitary environment of souls headed for eternal freedom from the banalities of life, it may well have been. We squealed in delight and took them in with us, making a sumptuous dinner of them.

Tish began to talk in her sleep: something about being sorry and how she was better now and would pay it all back. She had no memory of it in the morning. I tried talking to her as she slept, but she didn't seem to hear me. One night, she screamed. I woke up, petrified, then turned furious. Tish was fast asleep, mumbling about stupid people. I was really tempted to slap her, but I was scared to wake her up, because you know what they say about waking up sleepwalkers and I figured that sleep-talkers operated on the same concept. So, to take revenge, I went to the loo and emptied her shampoo into the toilet. I knew that she would just start using mine. But I still felt happy, anyway.

One thing I learnt at vipassana was to be achingly aware of the time. The number of times I opened my eyes to look at my watch during the long meditations was not funny. The worst was when, thinking I'd been focused for really long and feeling that I deserved a break, I would open my eyes to check the time, only to find that all of four minutes had passed since the last time I checked. The other thing vipassana taught me was to be completely aware of what day of the week it is. You know those times when you feel like it's a Friday and it's really a Thursday? That never happens at vipassana.

By the seventh day, I had begun to dream these really weird dreams about Arf. Obviously, I wasn't going to tell Tish about them, even though we had given up all pretence of keeping quiet and had begun to chat whenever we had a chance to be alone. It was probably some crazy behaviour that was coming up because of all the meditation. I had read somewhere that vipassana brings up some unexpected experiences in order to get them out of your system. My attraction to Arf was probably some weird Freudian quirk, like how some girls dream of having sex with their fathers and things. The bananas were still showing up at our door, so Tish figured it was some guy who had a crush on her who would probably come speak to her on the last day, when we'd be officially allowed to speak to each other. I couldn't wait for that day. I had had enough peace of mind, and now longed for the craziness of home and my sisters.

On the day before we were to break our vow of silence, Arf came to the pagoda and placed a red leaf by my hand. I smiled and picked it up and looked at it more closely. I gasped. In the light of the sun, it looked like a jewel, veins of purple and yellow and green glinting in the red. I don't know why, I slipped it into my pocket, assuming that he had given Tish one as well. I had actually made it through almost nine days of meditation, waking up at 4 a.m., and eating only two bananas, some puffed rice and a glass of lime juice for dinner. I felt unbelievably proud of myself, and my friends. But I was pretty sure that the next time we had a chance to get away together like this, I would be choosing the destination. I smiled to myself. I would miss looking at Arf so serious and meditative every day. Vipassana Arf was vulnerable and deep. Normal Arf was always saying things to me that I couldn't handle.

Our final meditation was on universal love and friendship. I let my mind wander, thinking about getting back home and wondering what things would be like there. Vipassana had been a real break in that sense. Surprisingly, I hadn't thought about Vyash or Mazher even once. I had thought of Arf a lot. And Sia and her love for Sunny. She kept saying she had fallen in love with her best friend, and that Sunny made her feel happy and like everything would be OK. Funnily, Pia said the same thing about Ant, when she wasn't accusing him of having an affair. I wondered if I had that with someone. I let myself fantasize that Arf was that someone. I visualized our lives together, full of good-natured name-calling and loud singing and watching movies—just this warm, peaceful, happy feeling all the time.

Suddenly, Tish, sitting behind me, began to cry loudly. Great, big, screaming sobs in between gusty intakes of air. I turned to look, but one of the Sevikas gestured to me to turn back. I couldn't see what was happening, but I could hear her

sob loudly about forgiveness and being sorry and how she had
seen the light. I decided that I wasn't going to ask her. We had
spent ten days together. Whatever issues hadn't been revealed
in these ten days were better off remaining unknown. I turned
my thoughts to the freedom we would have in just a few hours.
I couldn't wait to see Arf, look into his eyes and have him smile
his lazy, half-unsure smile at me. Soon, we would be on a train
back home together, and I would be able to talk to him, hear
his voice after so long. It was going to be a good day indeed.

I saw him as soon as he came out of his room, dangling his
knapsack by a strap. He stopped for a second, just outside the
door, looked up to the sun, inhaled and then straightened, his
eyes searching. They found me and he smiled. The most heart-
melting, tender smile I had ever seen. I smiled back and we
stood there for a moment, smiling at each other.

Suddenly, a streak of orange and pink winged across my
peripheral vision and I heard Tish sob 'ARF!!' She ran into
his arms and stood there, sobbing into his chest. He held her,
calmly, patting her back, and led her, still sobbing, back to the
place where her bags were. He picked them up and, gesturing
to me to come along, got us into the waiting taxi to take us to
the station.

I sat in front and leaned my head against the door. I could
see Tish and Arf in the side-view mirror. They were talking
softly to each other, Arf leaning his head against hers, holding
her hand pressed to his chest. My chest felt all constricted, I
wanted that to be me. It was also a bit scary. Was something
about to happen? On the train, Tish leaned against Arf and
fell asleep, he left one arm around her and looked out of the
window the whole way. They looked like a couple deeply in

love. I looked out of the window, watching the stations whizz past in a blur. My world, as I knew it, was falling apart. And I still didn't know whom I should choose: Vyash or Mazher. It was beginning to feel like it depended on who would choose me.

32

TEN DAYS AT VIPASSANA had given me absolutely no clarity on either man, but I did know one thing for sure, though. Mazher would give me the flexibility to do exactly what I wanted after marriage, but Vyash clearly wanted me to work. I decided to call Mazher. My parents were going to be out tonight. They had finally stopped fighting and made enough peace to be able to go out to the club and some friends' houses a few times a week. No one was saying anything upfront to Sia, but she had begun to go to college and out some evenings. She spent a lot of time on the phone as well as on Skype with Sunny, and my dad seemed to have come around and accepted it. My mother, on the other hand, would keep saying things like her health was failing and that her god-man had said that it was because her youngest was a sinner.

I decided to call Mazher over. I couldn't take watching another movie, and he hated partying, and it honestly felt like there was no other option. I asked him to come straight to my room, which he was not too kicked about, but I promised him I wouldn't touch him. Yes. This is a sentence I never thought

I'd say. But I never thought my two best-friends—the married one with children and a 38-inch waist, and the newly incredibly sexy one—would fall in love. Or in lust, whatever the case might be. I went down to organize some snacks for Mazher. Maybe slapping everything together with cheese would help calm me down.

Mazher arrived just as I was laying out a plate of Monaco biscuits topped with cheese and some random olives I found in the fridge, and these baby puffs Zara likes to eat that are really yummy. He smiled, the muscles in his throat flexing, drawing my attention to his collarbone.

Upstairs, he sat in the chair, while I sat cross-legged on my bed. We chatted about movies and music, and our childhoods. Mazher had been a shy child, completely in his brother's shadow. That had changed when he had got into athletics and become the class hero, finally ending up as the school captain. He got this really cute expression on his face when he talked about his friends from school. They were all still in touch, meeting almost every weekend, even though some of them had babies, there were still getting together to go to their school's founders' day, and then, he told me, they'd all get totally trashed and climb the school wall late at night, salute the clock tower and sing the school song as loudly as they could. Suddenly, he stood up, saluted and proceeded to sing the entire school-song, marching up and down my room during the chorus, till I collapsed on the bed, giggling.

He laughed and sat down on the bed next to me. 'Tell me about your schooldays,' he said, his face all earnest, flushed pink with laughing.

I told him about Tish, and our gang in school, and how we

used to get together on weekends and dress up in our parents' clothes, put on make-up and take pictures, and our cycling adventures, and the time Tish gave me my first sex talk. We had slipped into a really comfortable position on the bed—me, propped up against the headboard, knees bent, and him with his head on the pillow, looking up at me, his hand on my stomach. At some point he had slipped his hand under my T-shirt, his fingers warm against my belly, moving lightly across my belly button and above.

I kept talking as his hand cruised up to my breast, palming it. I shifted a bit, so he could get better access, and continued to talk, telling him about Slime and how we'd been together so long and how it all seemed so far away now. His hand stilled.

'What's wrong?'

He sat up, looking perturbed.

'What, Muzz?'

'Did you do . . . stuff . . . with him, too?'

'Stuff? You mean, did we make out?'

He nodded.

'Yeah . . . I guess . . . we were kids . . . I . . .'

'That's pretty sick, Rhea.'

'Mazher, it was years ago! How was I supposed to know . . . I mean . . . I thought I was going to marry him.'

His expression softened slightly.

I leaned forward, taking his tortured face in my hand. 'I'm with you now, right?'

I leaned forward to kiss him; taking his other hand, I slipped it under my T-shirt again. We kissed softly for a moment and then he tightened his arms around me. His breathing got heavier as he struggled with my bra hooks. As my bra came undone and slipped down my arms, he pulled away and moaned. Then, yanking off my T-shirt in desperation, he looked at me for a long moment and moaned again.

'Oh baby,' he said, before practically jumping on me. He attacked me with his mouth, biting and sucking, pushing his penis into me. He made this really frustrated sound and then pulled off his pants and underwear and fell on me again, trying to pull my pants off while his hips ground into me at the same time.

Suddenly, he grunted and said, 'Shit!' He jerked away from me, scrambling for his shirt.

'What are you doing?!' he yelled.

I flinched. I had never seen him so angry.

'Wha . . .?'

He was standing now, buttoning his shirt. He grabbed my T-shirt and threw it at me. 'You've done this before! You've done this with other men! You're loose!'

Something snapped inside me. I pulled on my T-shirt angrily. 'You started it!'

'You knew it was going to happen! You called me here when no one else was here.'

'So, why did you come, then? I told you I was home alone—you could have said no.'

'I'm a man. I have needs. You should be in control of this!'

I stared at him, my mouth open, waiting for all the venomous things I had to say in retaliation, but I was too incredulous for anything to actually come out. But as I looked at him, this gorgeous man furiously buckling his belt, it hit me that no matter what I said, it wasn't going to change the way he thought. A calm came over me. My mind stilled in a way it never had at vipassana.

'Get out,' I said.

He stopped dressing and looked at me. 'What makes you think I was going to stay?'

'No! I mean get out! For real! For good! And don't come back, you psycho! I'm calling Pammi Auntie and telling her I don't want to marry you! And,'—I added, as he opened his mouth and drew in a breath to speak—'if you say one more word, I will tell her that you're a no-good, pre-civilization Neanderthal, who can never make any woman happy, because you can't respect her in the first place! So, get the fuck out of my house right now, or I'll make sure you never get married to anyone!'

He stared at me for a long moment and then picked up his shoes and left without another word. I remained frozen in place till I heard his tires screech as he aggressively backed his car out of my driveway. And, then—for some reason I couldn't understand—quietly and methodically, I began cleaning my room.

I placed my old wastepaper basket in the middle of the floor and systematically chucked old make-up, single earrings that I had lost the pair of, broken pendants, deodorant cans with just enough for one spray left in them, comic books with their covers torn off . . . I spared nothing. An hour later, Sia came in with a tray and two large bowls of ice-cream, chopped bananas and a packet of fun-size Mars bars my mother had been saving for important guests. She sat on the bed and watched me clean, while she ate. A few minutes later, I picked up the other bowl and began to make my way through it. A few minutes after that, I put my bowl down, laid my head in my baby sister's lap and cried till I fell asleep.

33

THIS TIME AROUND, I wasn't going to take Pammi Auntie's nonsense about being desperate and taking anything that came my way. This time around, *I* was going to tell *her* what I wanted. I had thrown a man out of my house, made my own way back home from Goa, watched my best friends get together, even though one of them was a mother, and survived ten days of non-stop meditation. I had seen enough of life to not let people push me around. I was a bona fide badass. I straightened up as I walked up to Pammi Auntie's apartment behind Mummy, already forming what I was going to tell her in my head. As we entered, I heard Pammy Auntieji exclaim, 'Ah! Here she is!' Whom was she talking to? *The dog?*

I found out a second later. Sitting in Pammi Auntieji's profusion of flowered upholstery was a man about my age, cute in a skinny, nerdy way. He stood up and smiled this self-conscious smile.

'This is the beautiful Rhea! And her beautifuller Mummyji!' said Pammi Auntieji cheerfully. 'Sorry, ladies, but this is a serendipitous indeed occasion. Sid here is looking for a bride—caste, looks, size, height, colouring, complexion, cooking, earning NO BAR! And I thought, who better than our beautiful Rhea beti who has none of those things!'

Before I could react to that, she had plumped a flowery cushion, pushed my mother into its accompanying armchair, gestured that I sit next to Sid, and disappeared into the kitchen. Sid and I made eye contact and spontaneously giggled a bit.

'Don't believe her,' he said, his voice an unexpected baritone, 'you have all of those things, and more.'

I smiled.

'Actually, we weren't expecting to meet anyone today . . .' I said, hoping that my V-necked sweater, long skirt and boots with a bright-yellow scarf were enough to make an impression.

'Neither was I,' he whispered. 'But the old bat seems to have done a number on us, hasn't she?'

He had an American accent, which I had to admit was very sexy—even though it wasn't really fashionable to have an American accent any more. Plus, his eyes were blue. As he stood to help Pammy Auntieji with the tray, my mother pinched me and whispered, 'Is he Anglo??'

'Actually, Auntieji, I am,' said Sid, obviously amused. 'Half Norwegian-American, half Punjabi.' He said 'Punjabi' in the Punjabi way: 'Punjubby'. It was cute. 'I'm here on vacay, and thought it would be really nice to meet my soulmate.'

His eyes met mine and he smiled.

'You are vacant?' asked Mummy.

'He's come for a holiday, Mummy!'

'So, why don't you young people go see garden? Rhea beti, you know where it is.' Pammi Auntieji was back and shooing us out again.

I did the familiar journey round the back of the house to the little balcony that overlooked the garden and plonked on the swing. How many more times, Lord? I prayed silently.

'So, Rhea,' said Sid, pronouncing it *Ray-ah* in his unfashionable but sexy American accent, 'how's it going?'

I looked at him incredulously for a second and then cracked up. He looked upset for a moment and then grinned.

'Yeah, I get it, not the best opening line, it ain't. So,' he whispered, sitting next to me, 'why don't you tell me what it takes to impress a nice Indian girl?'

'How do you know I'm nice?' I said archly, flipping my hair a bit.

'Hey, what I do know, I'm just a stupid American dude, hanging out with a gorgeous Indian girl.'

'Half,' I said.

'You're half girl?'

'No,' I said, giggling, 'you're half American.'

'But only where it matters! You know, Indian men are too small for American condoms—they need to use Chinese ones. Just sayin'!' he said, raising his hands in the air, palms out. 'Just sayin', y'know.'

'Shaddup!' I swatted him.

'Wildcat.' He defended himself.

'Pervert!' I retorted.

'Have dinner with me. Make Pammi Auntieji happy.' He looked so earnest, his blue eyes wide behind his glasses. I liked the way he said; 'Pammi Auntie'—*Palmy antee gi* (as in Gigi). I smiled. Suddenly, things were looking a lot more hopeful.

'I'll think about it.'

'Don't think too long. I just might be Pammi Auntieji's

flagship product. You know, Amreekan boy and all that!'

'Not in Delhi. Here, everyone wants to go to our motherland, the UK,' I said, straight-faced. He cracked up at that.

'I like you, Rhea . . .?' he bopped his eyebrows.

'What?'

'You what. Rhea, what?'

I grinned. 'Rhea Your Majesty.'

'Ohhh I get it, you're royalty. All right, princess. We'll play it your way.' He jumped off the swing, knelt in front of me on one knee and swung his arm in an arc ending at his waist, 'Do me the honour of supping with me.'

'Well, when you ask that way . . .' I said, laughing, as he leapt up and began to do this weird chicken happy-dance. 'Oh, and by the way, people can see right into this balcony.' I laughed even harder as he turned his back to the 'audience' and shook his bum. How cute was this guy! I hadn't laughed this hard since Tish and I were in college and she was doing one of her impressions.

'Call me.' I smiled and swept out of the room. And couldn't stop smiling till we reached home.

Neither could my mother. She had already begun to plan two annual trips to America with my father. Sia, Mummy had decided with a dark look on her face, would stay right here, even though it would have been perfect for her to study in America, because God knows what else she would end up loving over there. Already she was behaving as if there were no limits! She even claimed that, if he wanted, she would be all right with a church wedding. She would even get the white frock stitched for me by her ladies' tailor.

When we got home, for some weird reason, I began to think about Tish and Arf. I wondered what they were up to. Were they a couple now? Tish had called a couple of times and I had told her about kicking Mazher out of my house. She acted as if she was expecting it. But that was Tish. She had always claimed to know me better than I knew myself. I was a bit hurt that she hadn't yet told me about Arf. And a bit jealous, too. But I figured that was because I just generally felt left out of the threesome. Tish and Arf had met through me. They had gotten along on sight. Arf wasn't great at getting along with women—he ended up making most of them hate him because he was so damn detached. But Tish saw something in him and he saw something in her, and she invited him to every snooty party at her house and he always mailed her his music and they smoked up together once in a while.

The funny thing was, Arf managed really well at Tish's parties. He was charming and chatty, and all the businessman-types would thump him on the back and Facebook him and set up golf games with him. Maybe Tish just brought out the best in him. Maybe they were meant to be. I don't know why that thought hurt so much. I shrugged it off. Chinky was planning some Mimosa Night at her place, so I supposed I would meet Tish there. And, maybe, she would spill the gory details after downing a few. Tish was unstoppable once she was nice and woozy.

My phone beeped. An SMS from a number I didn't recognize.

I hope Her Majesty has arrived safe at the castle. May I be so fortunate as to escort her to supper on Friday at sundown?

I smiled.

That was quick. We do not like cheese. Please reduce the copious lashings and arrive post haste. We do not sup past ten.

The phone beeped again.

Forsooth! The queen bestows favors and is kind and good! I shall have the carriage waiting at eight.

Since when did queens message in fake British accents? It was something to ponder about, while I checked Facebook on my phone. OK, so Chinky had confirmed mimosas at her house tomorrow night and everyone had accepted the invite except me and Freesia. So this was what not working was all about!—being available whenever your friends wanted to hang, mid-week mimosas, and all the time in the world to get your hair done. I accepted. And, then, not feeling silly at all, I put on my '90s mix and did my Michael Jackson moves all around the room.

34

THE NEXT DAY, I was at Chinky's place at 8 p.m. sharp. The others wouldn't be getting there for at least an hour or two, but I had nothing better to do and it was getting hard to hang around at home without a job or proposal in sight. Chinky answered the door in camouflage pyjamas and a black leather cap. She checked out my cleavage for a few seconds, then gave me a big smile.

'Come in, yaar!'

She had obviously been organizing stuff all morning. There was a pitcher of some violent-looking cocktail with a thick foliage of mint leaves on the dining table. She had done cheese-pineapple-cherry sticks sticking out of a pineapple shell—the cubes of all different sizes and suspicious shapes—and a serving plate full of kebabs. She looked around proudly. 'Cool, no? Champagne and orange juice are chilling.'

Within an hour, everyone had arrived. Everyone except Freesia. But that, as Tish informed us, was cool. Otherwise, whom would we bitch about? Saroj was, in her words, 'all ready to junky-funky!' When we asked her what that meant, she jiggled her eyebrows and said, 'Watch and see.' Tish arrived, looking all glow-y and breathless. Almost as if she were in love. I was dying to ask her about Arf, but a part of me didn't want to know.

And, then, squeaky-not-so-clean Freesia appeared—in a trench coat and the predictable baby-doll pyjamas underneath. 'Hey bitches!' she said, at a frequency that set a few dogs howling, raising an arm over her head and snapping her fingers. Where did she think we were spending the night, on a sitcom set?

According to tradition, girls' night had to begin with a movie. Chinky had downloaded *Jab Tak Hai Jaan* for the night. 'Oooh! Shah Rukh Khan!' Freesia clapped her hands together in glee. Chinky winked at me and rasped, 'Anushka Sharma. Bikini. File gets stuck at that scene. Repeats three times minimum. Happy birthday to Chinky!'

At Shah Rukh Khan's accident scene, Saroj began to sob, begging us to switch the film off because it was too sad. Tish got us to mix our third pitcher of virulent cocktail. By this time, we had no idea what we were drinking any more. It may have been one of the only two bad brands of gin we got in Delhi, but who knew? It was cloaked in an incompatible mixture of juices and buoyed with ice cubes, and, by now, we were eating ice-cream on pizza wedges and attempting to soothe Saroj, convince Chinky that no, she didn't need to rewind to the scene during which Anushka Sharma bursts out of the water in her underwear, Saroj that she would be fine as soon as Katrina Kaif came back.

Freesia was sitting on the exercycle, smoking a cigarette. She sat up suddenly, ash flying everywhere, 'Fuck this shit!'

'Eh?' Chinky was trying to get ash out of her cleavage.

'Fuck. This. Shit!' Freesia was now standing, her face bright-red, contrasting with her baby-blue satin shorts and frilly top. 'Let's get high.'

Saroj raised an eyebrow. 'What do you think we've being doing till now, fool? Drinking juice? This is bloody battery-acid!' she said, holding her glass high. 'Freakin' strrroong pegs!'

Freesia looked at her condescendingly. 'Listen, my sisters. There comes a time when alcohol is not enough.' She ran off and returned with her designer clutch. She reached in and pulled out a cosmetic pouch in leopard print. She unzipped it and retrieved a pale-pink satin pouch and, from it, a slim silver cigarette-case studded with diamantes.

'She's going to pull out a penis from there or what?' Chinky said sourly. But Freesia pulled out a cigarette with its top pinched and twisted.

'It's a happy ciggie!' shrieked Tish joyfully. She got down on her knees and bowed deep. 'I apologize for straying, my Lord Weed. I have seen the light. I have come back to thy fold. Light it! Quick!'

We shared the joint, then another, Tish leading us through the 'taxiing'—holding our breath till everyone had taken a deep drag and then exhaling in order of the joint being passed around. Tish and Freesia began to exchange knowing smiles. I felt nothing. Neither, apparently, did Saroj and Chinky. But my mouth was dry and I needed water. I stood to get some, but when I looked down at my feet, I saw something white and long wriggle. I screamed.

'Chinky! Worm!'

Chinky leaped on to all fours, staring at my feet. 'Show me!'

'Right there!' I pointed to the thing wriggling threateningly at my feet. 'Kill it, Chinks! Please!'

'Coming!!' she bellowed at my feet. She reached behind her and picked up a slipper and hit it hard. But it continued to wriggle. She hit it again, but it wouldn't die. She straightened, rearing up on her knees, her slipper held above her head in both hands and screamed loud and long from deep in her gut, bringing the slipper down with echoing force on the worm. She waited for a second, looking intently at all our faces, and then slowly raised the slipper. The worm moved.

Chinky screamed again and, lying on her stomach, began to repeatedly hit the creature, yelling loudly with each hit.

'Chinky!' Freesia yelled. 'You're killing Rhea's stole! Stop, I beg you!'

She was right. Chinky had been trying to murder a tassel on my stole. I found it hilarious and began to laugh. Chinky found it hilarious too and began to scream with laughter. In minutes, we were all screaming and laughing and clutching each other. But every time we calmed down, we would see Chinky, still smashing her slipper on my stole compulsively, laughing while she did it, and we would take off again.

My sides were beginning to ache with laughter, but no matter what I did, I couldn't stop. So I tried to think of the time my grandmother died to make myself stop. But, seriously, that was like the funniest thing ever. Imagine trying to think about your dead grandmother just so you could stop laughing. Her eyes were closed and covered with one-rupee coins. That was pretty hilarious. Hadn't God heard of inflation? Or maybe subsidies were available in heaven. Sure hope she had taken her ration card! I was breathless-laughing, and so were all the other girls. Freesia kept whacking Tish's boobs and yelling 'Booby-shake!' This was the funniest girls' night I had ever been a part of. I collapsed on the ground, far enough away from Freesia to keep my boobs safe, and picked up someone's cocktail glass. It was covered in condensation. I tried to lick it, so I could get some liquid in my mouth. Drinking made so much sense. Freesia's joint was such a waste. Maybe it was bad stuff.

I woke up a few hours later, because I couldn't breathe. I found Tish's arm flung over my face and Freesia's legs on my stomach. We all seemed to be sleeping on top of the other, like a pile of puppies. Only Chinky was awake, her eyes glued to the TV, as she played Anushka Sharma's bikini scene over and over. I stood up to go wash my face and get some water and Tish groaned and stretched. By the time I got back from the loo, Saroj was scrambling eggs at the stove, Tish was sitting at the dining table with a newspaper and coffee, and Freesia was groaning into a glass of orange juice. Chinky had popped some corn and plonked it on the table.

'At some point,' said Tish, 'we need to clean this pad.' We all nodded sagely.

'But first, we eat.' We finished the eggs, then Chinky brought out a whole brick of ice-cream we had forgotten to eat last night, and Freesia found a quart of rum we hadn't finished, and we poured it over the ice-cream and dug our spoons into the common bowl. 'Independent Woman' was playing on the radio, and we'd all take a moment to look up and yell 'I BOUGHT IT!' along with the song. Then, as the rum-drenched vanilla ice-cream began to loosen us up, Saroj asked the question everyone had been wondering about in their two seconds of sobriety since we had arrived at Chinky's. 'Freesia, tell about your pub *munda*.'

Freesia's face fell. She lit another cigarette and took a moody pull. 'We had sex.' She said it flat. No emotion, no inflection. There was a soft 'Oooohhh!' from one of us that trailed off when no one else joined in. Freesia let us watch her for a few minutes and then she put down her cigarette and shook her curls. 'He didn't want to marry me, or even date. He took me out for coffee once and we chatted. After that we hooked up a couple of times. That was it.'

'B-but arré! How come? I mean, didn't you ask him why?'

'Freesia, you're so stupid!'

We stared in shock at Tish, who had flung her spoon of ice-cream on the table, splattering bits of white everywhere.

'A man who picks you up in a bar is not looking for marriage. He wants to fuck you and leave you. He's probably married, with a fat wife and two stupid kids. Do you want to check?'

Freesia stared back, her jaw clenching and unclenching.

'Tish?' I put a hand on her arm. She flung my hand off her.

'I said, do you want to check?'

Freesia didn't reply.

'What's his name, Freesia?' Tish yanked Chinky's laptop towards herself. 'Give me his name!'

'Tish!' Chinky started towards Tish, but Freesia spoke. 'Aditya Mathur.'

'OK. Enough, Tish.' Chinky tried to pull the laptop away, but Freesia stopped her.

'Let her look, Chinky. She thinks she's so great because she's married. She thinks she knows everything. Go ahead. Find him on Facebook.'

'Fuck you.' Tish stood up, grabbed her bag and walked out.

Freesia spoke into the ironclad silence Tish had left behind.

'He's not married, you know.' Her face crumpled. 'That's what made it so bad. He didn't want me, anyway.'

Chinky came up to Freesia, picked her up and put her in her lap. Freesia cried into her chest like a little baby. It should have looked weird, our cropped-haired, lesbian friend, holding petite little Freesia in her arms, while Freesia nuzzled her face in Chinky's breasts. But it was the saddest thing, my two broken-hearted friends, illuminated by the half sunlight filtering through the beige curtains, holding on to each other. I looked around me and realized we were a roomful of broken hearts—even poor Tish, who had two men who loved her, but not enough for her to love herself. My eyes met Saroj's; silently we cleaned up, picked up our bags and left, hoping that we wouldn't see each other for at least a few months.

35

*M*ILADY, I DOTH DANCE *with curious achings of excitement. I despair that time doth passeth quite slowly.*

I couldn't help but laugh out loud. I had to say, there was something about Sid. Something I couldn't wait to see more of. He'd said eight, which, by Delhi standards, meant at least nine. So I curled my hair around strips of cloth and tied it in merry little bundles all over my head—I would let them down ten minutes before I left, so I'd have that just-out-of-bed look—and then settled down to waste more time on my laptop. I made sure I steered clear of all career sites. I wanted to get married. And *The Secret* claimed that if you wanted something, you had to prepare for it; you had to let nothing come in the way of your focus and your belief in it coming true. I had paid my dues. I had worked for six years, given it all I had, and maybe that's why I'd missed the marriage bus. But I wouldn't do that again.

My mind began to wander through my wedding, prettily done up in yellow and gold, flowers and sequins everywhere, winter sunshine creating spots of warmth on the grass, little kids running around . . . I was thirty, and turning thirty-one in a few months. I had four years to churn out two babies before my eggs got mouldy and I'd have to adopt some dark-skinned kid whom my mother would refer to as 'servant-baby' for the rest of my life. I sighed, my eyes flicking to the monitor where a large REGISTER FREE button was winking promisingly at me. There was a happy couple on the page, smiling at me. I bit my lower lip and decided. I had seen what Pammi Auntieji had to offer, I had met people through my parents' network, but maybe they were the wrong networks. I set about creating a profile on shaadi.com. Nobody had to know.

My phone beeped. Sid. He was . . . *here?* What?! What happened to Delhi Standard Time? Crap! And I had had so much planned. I was about to throw on a pair of jeans, when I realized that I didn't really have to give a damn. Sid was the fourth guy I'd met, so, obviously, my track record wasn't great. I decided to take my time.

The lady needs her time. Be so good as to while away some time, my good man.

I sent it, half expecting to be told to go fly a kite in a not-so-nice way. But a minute later I got a perfectly cheery response.

Certainly, my queen. I shall await thy entry soothing mine anxious heart. Mine eyes doth thirst for your visage.

A giggle burst out. Now I had no choice but to look stunning! I pulled out all the stops. It was a night that didn't just require make-up—it needed foundation! Half an hour later I looked drool-worthy, even if I say so myself. For once in my life, I hadn't turned the depression of being single and jobless into an excuse to eat everything in sight, including my mother's knick-knacks, and the weight had stayed off. In fact, on a good day, I would even say I was hot. On a normal day, I would say I had childbearing hips.

I skipped down the stairs in my version of 'Gangnam Style', the song blaring loudly in my brain. It was going to be a good night. I could hear my parents laughing in the kitchen—God knows how long it had been since I had heard that! I swung into the kitchen, one palm on the pillar, the other outstretched, and ended up giving Sid one resounding slap on the back. *Sid?* What was he doing in my kitchen. In my kitchen eating oily paratha with a fork. In my kitchen eating paratha and drinking whisky and chatting with my parents! My head felt simultaneously compressed and pulled in all directions till I felt like the screaming orange dude in that Edvard Munch painting.

'Er . . . hey, Sid.'

'Hey, hey, gorgeous!'

He stood and came over to me, kissing me on my cheek. I died. Then mumbled something about parents watching and tucked my hair self-consciously behind my ear. He turned to my parents.

'Mr and Mrs Kanwar,'—he pronounced it *Can War*, so cute!—'I just want to tell you that you have the most beautiful daughter in the world. And I can see where she gets it from.'

Papa grinned widely as if to say thank you, while Mummy looked like she was a moment away from flashing him in gratitude. Full frontal. I hurriedly waved goodbye to my parents and dragged Sid out the door.

'Easy, honey, do you have a room booked or something?' he said, laughing, his blonde-brown hair falling on his forehead. I smacked him, laughing.

'No, I just wanted you to stop charming my parents.'

'Jealous?'

'No, I just don't want them getting serious about you.'

'And if they do?' Suddenly he was staring intensely at me, voice dropped to a whisper. 'It doesn't scare me, you know. I make decisions fast.' Then he put his arm around my waist, pulling me to him and, bending me backwards, kissed me. Right there on my parents' front lawn. Thank God my sister was a lesbian. Because this was not going to be easy to explain to my folks. Especially with our neighbour Suraj Auntieji staring at me through her kitchen window, saucepan in one hand, paratha in another.

I pushed him away.

'Sid!! Not here! This is India . . .'

'Oh, phew! So the plane did drop me off at the right place. Two thousand dollars well spent!'

He looked like a naughty boy who'd just pulled off a prank—his cheeks flushed, his eyes shining, his grin wide and happy. I had to laugh. I grabbed him by the collar and pulled him towards the car.

'C'mon, you big oaf!'

He came along willingly, his hands up in front of his chest, flopped over like paws, panting, with his tongue hanging out, making puppy-dog noises.

Sid had to be the most fun person I'd ever met. He kept me in splits all through dinner—sushi, which I figured was completely low-calorie and safe to eat—drove me all the way to Nirula's for a hot-chocolate-fudge sundae, and then hatched this elaborate plan to drop me home and then climb into my balcony later at night. What can one do with a mad, romantic guy like that? He held my hand the whole evening, sometimes playing with my fingernails, sometimes just looking at it intensely.

'I like holding your hand, you know. It keeps me nice and warm and toasty. Your hand would be super-useful to me in the winters back home.'

He smiled at me and slipped my hand through the crook of his elbow, pressing it close to his body. Later, when we got to the car, he turned on the radio; old Hindi-film songs played softly, sadly in the cold night air. He hummed along, surprising me.

'How do you know these songs?'

He smiled at me. 'My father played them all the time. And I always felt that it was some of the most beautiful, most insightful poetry I'd ever heard.'

That was exactly the way I felt too. I nodded enthusiastically.

'*Yeh badan, yeh nigaahen . . .*'

'*Yeh meri amaanat hain . . .*' he finished, smiling broadly.

'My favourite too!'

We were both quiet for a moment, the sensuality of the lyrics suddenly embarrassingly obvious to both of us.

Before I knew it, we were parked outside my parents' garage. He looked at me sadly.

'I don't feel like letting you go,' he said, his eyes soft in the silver night lights.

'Me, neither.'

He smiled ruefully.

'So, in India, I don't get to kiss a girl I really, really like in public?'

'You wouldn't get to kiss your wife in public either,' I said to him, winking.

'But what if I thought she was the sexiest thing in the world and I was having trouble keeping my paws off of her?'

'Then,' I told him, 'you'd have to stay in bed all day. With the curtains drawn.'

I blew him a kiss before I burst out of the car and made a run for the front door, feeling a lightness I hadn't felt in years. 'Byeeee!' I yelled as I sprinted across the lawn. I felt like staying there and dancing under the stars. I couldn't explain it, but I just felt . . . *happy*. I sang to myself as I cleansed-toned-moisturized and combed out my hair. I changed into my softest flannel nightsuit and fell into bed with a smile on my face.

36

My phone tinged and I rolled over in bed to check the SMS. It was Sid.

The taste of thine sweet lips has kept me awake. I beseech thee, be mine. Come picnic with me at Lodhi Gardens today and shame nature with thy beauty.

OK. But you bring the food!

The phone tinged within two seconds.

I'd be honoured. See you at 12 sharp. Unless you want me to have a drink with your peeps again.

I felt wild and bohemian and exciting. No more lovingly de-crusted cheese sandwiches in hampers packed by me. This diva would be getting her smoked salmon fed to her on a cracker. I felt like dancing around in my towel the way Kajol did in *DDLJ*, but it looked pretty ridiculous even when she did it. So I just jumped up and down on my bed and started planning my outfit for the day and also my exit without my parents seeing. The barbed comments about not attending interviews or getting a job were beginning to come my way, and I really didn't want to deal with them.

How was my mother supposed to understand that over eight hours every day of working in the AC would dry my skin out and make me look old before my time? Aha! That reminded me—sunscreen. Even though it was still winter, experts said you needed sunscreen even at night.

My phone rang.

Arf? What the figgins was he doing calling me at . . . *10 a.m.?*

Jeez! Where had the time gone! It stopped ringing. Then began again.

'WHAT? *WHAT?*'

'Let me in.'

'What do you mean?'

'I mean open the door, so I can enter your bedroom.'

'It's open,' I said before I could stop myself, and in a second, the door burst open and Arf was standing there. I swallowed. He looked better than before, larger, somehow, and extremely sexy and *angry*.

'What are you doing, Rhea?'

'Ummm . . . Getting out of bed . . . uh . . . reading . . . uh, researching!' I said, drawing the blanket over my exposed legs. He looked as if he might laugh for a second, then his face darkened again.

'No, Rhea! What are doing with your life?'

Why was he yelling?

'Why are you yelling, Arf?'

He ran his hand through his hair in frustration.

'I'm not yelling, Rhea. You've turned yourself into this manic wannabe housewife. You're not doing anything about your career—which you used to be so good at. You're just obsessed with getting skinnier and skinnier and going to the parlour and . . . We used to make fun of those girls, Rhee. And, now, you're one of them!'

I was standing now, not caring that I was dressed in a heart-print flannel nightsuit.

'What's the big deal about being different, Arf?!' I yelled, trembling with fury. 'Those . . . those parlour girls are the ones that got married! What did I get? Bloody fired for being different! For having substance! Screw you and your fucking double-standards, Arf! We all know that men only want to marry helpless hot girls, who make them feel needed!!'

'I'm just telling you to be true to yourself, goddammit!' he yelled back. 'Be the person I knew and respected. Not this vacuous bimbo!'

'True to myself? True to myself?! What the fuck do you know anything about truth?! You and Tish and your . . . your . . . this *behaviour*! She's married, Arf! You're *disgusting*! Both of you!'

Everything I felt was in my face—my anger, my resentment, my disappointment, my jealousy. Arf had been the one pure thing in my life. The last good thing left. And, now, here he was in my room telling me how I had disappointed him.

He was still staring at me, his mouth half open. He started to say something and then stopped. He shook his head.

'Why do you have to feel that you can only be someone if you're married? Can't you see that you're already someone? Someone so fucking special . . . it . . .'

Were those tears in his eyes? He shrugged and turned away and walked out of my room, taking all my happy with him. I slumped back down on the bed. My mind was blank, yet there were so many thoughts racing around it. He hadn't denied his relationship with Tish. Should I just call her and ask her straight out? I was scared after the way she'd acted at Chinky's house. But then, this was Tish. My best friend, Tish. My first-period rescuer Tish. Of course, I could call her. Right? My finger hovered over the dial button. Wrong. Because I was in love with her boyfriend.

Stupid fuck Arf with his joint and his oh-I'm-so-in-tune-with-the-universe and his stupid gentle ways and the tender way he'd kissed me goodnight and his ridiculous always-being-there-for-me and his strong chest and V-shape and hazel eyes and all that I-love-you-just-the-way-you-are Archie-card nonsense.

What was I supposed to do now? Normally, I would call Tish. Or Arf. Guess those two weren't really going to be options this time! I felt like I'd been punched hard in the gut. So I did what I did best when confronted with a crisis situation. I avoided the matter.

I wore a pretty, filmy, flowered dress for the picnic, along with a wide-brimmed straw hat—just for the glam quotient. My mom says that if you're feeling low, dress up. You'll be high in no time. Trusting the outfit to do its job, I took a big shapeless powder-blue handbag and threw in some essentials. I was ready just moments before Sid sent me a warning message and then pulled into the driveway. I raced downstairs, barely waving at my parents and practically leapt from my front door, landing breathless in the front seat, one hand on the brim of my hat, trying to fit it inside the car. Sid did this purring thing and said, 'Nice moves, Catwoman! Plus you got Batman's new space missile on your head. I feel so secure now! Nobody can touch me.' He had a hand flopped on his chest, fingertips splayed. He looked so stupid and funny and adorable, I cracked up.

We reached Lodhi Gardens and he helped me out of the car and then went around to the back. He emerged with a foldable tent, a huge hamper and a boom box. This guy was straight out of *Archie* comics! He led me to a spot shaded by the one of the monuments and pitched the tent, a hardy-looking green structure large enough for both of us to sit in, and ushered me in, bowing low. 'My queen.'

'You look beautiful, by the way,' he said. 'Not pretty. Classically beautiful. Like an English painting.' His grey eyes turned earnest and intense and he looked at me gravely. 'Unbelievable.' He played with the hem of my dress, the sun through the tent dappling it turquoise. I tried to change the mood.

'So, serf, what did you cook?'

'Aha!' he sat up, charged with excitement. 'We must unpack!'

He rubbed his hands together and did some elaborate hand-movement above the hamper and then began to pull out in toe-curling succession: two adorable little pies, some skewered vegetable-and-fruit thing, a sweaty plastic jug of something pink, a small basket of strawberries, a tiny fondue pot with two long forks and a tea light, a bar of dark chocolate and something that looked like ham rolled around something. He then brought out two plates, two plastic champagne glasses, some paper napkins—and a condom. Which he then pretended to be very embarrassed about, looking around himself yelling, 'I've been framed! Framed, I tell you!' He then got down on his knees and pleaded, 'I swear I'm innocent! I care only for your mind! See?' He whipped out a book of poems with an I-told-you-so air, sending me off into giggles again.

He went about setting up the meal, breaking the chocolate

into the fondue pot, lighting the tea light underneath it, plating my meal—so carefully his forehead creased in deep concentration. He sat back, surveyed his work and handed me the plate, a searching, vulnerable look on his face, watching for my approval.

I bit into the pie. It was chicken-mince, still warm and flaky and moist and delicious! So was the pink lemonade. So were the fig-ham-and-mozzarella rolls, and so were the strawberries-and-chocolate fondue. It had to have been the best meal I'd ever eaten and I couldn't believe that it was this slightly insane man who had made it.

'Fess up, Sid. Which five-star did you order this meal from?'

He looked wounded. I expected another dramatic performance, another pretend-death-by-fatal-stab-wound scenario. But he looked at me straight, his eyes soft and serious, his mouth in a gentle smile.

'So, when I was sixteen, my mother took ill—with cancer. She told me one day, this big smile on her face: "Baby, turns out I have cancer. So I'm going to do the cooking at night, OK? So, no hanging around the kitchen with your friends. You'll have to take them straight up to your room." So she got lunch packed and ready every day, went down to the hospital after we had left for school and then came back and cooked for the next day. And then she started having bad days, and I began to do the cooking, and then she was in bed for three years and she got real fussy about food and she'd only eat what I cooked. Then, one day, she died. And I just kept cooking. 'Cause it was easier that way.'

He smiled self-consciously at me.

'TMI, huh? You think I just went for the sympathy vote?'

'Actually, no,' I said softly, smiling at him. 'I just think you're a really good cook.' He smiled widely back at me and we lay back in the tent, enjoying the spots of warmth through the canvas and the feeling of being out in the open, and yet totally alone. And I realized the most surprising thing, considering the morning I'd had: I was really comfortable being silent with Sid. I turned to look at him lying beside me, his blonde eyelashes flicking lazily in the afternoon cold, his hands clasped on his chest.

'Sid?'

'Hmm?'

'Are you a free spirit?'

'Lady, what have you been smoking?'

'No, seriously! Are you, like, all the world is all illusion and shit?'

He laughed.

'Well, I'd love to be. But, unfortunately, I want the babies and the little woman and the dog, you know? I'm an old-fashioned Indian guy at heart—I still believe that the woman of my dreams will float down from the clouds in a red sari and we'll kiss in a rainbow-coloured heart. So, if you want to backpack around Europe and meditate in the mountains, I'm not your man. But, if you're looking for a guy to massage your feet when you're eight months pregnant—well, all you have to do is say yes.'

I was about to roll over and kiss him. Just for giving me the most awesome picnic I'd ever had, when a baton slammed on the roof of our tent. 'Excuse me! No love-making in public place. Come out! Come out!'

We crawled out, trying not to giggle. The cops were super-upset with us for 'making romance' in our tent in a public place and 'performing nuisance'. They thought we were married and figured that Sid, being a foreigner, could be excused for thinking that every country was like 'England', but, I . . . I, at least, was a good Indian woman and it was my duty to 'explain my husband' the laws of India. Anyway, we were old enough to understand such things and they hoped we would pass on these good values to our children.

As soon as they left, Sid stared me incredulously and said, 'Are you serious?'

He was so shocked that I started giggling all over again. I put my arm around him and ruffled his hair.

'Yes. Yes! I'm afraid so, yes!'

He grinned at me. 'I like being held by you.' He put his arm around me and squeezed tight. 'You want to hang out here or you want to go to the mall or something?'

'Mall or something.' No cops there. And we could pretty much hang out as long as we wanted. I helped him pack and we traipsed back to the car, chatting easily.

Sid was turning out to be everything I hadn't expected him to be. He was surprisingly vulnerable and tender, sensitive at moments you didn't expect him to be. And he cooked! That was pretty sexy! I'd always fantasized about being in the kitchen with a man and ending up on the kitchen counter with mayonnaise or something smeared all over me.

He bought me a bracelet, smoothing his fingers over my wrist as he put it on. He smiled when he was done. 'You make it look pretty.'

That night, when he dropped me home, I really, really wanted to kiss him. But he didn't make a move, just stood opposite me, not touching—which was unfair, considering he had already jumped me twice, on my dad's lawn that too. He just looked at me for a long time, his eyes shining green in the street lights.

'That was my best date ever.'

'Me, too,' I said, not wanting to say goodbye.

His fingers were playing with my bracelet. Suddenly, he yanked it forward, jerking me towards him, till my nose was touching his. He laughed softly and kissed my nose, then dipped lower and sweetly kissed me.

'Goodnight, princess.' He winked. 'You'll hear from me.'

He got back in the car and sped away, and I watched him till he disappeared from sight.

The next morning, Pammi Auntieji called, insisting on being put on loudspeaker so she could talk to both of us 'same-timessly'.

'See, Cocoji, it's a good match. The boy is from foreign, where they don't care about age and oldness. And our Rhea beti is definitely aged. Just close your eyes and say yes, the rest will all be seen later. Hain, Rhea beti? And you're serving Horr-Doos, nahin?'

'Hainnn?' said my mother, her hackles up.

'Nothing ji, Cocoji, just a small joke between my daughter and me! But I'm telling you, this is the best from my range. And seems like he also likes her. After this, I have nothing better.'

Oh no. She had done it. She had pissed Mummy off.

'Pammiji, seems like your range is extremely small, then.'

She disconnected before Pammi Auntieji could answer, smiling triumphantly at me.

'Mummy! Why did you have to do that?'

'Who is she to tell me that after this she has nothing better! Then she should know that she has to work much harder, nahin?'

37

I SPENT ALMOST ALL of my time with Sid. We'd talk in the morning and fix a place and time to meet and then we'd spend the whole day together, often running in to dinner or a late movie. We had got a little physical, fooling around here and there if we got a chance, but, for once, it was nice to just take it as it came, without having to worry about being proposed to. Sid made me forget about everyone else and everything else. In fact, I was probably having the most fun I'd ever had.

One day, he and I were sharing an ice-cream and giggling over something gross he had said, and I looked up, and Tish was standing there with an orange parasol, one hand on her waist, staring at us. We hadn't spoken in a while, and I felt weirdly embarrassed, like I'd been caught doing something wrong, like hanging out with her boyfriend or something.

'Oh! Hey! Tish!' I said, sounding fake.

'Hi Rhea.' No acidic comment, no joke, no 'Who's your cute friend'. Nothing. Very un-Tish.

'How are things?' I was genuinely concerned.

'Good, I guess.'

Her face fell for a millisecond, then settled back into its customary cocky expression. I felt like shit. Tish, my best friend, had been going through God-knows-what in the last few months and I hadn't been there for her. I wanted to say something, but I felt really awkward. And that's when Sid did something I would never forget him for.

He stood up, reached out his hand and said, 'Hi, I'm Sid. Why don't you join us for some ice-cream or . . .' he looked around, 'I don't know—water?'

Tish began laughing at that and said, 'Sure.' And sat down.

He ran off to get her a chocolate-and-mint sundae—her favourite. I looked at his rushing-for-ice-cream back with a mixture of gratitude and almost-love. He had given me my Tish back. We smiled at each other.

'What's been going on, babe?' I asked her softly.

'Well, I was going to ask you the same question,' she answered bitterly.

'Why haven't you called?'

'Why haven't you?'

'I don't know. After that day at Chinky's . . .'

'When I threw a hissy fit and told poor Freesia a few home truths? Dude, I should just stop letting people tell me about their personal lives!'

I started laughing. 'Or . . . or . . . you could—just try this— just listen. Just for a change.'

She smiled. Sid came back with her ice-cream and another one for us to share and we sat there chatting and laughing till evening fell and it was time to go home for me, and for Tish to pretend she loved her babies—as she put it. We hugged, and she said, pulling me close, 'Rhee, we have to meet, OK?

When are you free?'

Sid and I were going to Old Delhi the next day because he wanted to take photographs and I really didn't want to cancel. 'Day-after lunch!' I said quickly.

'OK, deal! One o'clock!' she called over her shoulder.

I squeezed Sid's hand gratefully. I had my best friend back, and that meant the world to me.

'Sid?'

'Yes, princess?'

'Would you like to meet my sisters?'

He stopped to look at me, grinning.

'Is that a version of "meet my parents"?'

'Yeah, sort of.' I smiled.

'Well, then, hell yeah!'

'Tonight?'

'If it'll make you smile that gorgeous smile of yours.'

'OK!'

I called. Ant was willing to watch Zara, and Sia wanted to bring Sunny. I was about to say no, but, then, I figured, if he survived the lesbian sister as well as the neurotic one, I would know if he was a keeper. We decided to meet at a rooftop place at Hauz Khas Village. Pia wanted me to tell Sia that she was not allowed to touch Sunny sexually in front of us. We were her older sisters and it was not proper. Plus, she didn't want Zara to turn lesbian, and if she saw a lot of lesbianism from a young age, she might. Also, she thought it was proper that Sunny buy each of us a present. To which Sia said that I should tell Pia to fuck off. To which I said that I would show that text to Pia. To which Sia replied *Challenge*. Surprisingly, after all that, we were all still on time for dinner.

Watching them all together, I wondered why I was so worried in the first place. Of course my sisters would love Sid. He was charming and easy to be around. Sia and Sid ganged up on poor Sunny, ribbing her. Pia glanced at me and nodded and winked. I guess that meant she liked him and my mother would be getting a call soon.

Sid paid for dinner for the whole lot of us and then insisted on dropping everyone home. And even Sia wasn't all like oh-you're-challenging-my-manhood. She just smiled and kissed him on the cheek before going inside. Finally, it was just him and me in the car again.

'I . . .'

'Ummm . . . Hitchcock, you're killing me.'

'Sid . . . I . . . That was really sweet. What you did today—all of it.'

He smiled. 'Well, that was a lot of women for one day. What do you do, breed 'em?'

I swatted him on the chest. 'Stop making me sound like an idiot!'

His voice got low and growly, 'Why? 'Cause you do such a good job of it yourself?'

I grinned, 'No! Because you're doing a good job of it yourself! Wait . . . er . . . That didn't sound right.'

He laughed and tapped the tip of my nose with his index finger. 'Has anyone told you you're cute when you're mad? Your nose gets red.'

It did? Well, that was pretty cute. I hashtagged that one #whyIloveme and filed it away for when Oprah couldn't help drag my self-esteem out of the gutter.

'So, Queen Rhea, in case you haven't noticed, I really like you.'

This could go two ways, I thought . . .

'I . . . Look, I don't know how it's done over here, but over there, it's . . . it's important to know if we're compatible . . .' He began to speak hurriedly. 'Look, I get it if you don't want to or you don't like me, but I . . . The thing is, Rhea, you're pretty much it for me. And I . . . wanna take it to the next level, you know?'

He must have read something in my face, because he sighed.

'I'm talking about sex, Rhea,' he said softly.

He had both my hands held tight in his and, in a way, that was a good thing, because the slight pain of it was the only thing I could feel at that moment. For a millisecond, my heart splintered. Not again. I couldn't take another encounter, only to have it not work out. For the first time, I got to hang out with a guy who made me happy—just uncomplicatedly happy. And whom I actually liked being with. I didn't want the pressure of sex, the body-image issues, the fear that if he saw my inner thighs, he'd leave me. But, in America, they didn't even fall in love without having sex first. Well, in a world of free samples, what did I expect? I opened my mouth to answer, but Sid covered it with his hand and then slid it under my chin and tipped my face upwards.

'Rhea,' he whispered, 'I don't just think you're beautiful and fun and sweet. I think you're mad hot. And I want you. And that's a good thing. But that doesn't mean you have to say anything now. Just think about it. Because I'll be thinking about that beautiful . . . curvaceous . . . sexy . . . body . . . all night.'

He kissed my face between each word, ending at the corner of my mouth and then said goodnight.

I ran up to my room, my heart skidding around, bumping different organs in my body. I stared at said hot body for a while. What if this was the last time? What if Sid was going to be the guy I'd be having sex with for the rest of my life? Arf didn't love me—wouldn't love me—and Sid would never leave me for a long-haired, lungi-wearing baba in the Himalayas. Sid was the marrying kind. And I hated to say it, but the truth was, my parents' cachet would go up several notches if I married a half-white man and moved to America. Ant was a good catch, but he didn't have a patch on Sid in the class department. I heard Pammi Auntieji's shrill voice hissing 'Horr-Doos . . .' and my mind was made up. I texted him.

OK.

My phone tinged a second later.

Really?

Really.

The phone was silent for a long time. Then, just as I was thinking that he had probably changed his mind, or worse turned Mazher on me, my phone flashed, indicating that I had an email. It was from Sid.

Princess,

I know you're scared about what we talked about today. And I really do understand if you need to take your time. I know Indian girls are not the same as white ones. And that's why I wanted to marry one.

I think you're the most beautiful girl I've ever known, and if you're really, truly sure about things, then you've made me the luckiest man in the world!

Xxx

Sid

What a sweet email! I would have kissed it, but I wasn't sixteen any more. Sid didn't seem like a bastard, but I had to admit I was a little put off that he'd asked me to sleep with him. Especially since it had been going so well without sex. But he was half-American and he had met my parents and sisters and my best friend, so obviously he wasn't going to do and dash like Jay had.

I needed a friend.

38

I CALLED TISH, WHO heard me out patiently and, then, in a most uncharacteristic way, didn't start loading me up with advice. She asked me, 'So, what do you want to do?'

'I want to marry him.'

'Yes, but that's not going to happen until he sees you nekkid.'

I sighed, 'Tish!'

'Would how he is in bed make a difference to you?'

'Honestly, no.'

She was silent for a long time.

'You know, Arf would never ask you for sex.'

'Fuck off, Tish! What are you talking about! What the fuck does Arf have to do with this shit!'

'Will you calm the fuck down, Rhee? What's eating your ass?'

'Tish, I know.'

'Eh?'

'I know about you and Arf. I know you're in love or in sex or whatever you want to call it.'

She started laughing.

'Rhea, have you lost your fucking mind! What is it, too much sun? Or fucking old age?'

I was confused.

'Umm . . . Vipassana . . . You've been acting weird . . . It was all so obvious.'

'Babe, I love Arf. He's my best friend, apart from you. And, unlike you, he's been around. But, honey, I haven't seen another penis apart from my baby boy's in ten years. K and I had an accident earlier in the year and I freaked because I didn't want another baby, but then I had a miscarriage. And the guilt fuckin' killed me. And I feel like I've been dragged through mud for the last few months, Rhee. I just needed someone who could listen. And Arf was there.'

My eyes filled with tears.

'Tish, I'm so sorry,' I whispered. 'I've been a self-centred bitch.'

'That you have. But you have an agenda. So it's OK. Now, what you going to do with Mr Indecent Proposal?'

'Can I tell you something?'

'That you're in love with Arf? Sure.'

I gasped.

'How the fuck : . .?'

'I've known you since you wore Minnie Mouse undies, man. I can tell this much.'

'Why didn't you say anything?'

'I don't know. You were trying to marry anything with a dick.'

I burst out laughing at that. It was pretty funny.

'You think he loves me?'

'Only one way to find out.'

'So, I should talk to him?'

'Sure. There's just one thing, Rhee.' Her voice got serious. 'You need to stop playing with these guys. If you're going to talk to Arf, you have to be serious, Rhee. No Vyash, no Sid— no nobody in the background, 'just in case'. It has to be true between you both. You know Arf. And you know he'll call it if you try and play games with him.'

Break up with Vyash, and Sid, and then tell Arf that I was in love with him. Who did Tish think I was? Superman? But I knew she was right. If I really, really loved Arf, and no one else, it'd have to be all or nothing. The thing is, what I felt for Sid was beginning to feel a lot like love. I was confused. Maybe I should meet Arf first, but what if he threw me out or refused to pick up or something. And what was he going to do if I told him I loved him, anyway? Fall in love with me? He'd had years to do it and the fool hadn't even asked me out for coffee. Ass.

OK, now I hated him.

There was another way that I was avoiding thinking about—process of elimination. Choose the guy who was left at the end of it all. And at least Sid wasn't an emotionally distant insensitive asshole like Arf. I emailed Sid back.

Sid,

I'm really scared. But you make me feel safe. I trust you. Just don't let me down OK?

Rhea.

Within minutes, he called me. His voice was raspy and sleepy.

'Hey, baby,' he said, his voice smiling.

Before I knew it, we had chatted all night. It was five in the morning and there was no way I was sleeping now. In fact, I couldn't wait to see him.

'Babe?'

'Hmm?'

'Do you want some coffee?'

'Yeah.'

'OK, I'll be there in twenty.'

Twenty minutes! I ran into the loo to shower, defuzz, moisturize, pluck, perfume, blow-dry, and then met him at the front door with a minute to spare, in a pair of yoga pants and a sweater, as if I'd just woken up. He actually looked like he had just woken up. But his face lit up when he saw me, his grin wide in the Delhi morning, his breath misting, his hair ruffled. I left a note for my parents saying I'd gone to the gym in a friend's car and hurried out before they woke up.

'So, where are we going?' I asked once we were back in the warmth of the car.

'Well, actually, I thought you could come home,' he said self-consciously.

I had actually never thought about where Sid stayed. I knew he had an apartment in GK 1, but he had never asked me over and I had assumed it was a filthy bedsit shared by eight boys. It wasn't. He lived in a spotless one-bedroom with a bar kitchen stocked with spices. The counter had a bowl of fruit on it and his shoes were neatly lined up on a folded newspaper near the door. He caught me staring and grinned. 'I live alone in America, too, you know. I know how to look after myself. And you, too, for that matter.' He kissed the top of my head. 'Smoothie, eggs and toast.'

'Mmm,' I nodded, watching him as he threw fruit and curd around and served to me what tasted like fancy lassi. He expertly cut tomatoes, one chilli, onions and grated cheese, and made this fat, loaded omelette with hot toast. I liked watching him cook. His face was so relaxed, his muscles shifted under his T-shirt as he reached for this and that and hummed bad pop songs from the '90s. It was adorable.

'So, what are you doing here, Sid? I mean, when are you going back to the States?'

'I came here for six months on work, actually,' he said. 'But I've got just two weeks to go, and I've been trying for an extension, but they've said no.'

I looked at him in shock. Two weeks! Why hadn't he said anything before?

'That's why the pressure, Rhea,' he said softly, reading my expression. 'I would have waited for you for ever, but from the US to India is too long a distance, really.' He smiled and held my hand. 'Eat. We're here together now, right? That's all that matters.'

When we were done, I helped him wash up and then he led me to the sofa. The sun had kicked in, its rays trying to fight through the heavy drapes, and the room was dim and cosy. I cuddled up to him. He'd obviously spent the night on the sofa. His blanket was still on it and so was his pillow. I pulled the blanket over me and turned to face him, listening to his heart beat. He took his glasses off and put his arms around me.

One arm was around my shoulders, the other one on my knee. He pulled my knee up, so my foot was on the sofa, and slipped his hand straight in between my legs. Wow. That was a bit direct! I was used to kissing at least before. Then he pushed me back on my back, his hand pressing down between my legs, and lay on top of me. His other hand came up and pinched my nipples a bit and then my pants and underwear were off, and so were his, and he had rolled on a condom and slid inside me, and before I could fake a moan, he had sighed and collapsed. I wasn't sure how to react. Should I be sympathetic because it was premature, or should I pretend I enjoyed it or . . .?

Sid smiled at me, put his glasses back on, kissed me on the forehead and then disappeared into the bathroom for a shower. I shrugged. At least the food was good. When he got back, we hung out together some more and then he dropped me home. He was acting like he'd enjoyed it. How could he have? It would take me longer to eat a fun-size Mars bar.

Back home, I figured he'd cancel our trip to Old Delhi and never call me back. I'd know the truth then. I was beginning to feel like the expert at being *non-married*. Well, what's another heartbreak when you have so many?

But, to my surprise, he was back in my driveway, bang on time, grinning his mad-happy grin and cracking his stupid jokes, and before I knew it, another fun, joyous afternoon had passed in his company. I came home, dirty and tired and exhilarated and a bit confused, and collapsed into bed.

39

S<small>ID WANTED TO MEET</small> my parents formally and declare his intentions or something. I should have been ecstatic, but I wasn't. It felt like I had unfinished business. I went through the motions: helped Mummy in the kitchen, listened to her sing Punjabi wedding songs for two hours in a row, let her pick out an outfit for me and then went up to get ready as soon as Pia, Ant and Zara arrived.

The only person missing was Sunny. But expecting Mummy to have Sunny sitting at the dinner table with her baby granddaughter was like expecting Satan to serve a newborn lamb a bowl of grass and then kiss it on its forehead. She had supervised everyone's hair and outfits, down to our underwear—'Only control-panty, girls, Amreekans don't like poppings'—and my father's moustache—'Virji, please trim little, otherwise it floats in the soup spoon.' No amount of convincing could change Mummy's belief that he was a foreign-white, so he would eat only bland food, so instead of her delicious paneer-butter-masala, parathas and chicken curry, she had found some *Punjabi Ladies with International Tastes* cookbook and had roasted a chicken which still looked almost pure white and quite suspicious, and served it with mashed potatoes, carrots cut in a flower-shape and tomato roses. I figured I'd be taking Sid out to get a burger or something after dinner.

Sid arrived on time, with a bunch of roses for Mummy, and a bottle of whisky for Papa, who glared at the label and grunted, 'Good. Normally, I drink Pimm's. But this is good whisky.' Mummy, of course, was a blur of fluttering hands and chirps and *So sweet! Why did you? Sit here in this chair. Have some drinks. You must be tired*, et cetera, et cetera. Pia finally managed to calm her by asking her to bring the baby down. Mummy sighed with relief. 'With Indian food, you have to stand in the kitchen sweating and mixing till it's time to eat. With conti-cooking, there is too much free time!'

The moment Zara came down from her nap, all pink and gurgly, Sid gave her this wide grin and plucked her out of my mother's arms. We all steeled ourselves for a demonstration of her iron lungs, but, instead, she giggled and pulled his nose. And then proceeded to sit there extremely contentedly till dinner was served. Mummy looked as if she might burst from joy.

'So, Sid beta, you are half-Indian. And your mother?'

'She was Norwegian, Auntie.'

'Ah! So, do you still have relatives in Norwegia?'

There was a panicked moment of silence during which no one knew what to say or do, and we were all refusing to make eye contact in case we started laughing.

Sid finally cleared his throat and said, 'Actually she was from Norway, and we do have relatives there.'

'Ah!' said Mummy. 'Must be a different part then. So nice that you have nice Indian values also.'

'Well, my father had a lot of family living around us, and they kept me Indian. In fact, they used to call me albino because of my colour.'

'Arré! Don't say that, beta! You have beautiful white colour! It's better white than too much black, no?'

Sid smiled and then, transferring Zara to the crook of his arm, while she sucked on his glasses, he leaned forward. 'So, Uncle, actually, I was here to ask your permission to ask Rhea to marry me. That is, if she'll have me.' He glanced at me shyly and then smiled his full, slightly nerdy, totally adorable smile at me.

No one breathed. I could hear a faint buzzing somewhere. But the room seemed frozen. What was this? Purgatory? Shouldn't there be trumpets, drums, a liveried band? The buzzing got louder and transformed itself into loud, gasping sobs from Mummy.

'Somebody wants to marry my Rhea!' she said, her voice well scrambled with sobs. '*Hay Bhagwan*, I thought it would never happen!' She threw herself on my father. 'Please say yes, Virji! They are in love!'

My father cleared his throat. 'Cocoji. Please control yourself. Why don't you go and heat dinner or something? Girls?'

We herded our overcome Mummy out of the room and into the kitchen. But as soon as she got there, she straightened up, dusted herself and said, 'Come on, girls, chalo, let's heat and serve. Everyone take charge of one dish.'

As she bustled about, cheerfully humming 'Mahi Vey', stopping here and there to do a move from the song, I sat down on a stool in the corner and tried to tap into what I was feeling.

But every time I did, I just felt immense pressure and stress, as if I was on a train that refused to stop. Everyone around me was super-excited and chatting, and each time someone passed me, they patted me on the head or back or thigh, as if I had just achieved a major milestone by getting someone to marry me. I wanted to scream. I ran up to my room. As I did, I heard my mother tell my sisters how overcome I must be now that my dream was finally coming true.

My dream? It *had* become my dream, hadn't it? From being hurt and angry that my parents had started to look for someone to marry me, I had gotten so obsessed with getting married that I'd lost my job, my friends, my sense of self. I liked Sid. I really did. In fact, I may have been in love with him. But, seriously? This was something to get so excited about? We hadn't celebrated promotions, babies or academic achievements the way we had celebrated this. My dream coming true—a half-American boy proposing to me.

I went back down and suffered through dinner, but when it came to saying goodnight to Sid, I just waved. I didn't walk him out or kiss him and just went back to my room before anyone could ask me any questions.

I opened my laptop and randomly surfed Facebook, but my mind wasn't in it. I just wanted to lay my head in my hands and cry. I slept.

All night, I had the strangest dreams. Sid's face turning into snakes, Tish in a red sari sitting on top of a white Maruti pulled by me, snakes in my underwear, choking on snakes, my arms bleeding, weird images, screaming, crying. I woke up with tears on my face. There was already a text from Sid.

I want the rest of my life to start as soon as possible.

It was a quote from *When Harry Met Sally*. I had told him how much I loved that movie. I felt like a worm—because I was going to break up with him.

I wanted to be with Arf. And if he didn't want to be with me, that was fine. But I had to try. Arf felt normal. It felt right. Arf didn't need to sleep with me to know that he loved me. I texted Sid back.

Can we meet around four?

Sure. I'll pick you up. Wife-to-be. Xxx

Just in case I needed to feel worse.

I went over to Tish's. I needed her more than ever. I loved Sid. He was the perfect man. And the complete opposite of surly, moody Arf. Maybe if I married him, my life would turn out different. I would live in my mother's beloved Amreeka. We would have a cool apartment and edgy, artistic friends, and later, a nice house and garden with a yard and a dog and neighbours who waved while jogging past our gate. I would come to Delhi twice a year with bags of chocolates and bras, and go back with saris that I would use as curtains.

I couldn't even imagine what my life would be with Arf. I didn't know if he loved me back—obviously, he didn't. I didn't know what he saw his life as. I just knew that I had never felt as secure and right as I did when I was with him.

'Plus,' said Tish, 'maybe he can last longer than three minutes.'

I pinched her. Of course, the sex had nothing to do with me wanting to leave Sid. I mean, I hadn't even kissed Arf, and here I was, willing to give up lovely, loving Sid just to see if Arf would consider me.

~

Sid brought me back to his place. I think he wanted to cook me a celebratory meal or something. He had taken half a day off work, and looked gorgeous in a grey suit tailored for his lean body. He leaned up against a bar stool, a glass of milk in his hand.

'So, beautiful, what did you have to say to me?'

'I . . . er . . . I . . . Sid, I can't marry you!' I blurted.

He smiled and put his glass on the counter and then came over to squat in front of me, taking my hands in his.

'I know, baby. I know you're scared. But, no one, no one can love anyone the way I love you. You're the best thing to happen to me, Rhea. You're my angel. No one has made me this happy since my mom died. You gave me back my joy. And I'm going to spend the rest of my life saying thank you!'

He kissed my hands gently and looked into my face.

'I'm sorry, Sid, I can't. I just can't.'

'Take your time, babe. We don't have to rush. I haven't even proposed yet.'

'Sid, there's someone else!'

He jerked backwards, letting go of my hands.

'What?' he said softly.

'No, no. Not that way. I mean, he doesn't know. But I love him, Sid. And it wouldn't be fair to you to say yes.'

He laughed bitterly.

'So, let me get this straight. You like . . . love this guy, and he doesn't even know it. He probably doesn't love you, because if he did, you wouldn't be . . . wasting your time with a dumb dick like me . . . And you still want to dump me because . . . I don't know . . . ten years from now . . . he might notice that you exist?'

I nodded miserably.

He shook his head.

'Perfect. Just fuckin' perfect.'

He looked at me for a long moment and then took a small jewellery-box out of his pocket, opened it and slammed it down in front of me so hard that I flinched. It was the hugest, most perfect solitaire I had ever seen, set in a platinum band encrusted with diamonds.

'The doorman will get you a taxi,' he said.

40

I CRIED FOR THREE days. My biggest fear was that I had done the wrong thing. I missed Sid. I missed seeing his messages on my phone first thing in the morning. I missed being able to tell him anything without being judged. Mummy had stopped talking to me and wouldn't come around no matter what I did. Pia and my father kept things cordial, but never lost the opportunity to tell me how stupid I was. About the only two people talking to me were Sia, and Saro Didi, who had heard that I had refused an Amreekan, but privately felt that men with 'coloured-eyes' were not to be trusted and that it was actually better that I had let him go before I found out about his yellow-haired 'mem' and three 'coloured-eyed children in Amreeka'.

I still wasn't sure if I'd done the right thing. I missed the outings and the eating and the laughing. But I had to speak to Arf. Before that, though, I had to cut ties with Vyash. I didn't think I could do it in person, though, and I didn't think he deserved it either. We hadn't really been in touch for a couple of months, anyway. So I sent him an email which took an entire day to write. Finally, I settled for:

Vyash,

I don't think it's going to work out between us. But I would love to stay friends. Keep in touch?

Cheers!

R

I thought that sounded breezy and worldly enough. Plus, I'd kind of gone past Vyash sometime between Mazher and Sid. I really did wish him well. He was my first after all. And now that my slate was wiped clean, I mustered up the courage to call Arf. He answered on the first ring, his voice warm and husky, the way I'd always remembered but not paid attention to.

'Hey, Rheeses-Pieces.'

'Hi Arf!' I almost shrieked, trying hard to sound cheerful and not like I was going to show up at his door with a bottle full of poison and drink it if it came to that, like I had earlier planned. 'Arf, I need you . . . I mean I need to see you—now . . . er . . . today, if possible.'

'You OK?'

'Yes! I just need . . .'

'You want to come home? Should be home like eight-ish.'

'Yes! I . . . sure!'

I'd wanted to think about what I would wear, how I would look, what my hair would smell like, but finally I was in this weird space between meeting good old Arf and meeting the man I had been in love with for at least the last two years. Tish was no help—she kept quoting Kahlil Gibran and Oprah and Louise Hay at me—trust her to turn philosophical at a time when I needed her to stay at *Cosmopolitan* level. But just before I left for his house, she sent me a text.

The bananas at vipassana were from Arf.

The bananas at vipassana were from Arf?? It made sense. He must have saved his share up every day, so we wouldn't have to go to bed hungry. Suddenly, I felt like smiling again. He must love me, right?

I landed up at his place in jeans and a pretty top, and chatted with his mother because he was late. Arf's mom had been the go-to person when we were younger. She smoked, wore shorts and cursed at everyone. She had once bashed a watchman's head in because he had tried to feel her maid up. When they finally pulled her off him, she told him that if she even sensed his shadow in the area, she would kill him and feed him to her dog. She had also told Arf's school principal to go fuck himself. Obviously, she was our favourite mother.

Arf arrived when his mother was on her fourth cigarette and we were both on our third vodka-iced-tea. He smiled at both of us and then came over and put his arm around me.

'Come on, skank!' he said affectionately. 'Let's talk.'

'Bye, kids! If you want dinner, order me some as well!' She winked and then wandered off inside the house. She usually waited up for Arf's sister and dad and had dinner with them. Arf rarely joined them. He led me upstairs, opened his mini-fridge, pulled out a beer and threw me a bottle of water.

'Hydrate.'

He sat on a bar stool and looked at me expectantly.

'So?'

'So, what?' I said, trying to act aggressive and playful and basically undrunk.

'You OK?'

I looked into his eyes, all concerned, and soft, pale circles

around them, and I was slain. Suddenly, I felt as though I had
to say what I had to say. Should I hold his hands? Should I
open a button or two? It felt like I had a lot of experience in
these matters, but it had never felt like it meant so much before.

'Arf, I . . . I'm in love with you.'

'Oh shit.'

'What?'

He rubbed his hands over his eyes, looking even more tired
than when he first walked in. I should have left then, kept the
explosive confessions for a Sunday or a time when he was less
tired. But the words had long stopped listening to me.

'Arf, I tried, OK? I met other guys, I went out with them,
tried to get married, did everything, but it just comes back to
you, Arf. I . . . I feel safest . . . happiest . . . rightest when I'm
with you. And I really need you to love me back, because I
think I've loved you for years and the only way my life is going
to have any meaning is if it's with you.'

My nose had got too blocked for me to speak now, because
the tears were running down my face and I was seeing two Arfs
and they both looked dismayed and un-in-love.

'Arf?'

He put down his beer and ran both his hands through his
hair and sighed.

'Aww, babe . . . Rhee, I love you too. I've loved you since
you were my best friend's girl. Why do you think I've stayed
single all this while? But . . . I can't give you what you want,
Rhee. I never could. I'm not the marrying kind.'

'I don't have to marry you!' I managed to wrench out
through tears and sobs and heart-twisting pain.

He smiled bitterly.

'Yes, you do. You want marriage and babies and anniversary parties and EMIs, Rhea. And I'm not that man.'

'I don't understand. You're saying you love me.'

'More than I thought I could love another person. So much so that I've wanted to kill myself over this past year.'

'Then, what's in it for me?'

He shrugged.

'I don't know. There were days when I was afraid to come near you, because I wouldn't be able to help myself but kiss you, touch you, tell you that you belonged with me. And I watched you. I watched you with those idiots . . .' His voice broke and he turned his back. I got up to go to him, but he whipped back around. 'Rhee. I can't do it. I'm sorry, but no.'

I sobbed out loud, wanting to scream, but through the drunken haze and the pain of the things he was saying, I was also aware of his mother downstairs. I held my face in my hands, not wanting to look at his tortured face. Not believing he had a right to feel this bad, because, right now, I was alone. No backup. No security system. Just me. Facing a life living at my house, forever having to listen to how I said no to perfect Sid, for Arf—who anyone could have told me was not interested in marriage. In fact, Pia had always said she thought he was gay.

I looked up. He had his back to me, his shirt stretched tight over his muscled back, his thighs straining against his jeans, his hair curling on his collar. Maybe . . . maybe, if I could just touch him, show him how much I loved him, maybe he would understand that I was willing to be with him in any way he needed. In this barsati, in a shack in Goa, backpacking around the world. I would be happy anywhere, as long as he was with me. I took off my top and slipped my hands under his arms, from behind him, and felt him stiffen. I pressed myself to his back, wrapping my arms tightly around him, feeling every muscle in his chest with my palms. He held my hand against his chest, pushing down firmly. Then I felt him exhale and heard his whisper, 'So help me God.'

He pulled the hand he was holding, bringing me around to face him. I couldn't meet his eyes, so I just stared at his chest, feeling the embarrassed blush slowly burn my face to ashes. He kept my hand held against his chest for a long time, looking at me in my white-lace bra and jeans. Then I felt him pull away slightly.

'No!' Not realizing I had said it out loud, I let the alcohol move me, grabbing a handful of his shirt, I pulled him nearer, rising on my toes, I pressed my lips against his. He took a swift shocked breath and then he was kissing me, his palms coming up the sides of my body, holding me tight against him. I managed to pull his shirt out of his jeans and my fingers raced all over his torso, almost hurting him in their desperation to feel every bit of skin, touch every inch of this man I had loved and, without realizing it, lusted after for so long.

We were touching and whispering and looking at each other, never a moment when we weren't connecting with each other in some way. Somehow, naturally, we were rocking together, his hand cupping my head, so it wouldn't bang against the headboard, my legs wrapped around his, trying to get as close to him as I could. I felt it just as he did, a sudden tidal wave of sensation, our arms tightening around each other at the same time and then we were kissing and slowly disentangling ourselves and falling asleep, content and whole again.

I awoke while it was still dark, thinking that I was going to get murdered at home. The bed was empty. Arf was standing at the door, looking out over the terrace.

'Arf?' I said uncertainly, trying to get the blanket to wrap modestly enough around me.

He turned and leaned against the door frame, looking at me for a while. Then he came over to the bed, sat across from me and drew my legs over his, holding my hips.

'Rhee, last night was the most perfect thing that's ever happened to me. I've thought about that moment for so long. But it shouldn't have happened . . .' I started to speak, but he placed a finger on my lips, smoothing my hair away from my face with his other hand. 'It shouldn't have happened, because I don't have anything more to give. You deserve your dream, Rhea, and I'm not the man who can give it to you. I'm sorry. You better get ready quick before everyone wakes up. I'll get you home.'

I felt a weird mix of hungover and numb. For the first time since this whole circus had begun, I'd felt right about something. Sex with Arf had felt right. Sleeping in his arms had felt right. Waking up in his bed, even though he wasn't in it, had felt right. How could I be wrong, then? I searched and searched his face for a clue, for an answer, but his face looked as tortured as I felt. Why couldn't he abandon his stupid free-spiritedness, his spirituality? Was it that important to him?

I carried my shoes in my hand as we walked across the living room, trying to be as quiet as I could. As we closed the front door, his mother called out from the dark, making me jump, 'Rhea, there's a magazine I've left in Arf's car to pass on to your mother. Don't forget, OK?'

41

MY DAYS HAD BEGUN to pass in a grey blur. I'd heard stuff about Zara being ill and had gone to babysit, but spoke very little to my sister. Then Sia tried to confide in me about her and Sunny, but I didn't register much—just some stuff about them having problems. The world was turning, but, honestly, I didn't care any more. Because mine had stopped.

My mother began to come up to my room, talking about repainting and buying new curtains now that summer had come and I had grown up. My dad said nothing, but came and sat around for fifteen minutes at a time, looking tortured. Ant came up one day and tried to get me to watch a movie with them, but I really didn't feel like going out any more. 'Main Pareshaan' played over and over in my head.

Tish had called a couple of times. She had to go in for a surgical procedure after her miscarriage and spend some time in the hospital. I didn't go to see her.

Then, one day, Chinky and Freesia came to see me. Chinky looked great. She had lost weight, coloured her hair purple and green and got a new tattoo on her neck. Freesia wore a blue dress and carried a frou-frou white bag and literally glowed with well-being. They came and sat on my bed. Then Freesia giggled and took out a gift-wrapped parcel from under her T-shirt. 'This is for you,' she said. It was a vibrator—a realistic-looking pink penis, with four speeds. 'It'll set you free, Rhea.'

I stared at it for a long time and began to laugh. And then we were all laughing.

'Sleepover at my place,' Chinky said. 'With drinks.'

I wanted to say no. I felt ashamed. What if they called me out for being the failure that I was? Plus Tish was probably mad at me and, by now, I'm sure I'd been discussed to death for my desperate attempt to get married and then my loud proclamation of being in love with Arf—the guy I'd made fun of at every sleepover. Man, I wanted to slap myself. I didn't even want to think about what my friends thought of me!

But I went. Because to not go would (a) make me lose all my friends forever and (b) give them even more to bitch about.

When I arrived, they were all there, their faces solemn and even woebegone. They all said hi in whispers and moved around me very carefully as if I was injured or mentally unstable. I tolerated being served and wrapped in a blanket and being spoken to softly for about half an hour. After that it all got too Simi Garewal for me. It was like I was expected to start talking about my childhood or something.

'Guys, don't you think this scenario is getting a bit pathetic?'

There was dead silence. Then, Tish spoke, 'Rhea, we're a bunch of thirty-year-old women who still have sleepovers. I think we stopped worrying about being pathetic a while ago.'

Then we were all laughing and I was being called all sorts of names, and it turned out that Freesia's bar guy had turned out exactly the way Tish had predicted, but Freesia had just started going back to the bars to find a husband. Chinky was rooming with Freesia and enjoying living with a straight girl for once, and Saroj was engaged to a man who had no connection to her high-society sister-in-law. Tish was eating a tub of hot popcorn with peanut butter because it tasted great and she had lost two kilos so she was treating herself. It was time to move on. My friends had done it. They had taken their personal tragedies, mourned, dusted themselves off and then carried on living. It was time for me to do the same. I needed a job. I needed a man. And I needed a proposal.

Surrounded by my friends, I logged into shaadi.com for the first time since I'd registered.

'Wait, wait!' Freesia yelled in her squeaky voice. 'Shouldn't we, like, pray or something?'

'Dude, it's the Internet, not some swayamvar!'

'Ya, but what if there are no . . . options? It's a big rejection!'

'Are you saying our Rhea cannot get a proposal? So far all the men have been interested!' Saroj seemed to be taking things quite personally, but I had to agree. And I had to agree again when she said, 'Arré, everyone wants her jelly, yaar!'

Freesia sighed in exasperation, 'All she has is a picture up, Saroj! With some poem or something. Be someone with brains, no!'

We turned to the laptop and said a quick prayer led by Freesia and then restored the screen. I had some 'expressions of interest'.

Ronald McDonald, 44, loves to party, wants a happy woman.

'Oh great! You can sell burgers together for the rest of your life,' Tish said. 'Hope you look good in yellow!'

Adarsh Malhotra, 34, looking for a tall Punjabi girl, up to 28 years.

Chinky said, 'Why did he think you've written thirty there? It's your waist-size or what? Fool! Express interest elsewhere, idiot!'

Freesia: 'Chinky, you're being rude!'

Chinky: 'I didn't say waist-size!'

Freesia: 'You did—if he had said it, it would be written there!'

Ayushman Roy, 38 years old, looking for a soulmate who loves to travel, read and dance.

'Hello!!!' Freesia, Chinky and Saroj said it together. We all looked at each other. Tish squeezed my hand. 'Ready?'

I took a deep breath.

'Ready.'

First, we created a new email address because Tish said we should have a general slimeball landfill. Then, we wrote an email.

Hi Ayushman

I loved your email. I'm 31 30, and I work in IT as a project manager. I've travelled a lot on work and when I've been able to, taken vacations with my girlfriends. I love experiencing new cultures and seeing new places.

['Just write it, you need to sound interesting!' Tish said, flicking me on the hand.]

I'd love to meet—I feel we'd have a lot to talk about. Shall we do coffee?

['He sounds Bengali. Bengalis do a lot of coffee.' 'Don't say "drink"—he'll think you're a slut.' Saroj was doing the typing.]

Hoping to hear from you, Rhea.

We looked at each other and then Chinky said we must pray, so we linked hands, closed our eyes and prayed, and then hit send.

Then Chinky found a two-litre bottle of Coke and shook it and popped it like a champagne bottle and sprayed all of us till we were a giggling, sticky mess on the floor and all needed to take showers. Tish was convinced that Chinky had video cameras in the loos and then Saroj lectured us about being politically incorrect and LGBT-insensitive, and then Tish asked her why she was upset when Chinky was the big fat lesbian anyway, and then we were all laughing again. So much so that after we were cleaned up and were lying around the living room again, we began to have this serious conversation about careers and jobs and futures, and I realized that I needed to start interviewing again, too. Just suppose I didn't get married. I needed something in my life. Whether it was IT or teaching or baking cakes or walking dogs, it was time to find purpose. Plus, marriages cost money and I didn't know how much of it my parents had left after supporting me for four months.

With that thought I drifted off to sleep with my head on Chinky's legs. I had a lot of work to do tomorrow.

42

I GOT HOME THE next day and began spring-cleaning with a purpose. I began with buying new curtains for my bedroom. Even if I was getting married in one day, there was no way I was going to look at those stupid mice floating on rainbows for another minute.

Then I took down all the posters from my hormonal teen years. Off came poor Michael J. Fox, New Kids on the Block, Patrick Dempsey and Bon Jovi. Every heart-shaped sticker I had ever stuck on any surface was pulled off, crumpled and chucked. I, Rhea Kanwar, was finally moving on—starting with moving into my room.

Then, it was time to check my mail. I hadn't done that since I had broken up with Sid and Vyash. I was scared. I hated the way it had ended between Sid and me. I really had been fond of him and could have grown to love him—really love him—I guess . . . in about twenty years. We would have had fun together, Sid and I. He was so funny. I smiled to myself. I wonder if he had met someone else. It had been a month. He'd probably have gone back to the US by now. Maybe, someday, we could be friends. Maybe.

I logged in. Mostly grow-a-bigger-penis trash, some miracle drug to last longer, some more stuff about my penis and, then:

RE:

It was from Vyash. I braced myself and opened the mail.

Hello Rhea,

Well, you beat me to it. I was going to write you but I'm glad you did. I actually met this beautiful, intelligent twenty-eight-year-old woman who's a dancer. She's graceful, successful, gorgeous and creative and she's agreed to be my wife. I hope you'll be there for the wedding.

Vyash

He'd attached a photo, but I didn't want to see it. I wished him well with his dancer chick who, he hadn't omitted to inform me, was twenty-eight and not thirty-plus like me. Well, that was one chapter closed. I hope she likes the name Gina. Because she would be hearing it a LOT from now on.

I saw another mail from Pammi Auntieji, but it was some offer-mailer-discount if you had an unmarried younger sister—Pammi Auntieji would find you two grooms for the price of one and a half. I reminded myself to ask my mother what had finally happened to Pammi Auntieji after I broke up with not one but two of her prized candidates—one, a flagship product.

Then there were some other general emails about job vacancies and reunions and stuff. I applied for a few, sent out some emails to former colleagues and then had a shower and went down to see Mummy, who was making karonda jam.

'Mummy?'

'Hullo, my beta!'

Her voice was wobbly. I knew it had been hard for her this past year, dealing with all the ups and downs, and then having to handle me not talking to anyone for the last few months. This, too, when she felt that she was the one who had been wronged and should be the one freezing everyone else out. I went and put my arms around her waist.

'Sorry, Mummy.'

She held my arms for a while and then turned around to face me.

'Koi nahin, beta. But now you must be a sher, OK? No more this crying in your cave. Be strong. Be brave. So what if you don't get married. See Bubbles Auntie.'

Oh yeah. That. I grabbed a piece of bread and settled down to eat it with Mummy's not-quite-ready jam. There was still the danger of turning into the woman who came for all celebrations of all festivals at our house and spent the first hour yelling because the maid was stupid, Indian men were stupid, the food was stupid and India was stupid. And then made body-part jokes for the rest of the day.

I imagined myself at the tables of Saroj, Chinky, Freesia and Tish during the next Lohri or Baisakhi, and shuddered. Oh well. Job first. Gym next. Marriage—if possible.

43

I WAS ON MY way back from an interview when my phone
tinged. It was Saroj.

He replied.

Ah. Ayushman. Well, that was good. I knew in my heart
that if he said yes, I would too. Marriage was never about love,
anyway. It was a deal between two people. The man I loved
didn't want me, anyway, so all that 'He's just not that into you'
shit was true. Even if the men claimed they'd kill for you, they
didn't exactly want to take you home for good.

If Sid were to come back, I would have said yes. But I didn't
know how to get in touch with him. Yes, there was Facebook,
but what was I supposed to say? 'Hey, do you still have that
ring, because . . .'?

I had had to deal with the consequences of my decisions. It
had been ten long months of meeting men, sleeping with them,
thinking I was in love, and breaking their hearts, and, finally,
one big, devastating blow to mine. Administered by my best
friend, who, I should have known, just wanted to die alone in

the Himalayas somewhere, with the Dalai Lama personally meditating over his remains.

I checked the email on my phone. Ayushman wanted to meet for coffee tomorrow at the Taj Palace coffee shop. That seemed doable. I had an interview right before that. I could finish that and go straight to meet him. I had a nice skirt-suit that I could wear with a flouncy top that could look both interview-y and date-y so I didn't show up at either looking strange.

I had seen a picture of Ayushman. He was no Mazher, but he was pleasant enough. Glasses, chubby face, serious-looking. He looked like a guy who would marry a girl and produce two babies with her. I spotted him immediately. Black suit and blue shirt and taller than he looked in his picture. I waved, and he waved back, smiling. OK. He seemed nice.

He stood and pulled out a chair for me when I arrived.

'You're even prettier in person, Rhea.' He had a gentle voice, soft and low.

I smiled, 'You're very charming.'

He tugged at the front of his suit-jacket self-consciously and laughed softly. 'I've actually been rehearsing that line.'

I laughed at that, 'So . . . that means . . .'

He grinned widely and patted my hand. 'It means I meant what I said the first time!'

Ayushman was the CEO of a packaged foods company. Apparently, he worked crazy hours—sleeping just six hours a night, so he could fit in a game of tennis before his day started. On Sundays, he liked to play golf. Obviously, with a schedule like that, he had trouble meeting women. He had met some girls through matchmakers and his mother's network, but he was sick of the twenty-three-year-olds whose only impression of marriage was going out 'roaming' in the evenings. He wanted someone real, someone he could talk to.

I found myself telling him that I didn't have a job and that I was interviewing at the moment. He gave me some advice on job-hunting. The evening seemed to go well. We hung out for about two or three hours and then we stood to leave.

'I'd like to see you again, Rhea.'

I smiled. I felt the same way. He was a nice guy—polite, decent, gentlemanly.

'Me, too,' I said shyly.

He smiled widely. 'That's good news.' He grasped my hand warmly and led me out to my car.

I checked my emails as soon as I got in. I had a callback from an interview. Joy surged through me like a third drink. It was a sign. A sign that life was going to change for the better.

I replied to the email, fixing an appointment for the next day. Then I went to Tish's to fulfil my babysitting promise, so she and K could get some time alone. I made the kids dinner, gave them their baths and changed them for the night. And as their little bodies got heavy with sleep, one on either side of me, I hoped, really hoped, that I would get to be a mother someday—even if I was unable to have my own, I hoped I would at least be able to adopt.

I brushed Kahani's hair away from her forehead and whispered, 'Don't wait for your prince, li'l girl. They don't exist. Say yes to the guy with the house and the car. And hold on to your girlfriends. They're the only thing that will get you through life.'

44

WE RECEIVED THE INVITATION to Saroj's engagement. One shiny bronze number with a silver Ganesh on it and hearts on the inside cover. My mother got all upset about it.

'Haye! Why do they put Gods on their cards? Then we can't throw away the card and for months are looking at it thinking we have to go for a function even five years after it is over!'

Saroj was getting formally engaged at the India International Centre to a guy named Papplu. My 'fly' was not coming, but Chinky-Freesia-Tish had decided we must go en masse. Freesia had bought Saroj two Madhubani paintings.

'Seriously? And where is she going to hang them? In the no man's land in between their two houses? It's an engagement, not a marriage, Floosia!'

'We can't go to a party without a gift, Tish!'

'So get her some body butter, no, Of-Very-Less-Brain Person!'

'OK, she can keep it in her Troos. Leave it, let's go! My pant is choking me!' Chinky was dressed in a blue suit and red bow-tie—which Tish made into a flouncy thing just in case people started calling Chinky 'dyke' or something.

Then we saw Saroj and we all started crying. She was dressed in a pista-green sharara embroidered with pearls and silver threads, her cheeks were dewy and her hair was all stiff and hairspray-ed, and suddenly we were all tightly holding hands, whispering to each other that Saroj had never looked prettier. Except for Chinky, who said that she had seen Saroj in her underwear during a girls' night and the woman had a 'serious body'.

We kept looking around for Papplu, but we couldn't see him. At one point, Tish pointed out a really dressed-up guy likely to be him, but before we could see him, our view was completely obscured by a woman in a lurid purple salwar-kameez embroidered with bright-green leaves, carrying a humungous plate piled high with laddus.

'Betis!!' she screamed. 'Arré, my beti!'

It was Pammi Auntieji.

'Didn't you know it was my only *rishta* today? It's a big day indeed! The boy is an NRI from UK. Arré, *sochon*! Dhi UK! The world's best Punjabi culture is there! And you know,' she sidled up to us, grinning slyly, 'it was first time accept. Not like you. Too fussy I tell you.' She turned to my friends, balancing the laddus on a shoulder and pulling out business cards from her bra, 'I think so ki she is too picky. My best boys she said no to. And, trust me, Pammi Auntieji has the best available in India. Call me, OK? I can get you all married. One week guaranteed. Plus, discount because of your friends!' She stopped to appraise Tish. 'You, beta, I am very sorry, but we will have to do some exercise-*kushti* first. Girls, I don't want her to feel bad, but there is only so much Pammi Auntieji can do!' She turned to leave, stood still for a second and then did this dramatic Bollywood turn-chin first, then waist, then the rest of her, brought to momentum led by her hips.

'Arré, the biggest news I forgot to tell! Remember Sid? My flagship?' she addressed us again. 'That he only used to say—so cute! "Palmy Antee, I'm your flagship product!" He's getting engaged! To one of my daughters only! It's next month—he's coming down.'

I stayed motionless, not attempting to dodge the million blades flying at me, lodging themselves in my body. My eyes felt warm, reminding me that if I didn't turn away quickly, Pammi Auntieji, the heartless bitch, would see me crying. Sid? My Sid? That was quick! I had a sudden vision of us that day in Lodhi Gardens in the golden-green tent. Us getting so close to each other that day on the grass. The way his blue eyes looked so earnest and the way they went dark the day I told him I couldn't marry him. I wanted to turn and run from there, but Tish stepped in.

'Auntieji, I'm so glad your business is getting other girls married and not yourself, because I really feel that you are the rudest, most unpleasant woman I have ever met. And *you* get *me* married? You'd have to pay me to even acknowledge you and increase your worth in society. So take your laddus,' she eyed Pammi Auntie's robust breasts and butt meaningfully, 'and those sweets you're carrying and stay as far the fuck away from us as you can. OK?'

Pammi Auntieji burst into tears and ran away, laddus dropping from all sides, and disappeared somewhere behind the trees. As Tish turned towards me with her arms stretched out and her face all sad-smiley, Freesia hissed, 'Tish, you bitch! I was planning to contact her and get a discount!' She stomped away towards the crowd and, as Tish and I hugged, we all giggled till our stomachs ached.

We met Papplu later that night. He was short, but cute, and had this whole British-humour thing going on. He was a school teacher in Rotherham—some boondocks place with a population of three hundred or something, but apparently he was a good person and he really liked Saroj, and Saroj really liked him, and the fact that she didn't have to feel indebted to her sister-in-law for an introduction, freeing her from any future judgement by the wretched woman. Plus, her mother told us, she had given Saroj so much jewellery that if she was not happy, she could run away and use the jewellery to start off anything she wanted and be happy. Plus, if this was the engagement with three live-food counters, could you imagine the wedding? Nothing compared to even her own son, Saroj's older brother.

We landed up in Saroj's room after the party had ended. She was wiped. She had spent four hours at the beauty parlour, three at the puja, and her reception outfit weighed 25 kilos. She collapsed on the bed after changing into a pair of shorts, her feet in Chinky's lap, and Freesia pulling pins out of her hair, like you see street children having lice plucked. Tish and I tried to fold The Hulk, which is what Tish called the huge green confection of an outfit.

'Yes, I'm happy, guys,' Saroj spoke into the silent room which was positively noisy with the unasked questions straining at the leashes. 'He's nice. Really. And he loves me. Aaand,' she asked us to shut up with her tired gaze, 'it worked out, OK? It's happening. I'm getting married! Before I turn thirty.' And then she bit her lip and lowered her eyelids before I could say anything.

It was only the next morning before I thought of Sid. My sweet Sid was getting married. I had been so cut-up the night before, I hadn't even asked Pammi Auntieji who the girl was. I checked out his Facebook page. His relationship status still read 'single'.

Shits! This called for some intelligent sleuthing.

I checked his 'recently added' friends. Aha! He'd added four friends in the last month, two guys—one white Barnard something, one Sean Crasta, whose picture looked really familiar, one Gina Crasta, who was gorgeous and familiar, and one Sonia, nondescript Punjabi chick. So it was Gina, I thought, while skimming through her profile, was hot; she listed cooking as one of her likes and Harper Lee and Sartre as her favourite auth . . .

HULLO! What the fuck was this? My life as a Hindi movie? Fucking *Life is Strange* in ultra-real execution??! And Sean! I hit my head! I had met Sean at that art gallery! Don't tell me Gina was seeing Pammi Auntieji! She hardly seemed the type! And as Vyash's ex-wife, would she be older than Sid? But then Sid was the age-size-sex-no-bar variety, right? I remember Pammi Auntieji telling me that the first time I met him. But, Gina? It still didn't fit. I went back and checked out Nondescript Punjabi Girl's profile. It was weird, but she looked a lot like me. And he had asked her to marry him right after he asked me. So what if Sonia was his Rhea substitute and he really couldn't get over me? I couldn't make out much from Nondescript Punjabi Girl's profile, except for the fact that she seemed to spell decently and she was from some school in Shimla. This got me thinking that if Sid was marrying someone so much like me, there was a good chance he'd still be in love with me. And that was a pretty nice feeling. It was nice to feel that someone still wanted me after a string of rejections from already desperate boys! (I mean, if they were in the arranged-marriage circuit, they were obviously desperate!)

I had to find a way to get to the Sid–Sonia engagement. But, how?

'So, what are you saying? That you want Sid back now?' Tish was sitting at my dressing table, going through my make-up. Did I want Sid back? I had a Shakespeare-in-twenty-seven-seconds experience, where my mind zipped through stomach-clenching scenes of Arf's eyes, his mouth, his hands on my skin, that awful dark morning, and the pulsing hatred I felt for him at what he'd put me through. I sighed.

'Yeah. I do, actually.'

Tish swivelled around to look at me.

'You stupid fuck. So, what now? You're going to land up at his engagement crying "Wait-wait, marry me!"? "I'm the mother of his unborn child"? In real life, people just call the cops on that chick and she lands up picking lice out of her vagina in jail.'

'Ewww! What's wrong with you!' I disgustedly threw a pillow at Tish.

'Seriously, though, dude. Isn't it time you made a decision? And what about Ayushman?'

I sighed. 'Maybe I just want to say goodbye, Tish. Maybe I just want closure. I mean, Ayushman is nice, but maybe Sid was the one. Or maybe he wasn't. But I just need to see him and make sure of it myself.'

'Cool, so let's go.'

'Eh? Meaning, crash it?'

'No, muffin top. Saroj got an invite from dhi Pammi dhi Auntieji.'

In all the years I had known Tish, hung out with her, seen her naked, etc., if there was ever a time I had wanted to really plant a wet one on her, it was now. My fighter-friend who always came through. I looked at her with all the love I felt for her.

'Pea-brained bimbo,' I said.

45

BETWEEN HEARING THAT SAROJ had an invite to Sid's engagement and the actual event, I ate a total of eight grapes. Even though I (probably) didn't want Sid, there was no rule in the rule book that said he shouldn't want me. And Tish always says, 'If you meet your ex, you should either be looking fantastic, or you should be with your super-hot, super-rich current.' There was Ayushman, but he wasn't exactly my current, and worse, he wasn't super-hot. He was super-rich, but you can't always make that out the first time you see someone. Plus, I just wanted to see Nondescript Punjabi Girl and figure out if she was super-intelligent or super-funny or something, or that I had nothing to feel jealous about. It was a quick peek; no strings, no expectations dangled from it.

I borrowed one of Pia's wedding-function outfits. She'd had it done designer and exclusive and expensive, and I still didn't have a job, so I sneaked it out of my mom's cupboard, where she had lovingly wrapped it in tissue, kissed it and put it to bed. I would stuff it back in its wrapper and chuck it in the back when I was done. 'Borrowing' in sisterly parlance.

Saroj and Tish came to get me. Tish had a pack of cigarettes and a hip flask in her bag, in case things got bad. Saroj pulled out a coconut from her bag, moved it around my head in circles, surreptitiously, so the driver couldn't see, and then cracked it on the pavement. 'Taking no chances!' she said to Tish, who nodded vigorously.

We walked into my engagement. Or rather, the one I had dreamed of all my life. It was in a garden lit completely with candles. The wax had dripped and made funny shapes everywhere, making it seem like we were in a stalactite cave, or, as Saroj said, 'All fire and icey.'

People appeared and disappeared in the dim, flickering light, an occasional diamond or bit of gold detail throwing reflections everywhere. I looked around for the couple, but could see no red-velvet thrones or flowery stages anywhere. The music was some New Age crap. It reminded me of Sid. Indie Pop. He used to go on about it. I always thought Indie Pop was stuff like Remo Fernandes and Sunita Rao and stuff. Turns out, that was just what old-time TV stars like VJ Nonie and VJ Sophiya used to call it. In the US, Indie Pop is Sid-type music. Also, people who introduce music videos on TV are RJs.

I lazily looked around the cross between a candlelit wonderland and a Satan-worshipping cult and then my eyes landed about two inches from my nose, looking right into Sid's solemn-and-blue ones. My heart did two pole-vaults and stopped short of my throat before falling back into its cavity. Those blue eyes felt like home, like I was never supposed to have looked into any other eyes. They crinkled at the edges, getting those crow's-feet only white guys seem to get, and as my eyes refocused and took in his whole face, I realized he was smiling at me.

'Rhea.' (Ray-ah)

'Sid,' I whispered.

'So, you know Gina?'

'Huh?' That came out a bit like Lurch from *The Addams Family*, but I couldn't help it.

'I'm sorry. I mean, I don't remember sending you an invite . . .'

'Gina?' I said stupidly.

'My fiancée,' he said, drawing a stunning, fresh-from-the-parlour-coloured-hair, painfully-thin-eyebrows, twenty-two-inch-waisted woman to him.

Gina. It was Vyash's Gina. And she looked like she was born in a salon, incubated under those space-age hair dryers, and then fully made up before she was handed over to her mother. What was this Sartre-loving hot chick doing constantly entangling with men that I entangled with.

'Heya!'

She had an American accent. And an IQ of two, I thought viciously. I seriously hoped her designer outfit ripped that night, specifically in the arm-area where her biceps were bulging because she was holding on to Sid so tight.

The party was the classiest I'd ever attended. They had a champagne fountain, servers who flambé-d things at every table, personalized silver trays of chocolates as giveaways, Egyptian belly dancers who were *not* vulgar . . . It was the worst evening I'd spent in my life.

It's a night for Pimm's, I thought gloomily. But with a job interview to discuss money and hopefully sign an offer letter happening the next day, I'd just have to suck it up and deal. I'd give anything to be eighteen and French-kissing my Jon Knight poster again. I gestured to Tish that I wanted to leave this scene of pure and unconditional love. I mean, didn't Sid know that Gina was older than him? And that she'd been married, too? The used witch! Tish caught my look, fished Saroj out of a pool of aunties discussing her wedding mehndi and the theme—'How about *gendaphool*-wallah theme? How about a Harry Potter fantasy wedding theme?'—and shuttled us back home.

Coming back to my room was a depressing and over-familiar sight now. But at least the psychotic Minnie Mouses were gone.

46

I WOKE UP TO an email from Ayushman. Actually, it was from his personal assistant.

Mr Ayushman sir would like to know if you will be able to join him for supper at Masala Art. Today night. 8:00 p.m.

Oh right. Ayushman loved Indian food. And only went out for Indian food. I wrote back that I would go. Then got up to ready myself and get back into the world of people. And of course, I had to get ready to meet Ayushman 'today night'. Maybe I'd grow to love him in time. He was a good, decent man. Maybe we'd go to Switzerland on our honeymoon and I'd see him feed a sick puppy and have a turn of heart.

I went downstairs in my floral pyjamas and an old rugby T-shirt I had slept in. I went around the pillar at the bottom of the stairs, and stopped, staring wordlessly at an unshaven Sid, with bloodshot eyes, sitting at the counter, wearing a crumpled silk kurta from the night before, playing with the salt and pepper shakers. 'Wha . . .?'

'The door was open.' He shrugged.

Oh right. It was my parents' temple morning. Saro Didi must have left the screen door open.

'Okaaay,' I said slowly. 'But what are you doing here?'

He slid off the chair and took me by the hand, pulling me towards him so he was backed up against the wall, holding both my hands.

'Just say the word,' he said desperately. 'I'd walk out even now. You're my dream, Rhea. I'd . . . I'd do anything!' His voice caught and he wiped his eyes on his sleeve and looked up at me again. I wanted to say something. I wanted to speak. But I didn't know what I wanted to say. I opened my mouth and then closed it again, seeing the flicker of hope and its instant death in his eyes. I . . .

He dropped my hands and turned away. He stopped near the door and looked at me.

'Rhea. I'm the only man who didn't make you wait. Remember that.'

As he walked across the lawn, I saw him scrape his forearm across his eyes and then break into a sprint to the waiting taxi.

I ran upstairs, turned the bathwater to boiling and washed myself until the tears were no longer coming and the burning of my skin was more than the emotional twister that was wringing my insides to tatters.

Over dinner with Ayushman, I watched his mouth form words as I replayed my morning with Sid over and over again. He was the only man who never made me wait. But why couldn't I say anything? Why didn't I throw myself into his arms? I wondered if I had turned schizophrenic. Did I really not want to get married? Did I hate men, but wanted to keep them all preserved in a wardrobe like Norman Bates and his mother?

'No, no! Just toast it lightly, please!' I focused on Ayushman, who was tapping the chef on the shoulder, directing him as he roasted our parathas on the griddle. I watched as he gave long and detailed instructions on how the spots on the paratha should be medium-brown, because a lighter roti meant it was raw, and darker meant it was overcooked. And the perfect level of cooking heat created the perfect paratha. If I was going to be marrying this man, I sure as hell wouldn't be doing the cooking at home!

Over coffee, Ayushman had 'the talk' with me. 'Rhea, if you'd be OK with it, I'd like to meet your parents and . . . you know . . .'

I shrugged and looked down. I guess he took that for a yes, because he smiled and held my hand as he walked us to the valet desk. I looked at my watch surreptitiously. It was eleven. That meant my parents would be fast asleep by the time I got home. That was good, I guess. I needed some time before I could have the conversation with my parents. I wish we had done all this on email. Then I could've just copy-pasted words and not have to go through total embarrassment again.

My phone rang. Sia. I cut the call. She called back again. Such an impatient little shit. I cut the call again. We were almost home when my phone rang again. It was Pia. What, now? Couldn't my sisters leave me alone? I would be home in ten minutes for Godsakes! They were probably together, trying to bug me. Then my phone rang again. It was my father.

'Papa?'

'Beta. Sia's had an accident.'

My heart began to fight its way outside my chest, painfully clawing at my insides. I must have heard what Papa said through the throbbing in my ears and head and said something to Ayushman, because the next thing I knew, we were standing near my little sister's broken body covered by a bloodstained sheet, her face white and barely visible through the tubes inserted all over it. Pia was talking to the nurses and doctors, and my mother was crying. In a corner was Sunny, her face full of bruises, blood dripping from a gash in her arm. Nobody was paying attention to her. Before I could ask her what had happened, my father walked in and took in the scene. He then looked at Sunny looking like a scared child and went to her.

'*Ao, bachche*,' he said quietly and led her to the nurses outside.

She stopped, turned to him, put her arms around him and started sobbing.

'Sorry, Uncle,' she kept repeating.

My father patted her on the back and then, murmuring soothingly to her, took her outside, leading her towards the emergency area.

I looked at Sia. Her chest barely moved with her breath. She looked like she was going to die. My throat closed. I didn't want my baby sister to die. When she was little, we used to play this game where I was the mummy and she was my baby, and we'd go everywhere together—me, carrying this skinny, huge-eyed kid everywhere on my hip. Sometimes, we'd be beggars and I'd wrap a tablecloth around me like a tattered sari and she'd cry on cue and we'd beg from our parents' guests until my mother couldn't take the embarrassment any more and she'd shoo us off and tell us to come do ballet instead for her friends.

And in a weird way, Sia *was* kind of like my kid. I was eight when she was born and she was the pooping-crying-drinking-doll I'd wanted my Singapore uncle to get me, but my mother felt it was bad manners to ask.

Please, God, don't let her die!

When Pia came back, she told us what had happened. Sia and Sunny had been out with some friends. They were sitting in the back. A truck came and rammed them on the side Sia was sitting in. The driver and passenger just had some minor bruises, but had left after putting them in hospital and giving them some money, because they didn't want to be questioned about their sexuality—they were two drag queens who were Sunny's close friends.

Sia, on the other hand, had a fifty-fifty chance of survival. Only the next three days would tell.

On hearing this, Mummy fainted, her head knocking against the side of the hospital bed. Pia took in a deep, jagged breath and set about telling everyone what they would be doing over the next few days. My father was to take Mummy home. Pia would drop Sunny, who was refusing to leave the hospital, home herself. I would be staying with Sia that night. Pia would take my place in the morning.

As they were leaving, Sunny suddenly broke away and ran back to the bed. She bent and kissed Sia tenderly on the hand. 'I'm right here where you left me, love,' she whispered.

Tears bashed against my eyelids. I thought I saw Sia's eyelids flicker, but I wasn't sure. Then, everyone had gone and it was just me, my breathing, and the beeping machines keeping Sia alive. My eyes widened against the darkness, making my head hurt. I was so afraid. What if something happened? I would be all alone here. I held my sister's hand, so I could feel her faint pulse bob against my fingers, and leaned my head forward on the rail forming my headboard.

'Please don't die, Soo-Soo,' I whispered. 'It's not allowed in this game, OK?'

I woke up because someone tapped me on the shoulder. It was a nurse. My heart clenched.

'Didi,' she whispered, 'a gents has come. I not allowing him if you don't know him.'

I looked up, expecting Ant, but it was Arf, carrying a knapsack. My eyes had that crusty-crystal feeling you have when you've been crying all night, even in your sleep, so it was difficult to open them too wide. But Arf pulled me into his arms and kissed my hair. Then he opened his knapsack, pulled out a mouthwash, a new toothbrush and a T-shirt.

'Get *fareghaat*,' he said.

'Fareghaat' was a Tishism. It meant: Get into your underwear and relax; scratch your privates if you need too—whatever it takes to feel deep relaxation.

When I got back from the loo, Arf had spread a sheet on the floor and was lying down, his head on his knapsack. He had blown up a neck pillow and put that and a sheet on the chair I was sleeping in for me, there was a *Cosmopolitan* magazine too. I smiled at him and he winked at me.

At six in the morning, Sunny arrived. She settled down next to Sia, playing rock ballads on her iPod for Sia to hear. Pia arrived at eight, with a change and breakfast for Arf and me. At nine, just as we were leaving, a huge, gaudy bouquet of flowers arranged in a heart-shape arrived from the Kapoors, along with a huge tiffin-carrier filled with enough food to feed the entire hospital. Along with it, a note that said: *Linnyji would be coming to the hospital for a visit, after she has offered prayers at the temple.*

I was back in the hospital by 2 p.m. Mummy still couldn't handle the sight of her baby in hospital, Papa couldn't leave work, Pia had to get back to Zara because Ant had to get back to work, so it was just me. Tish had said she'd do night duty for Choohee, which is what she used to call Sia when she was a kid—mouse—because she was so tiny and squeaky. There was a tasteful spray of lilies from 'Sid and Gina', and I received an email on my phone from the new place that they wanted to make me an offer and would send me one in a few days.

The doctors said Sia was stable, but there was no way of knowing the extent of the damage until she opened her eyes. Sunny lurked in a corner, looking up desperately whenever a doctor or nurse passed the room. At seven in the evening, Arf was back; he brought Tish. Tish bustled about, getting people to clean the room, take out the flowers and arrange a bed for the 'attenders'. That was us. Imagine being called an attender when what you really were was a person whose life was slowly falling apart as you watched the one little baby, who had grown into a young woman, with her own battles and opinions, and who was so beautiful, your breath sometimes caught in your throat when you saw her, lying with her face all grey and mottled, barely breathing, on the hospital bed.

Tish and Arf slept on the floor, I slept in the chair like the night before. I could have stayed home, but I needed to feel Sia's hand in mine. The next morning, the doctors told us that if Sia didn't open her eyes at some point during the day, there was a good chance she'd slip into a coma and maybe never wake up. Every time he said words like 'coma' or 'death' or 'serious', he'd look away, his eyes skittering along the floor till he picked up his thread again. Arf caught my mother as she gasped and fell against him. Tish had her arm firm around me. That day, everyone came to the hospital, except for Zara, who, being an infant, wasn't allowed. Pia and Mummy held hands, their lips moving in perfect synchrony, praying. Ant ran up and down, buying everything the nurses asked for; Papa stood at the window, looking out in silence. Arf stood outside the room asking visitors to leave. Tish stood on guard, offering tissues, juice and biscuits to anyone who needed it. Sunny stood by her bed, singing 'Love Bites' to Sia over and over again, her voice cracking.

By four in the evening, the doctors came in to say that things were not looking good and that we should prepare ourselves. We gathered around Sia's bed. They had removed the tubes from her nose and mouth, and we could see her heart-shaped little face with its yellow-blue bruises. Her features had settled into a sort of peace, her mouth curved slightly in a smile. I sighed inwardly, saying goodbye to my first baby.

And, then, my mother began to sing. It was a Punjabi lullaby she used to sing to us when we were little. Her voice was clear and strong as she sang about the little princess, and her friend, the sparrow. Pia and I joined her, silent during the bits we didn't remember, but humming the melody. Mummy bent and kissed Sia, and then, for the first time since we had met her, looked directly at Sunny and said, 'I know you loved her, beta. Thank you.' And then she turned and went outside, holding Papa's hand, as Sunny began to cry.

I looked at Sia and I swear I saw her eyelids flicker. Just like in the movies. Wishful thinking can be cruel on the heart. But, then, I saw it again, and Sia opened her eyes and looked directly at me and croaked, 'Aargh,' just like Lurch. As the family jerked into ecstasy, Mummy came in running, shouting, 'Thank you, God! I will never say bad things about people again!'

Sia kept looking at me, trying to say something. Finally, Sunny realized what was happening and went close to her. She bent down to listen to Sia and then straightened.

'She's asking if you and Arf got married,' said Sunny quietly.

The room went silent.

Then Papa spoke, 'Children, please, all of you, go home. Sia needs to rest.'

47

It had been three days of stress and misery, not knowing what had happened. Coming back to my room was strange, especially when my parents were still at the hospital and I was home alone without Sia next door. I wandered aimlessly from room to room, then finally found a bag of M&Ms, settled down in my parents' bed, under the covers, and turned on the TV. It was like being thirteen with measles all over again.

When I woke up, it was dark and my father was just walking out of the room in his pyjamas.

'Papa?'

'Sleep, beta. I'll sleep in the study. Mummy is staying in the hospital tonight.'

'No, no, I'll go to my room, Papa. Have you had dinner?'

'Not really. Shall we see what there is?'

I followed him down to the kitchen, where he drew up a stool to the counter and I pulled out whatever leftovers I could find. As I heated them up, he spoke, 'Beta, have you thought about your marriage?'

I froze.

This was the first time in all my life that my father had begun a personal conversation with me. In fact, this may have been the most he had ever said to me. I brought the food to the counter in silence and sat down opposite him.

'Choochoo, I know you are a big feminist, and now you think that men, especially old men, know nothing.'

He used my baby-name. I had forgotten I used to be called that. I kept quiet. I didn't want to implicate myself.

'But, in my years of life, I, too, have learned something. It is my experience that a gentleman does not make you wait. A gentleman does not make you wonder about what you mean to him. And in a lifetime of forty to sixty years, it would have been better to have spent it with a gentleman than with a man who has too many problems to care about yours. No matter how nice, how kind, how helpful he is to your family.'

He then stood up from the counter, smiled and said, 'Thanks for dinner, my little girl.' He washed his plate and left, while I sat with my food untouched, the dal beginning to dry around the edges, my mind a whirring, clicking, deafening clash of colours, images and sounds.

And, then, Sid's voice echoed in my mind: 'I'm the only man who didn't make you wait.'

Was it too late? How was I going to find him? I called Tish. 'Ask Saroj to call Pammi Auntieji, she might have his number.'

I called Saroj. 'Give me two minutes, I had a Brazilian for the wedding and I can't walk fast now.'

I paced up and down, texting Chinky and Freesia, just so they were in the loop.

Chinky: *Ask if he has a hot sister for me ;) – just joke OK?*

Freesia: *OMG!!! That's so kewl! How exciting. BTW I'm also marrying a foreigner: Dave. He's Canadian, blue eyes. Keep in touch in America OK?*

Just as I was trying to access his Facebook profile on my phone, Saroj called. Gina's family was giving Sid, his brother and father a welcome dinner at The Qube in The Leela Palace. *Fuck.* All those big windows. All that zero-privacy. Well, there was no option. I had to go.

Tish drove up with Saroj, Freesia and Chinky. They were coming, newly balded vaginas and recent engagements notwithstanding. I looked at my friends in hastily-put-together-Leela-appropriate outfits, recognized a pyjama top or two under a jacket, and tears sprung to my eyes.

'I love you Fucks.'

'Fuck that, bitch, you need to get in the car, it's a long way.'

It's only once I was in that I realized that I was still in my hospital-crushed clothes. Freesia whipped out a brush and began doing my hair; Chinky rummaged in Tish's bag and pulled out a green eye-pencil and prostitute-red lipstick. By the time we reached the hotel, I looked like a rumpled clown, but we had a plan in place. We were going to go sit down as if we had come for a meal, then signal to Sid from our table. And then Freesia and Tish would go chat with the families to distract them from how long Sid was taking to come back, while I grovelled for his forgiveness.

We tried to walk as fast and calmly and unobtrusively as we could. The restaurant was almost full, with people sitting in those booths, eating their fancy food and being quite loud. We spotted Sid's group at the exact same time I spotted Vyash at their table. I pulled Saroj and Chinky, who had taken the lead, back with their waistbands.

'Change of plan!' I hissed. I would wait near the door, while the others went in, and Tish would tell Sid that there was a parcel for him at the reception.

I hovered outside, refusing ten waiters who offered to seat me and being looked up and down by every single person who entered The Qube or the restaurant opposite it. I sensed some movement from the corner of my eye. It was Freesia, gesturing to me hysterically from the table. She kept mouthing *Coming!* This was it, then. I smoothed down my hair, smelt my breath on my palm and mentally prepared myself to face him.

'Vyash?'

He looked confused, then shocked, then amused. Shit! Green eyeliner!

'Rhea? I see you're doing . . . umm . . . living your usual colourful life?'

I grunted. 'You look older,' I said. I didn't want to be bitchy, in case Sid decided to invite them to our wedding, but Vyash was being pretty shitty.

'So, you are here . . . to meet someone?'

'What are you doing here?' I blurted out. I mean, how very Ashton Kutcher of him, hanging with the ex's current and all that.

'Well, Gina, my ex-wife?'

'How could I forget?'

'She's getting married again, and she asked me to be there for her as her oldest friend, and I thought, Why not, you know? Life goes on . . .' He finally softened and smiled kindly. 'What about you, Rhee? Are you OK? Have you found a guy?'

'I . . . er . . . ummm.' I sighed. 'Look, Vee, it's complicated. In fact . . . I . . . er . . .'

I saw some movement again. It was Freesia practically falling out of the booth. Shit.

'I got to go! Bye!'

I ran out into the reception, looking around for a slightly more private place. Then I remembered passing a small alcove, so I stepped backwards and slammed into Sid. His arms went up around me to break my fall. Then he saw my face and went completely white.

'Rhea?'

'Sid, I . . .' To my horror, I began to cry, probably sending green eyeliner down my face in thick rivers.

'Is everything all right? Is Sia . . .?'

I nodded.

'She's fine. She opened her eyes today.' And then I started crying even louder.

'Rhea, babe. You're scaring the goldfish.'

I smiled and then laughed sadly through my tears.

'Sid, can we go somewhere? I mean, can we talk?'

He looked uncomfortable.

'Rhea, I'm not sure that's a good idea. I'm marrying Gina in a few weeks. And I don't think I want to be your friend.'

I shook my head.

'Please? Sid, I don't want to be your friend. I . . . I . . . You're the one, Sid. The one I choose. You . . . I love you.'

I looked up at him, seeing my reflection in his glasses. He took them off and rubbed his eyes, looking at the ceiling for a few moments, blinking furiously. Oh shit. *Was he crying?*

I took his hand in mine. 'I'm sorry. I'm sorry for everything. I didn't know . . .'

He laughed bitterly.

'And now you do? And, now, suddenly, it's all clear, and of course it must be, just as I get my life in order and ask another girl to marry me.'

'Do you love her, Sid? Do you really love her?'

He stared at me, his blue eyes almost black. 'Rhea Kanwar, you can really piss me off, you know that?'

'I suggest you decide fast, because your in-laws-to-be are planning to come out looking for you.' Tish and the girls were standing behind us, looking like a bunch of slutty rag dolls in their red lipstick and mismatched clothes.

Sid looked at me in panic.

'Please, Jeejaji, please do not forsake our sister.' Chinky was kneeling on the floor of The Leela Palace lobby.

'Chinky?? Have you been drinking?'

'Little,' she said, with a finger on her lips.

I looked at Tish, who rolled her eyes.

'I couldn't stop her. She kept saying she didn't want the pitcher to go to waste.'

Saroj said, 'Should I get her a coffee or something?'

'She'll be fine when she gets home.' Freesia was nonchalantly wandering around the lobby, admiring the flower arrangements.

'Maybe we should all crash at yours tonight,' Tish was talking to Freesia, 'we can make a party of it.'

'Umm . . . ladies?' Sid was looking at us a bit bemused. 'Do you all have to be here?'

'Oh yes, brotherji. Will you please accept our sister's love. She is pure and good.' Chinky had her hands clasped now. Tish rushed over and tried to get Chinky to move with Saroj and Freesia's help. As they talked her into sitting on a chair, I turned to Sid.

'Sid, I'm sorry about this . . . this . . . craziness, but this is what I have to offer. My crazy friends and my crazy life and my crazy family, and I love them all more than anything in the world. Except for . . . you. And I know I broke your heart, but if you give me a chance, I'll . . . I'll spend the rest of my life—our lives—making it up to you.'

He stared at me, fear and confusion on his face. My heart seemed to stop beating.

'What about Gina? I committed to her.'

'Fuck Gina!' I was desperate. 'For once, Sid, fuck Gina! OK?'

'Please, Jeejoo! Fuck her!' Chinky was now swinging from an antique *jhula*, her legs stuck straight out in front of her.

'Guys, please!' I hissed at Tish, who promptly tried to stop the swing and get Chinky down.

'Sid?'

Gina was standing there, in a little black dress and heels, with all the dinner guests behind her. Vyash was looking at me and smirking.

'Fuck,' Sid muttered under his breath. 'Umm . . . This is Rhea . . .'

'Oh, cheers, mate! This is the girl you told me about. Pleased to meetcha!' exclaimed a guy, obviously Sid's brother.

Sid grimaced as Gina's face began to tremble. 'Gina, I'm sorry! I . . .'

'No, Gina, I'm sorry.' Was that really me speaking? 'Look, I love this man. More than you ever can. More than anybody can,' I said fiercely, positioning myself between them. 'And I'm really sorry you're engaged to him and all, but he's never going to be happy with you, OK? So . . . umm . . . I'm sorry . . .' I trailed off lamely.

'Right on!' Sid's brother pumped his fist in the air, breaking the silence.

Gina cleared her throat. 'Sid, if you come to your senses and realize that you want me, you know where to find me.' She sashayed off, followed by her brother, Sean; Vyash, who kept looking back at me, completely confused; and two other people—probably Gina's parents; and another youngish woman, probably Vyash's dancer. I exhaled. Now that was some classy shit. No wonder she had Vyash mooning over her for so long.

'Ladies, maybe it's time you left us alone, too.' Sid was looking straight into my eyes.

'Oh! Yeah! Sure! Umm . . . Sorry!'

Tish began to round everyone up. Chinky ran to Sid and collared him. 'Don't say no, OK? I know people.' Freesia rushed up and disengaged Chinky, who was still showing Sid her middle finger, and pulled her away.

As I watched them walking away, Tish, with her arms around Freesia and Saroj; Chinky, walking on ahead singing the title track from *Hum* loudly, her arms in the air, I couldn't help smiling. When I looked back at Sid, he was looking at me, this bemused expression on his face.

'So, the crazy's never going to stop, is it?'

I smiled and shook my head. 'This is me. These are my peeps. This is what I bring.'

He grinned that adorable grin of his. 'Well, I guess, I'm going to have to buy you a new ring. Or get the one I bought for you back from Gina.'

I shook my head. 'We'll let Gina keep it in place of you. I think it's a fair trade.'

Then I put my arms around him and kissed him with all the love, all the relief, all the need I felt for him. Tomorrow was my thirty-first birthday. It had taken me a year to find my way back home. And this quirky, funny, loving, geekily handsome man was it.

Ah, that reminded me. We'd have to see a counsellor about the sex to ensure it lasts more than a minute.

But that is another story.

ONE YEAR LATER

Gina and vyash remarried. They're both our Facebook friends now and keep promising to come stay with us in San Francisco where we now live. They're expecting twins—two boys; they went to London to find out the sex of the babies, and have done up a room entirely in blue, studded with toy Audis and Maseratis. I hear that Vyash has barred all connections to the Internet in his house and Gina is not encouraged to chat online at any time.

Arf didn't come to our wedding. Tish told me he came to her place and cried for a week. Apparently, he was going to propose the moment Sia came out of hospital. I couldn't keep in touch with Arf. I know I loved him once, but it was what my dad said—he wasn't a gentleman. He now lives in Munger in the Swami Satyananda Saraswati Ashram teaching yoga and leading their music sessions.

Saroj turned out to be really, really happy with her husband. She's a stay-at-home mom to a baby boy she delivered exactly nine months from the date of her wedding. She keeps writing to us about the real Punjab she experiences in the UK.

Freesia got married to her foreign fiancé last month. It was a destination wedding in Bali, but none of us could attend. She sent pictures though. About five hundred, just of her close-ups. And, of course, she looked gorgeous. After her honeymoon, she'll settle in Newfoundland, Canada, which she thinks is America.

Chinky is seeing someone new—her name is Honey and she's a fashion designer. They're living together and Chinky feels it's really serious. She still has her copy of *Jab Tak Hain Jaan* though.

Tish and K are 'chugging along' as she puts it. Tish hasn't been happy for a long time now, and with just Chinky left in Delhi, it gets lonely for her; but she's joined a moms' group where they all find her hugely scandalous and bitch about her all the time, and that makes Tish extremely happy.

Jay was in the papers a few months ago for drunken driving. As far as I could tell, he's still single, but trying to be an actor in Bollywood. He certainly has the behavioural quirks for it!

Mazhar is married to Noor Banu—a beautiful thirty-two-year-old divorcee, who is a brain surgeon. I wonder what he feels about all the sex she had during her first marriage. Or maybe he thinks it wasn't consummated?

Poor Ayushman. I forgot all about him in the chaos of Sia, Sid, and the craziness that surrounded our wedding. He sent me a few emails, which I never managed to answer. He gave up. I guess he saw the wedding pictures on Facebook. I really don't know what he's up to now.

Sia recovered fully, and she and Sunny have been seeing each other for close to a year and a half now. She'll be coming to California in June to start her film studies course. Sunny and her are still deciding whether they should carry on a long-distance thing or take a break until Sia's done with her degree. Mummy thinks they should stay together—she really likes Sunny and is willing to turn a blind eye to her 'robber-brother'. But Sia wants to explore; she feels she might be bisexual.

Pia now has Zane—a beautiful baby boy who smiles all the time. She's the only sister still living in India and keeps reminding us that we've skipped on our responsibilities and therefore should buy her lots of gifts to compensate her for it. Sia has asked me to tell her to fuck off. I said I'd forward her email to which she replied: *Challenge.*

Pammi Auntieji attended our wedding and distributed her business cards to everyone. Mummy grudgingly gifted her a sari and some money. But she does not invite her for kitty-parties. Mummy now, in fact, recommends Auntieji's biggest competitor to people: Fun with Fenny: Flow into Love with Fabulous Fastness.

People ask me how Sid and I met. I smile and say, 'Half love, half arranged.'

We're expecting our first baby in four months. Obviously, Sid got better at the sex. The songs still play in my head. But now I sing them to my belly. I'm hoping my baby will sing them all back to me someday.

ACKNOWLEDGEMENTS

Anyone who's written a book knows that writing this section is the one they've fantasized most about. After formulating and reformulating this page in my head, I've come to the conclusion that this is my superhero moment. You know the one. The one in which you stand, legs apart, chest sticking out, hands on waist, and then, squirming a bit to get the *chaddi* to fit right, you pick up the shampoo bottle and begin: 'I'd like to thank . . .'

I've been fortunate to live my life in the presence of real superheroes—special and incredible human beings—who shared their own brilliance with me so generously that, today, in their reflected light, I am able have this incredible moment. Thank you to:

Saugata Mukherjee, for an 'unexpected email' two years ago; for his formidable eye, his patient ear, and for being the man who 'discovered' me.

My BFF, Naomi George, author of *Mum-Me*, for unsticking me each and every time over coffee, a few lunches and several crazy playdates ('No! Stop killing each other!', 'Izzy, your characterization is far-fetched. Stop! STOP!') She, alone, bears the credit for yoking me to her shoulders and hauling me over every paralysing rock. And for always striking a match to my flagging creativity.

Gudrun Seth and Aviva Dharmaraj, for their oceans of love, ready ears, and for being exactly where they said they would be whenever I needed them. Jane DeSuza, author of *The Spy Who Lost Her Head*, for being my writing buddy, my C'MON-YOU-CAN-DO-IT-wallah friend, and the nicest critic I have ever had. Niyati Dhuldhoya, for not giving up on me even after a disastrous Goa holiday, and for teaching me that I know fuck-all about love. You girls are my tribe. And my reason for being.

My wonderful, vivacious editor, Ameya Nagarajan, who went out on a limb for me, stuck by me, and who is such fun that she's going to make an appearance in my next book, editorial comments and all!—'Whut?', 'Eh?', 'Not possible, no?'

My incredibly warm, understanding copy editor, Rachita Raj, who allowed me three months to complete a one-month one, and who has added infinite class to my book.

My incandescent agent, Urmila Dasgupta of Purple Folio, who has juggled a cross-country move, a city she hates and almost two months without the Internet, and still managed to be there for me.

My dearest friend and mentor, Noel Godin, who is an inseparable part of all the work I do, and whose infinite wisdom, humour and unyielding belief that I can do better, has saved me, time and time again.

The indomitable Niloufer Patel, who teaches me more than the Buddha, from her every gesture, every word, and every decision she makes. She changed my life, and continues to do so. I am so grateful that she is a part of it.

My father, Sajid Peerbhoy, who will not appreciate this mention right at the end, but will have to understand that the largeness of his influence, his belief in me and his continual flogging of me into a person of some worth, needs some courage to be put into words. Above all, thank you, Baaps, for not being the least bit surprised when I broke the news of the impending book. And for always giving me your best. I am proud to be your product.

My husband, Ashish D'Abreo, for being the gentleman who never made me wait. For getting my jokes, and for twelve of the most alive years of my life. Aal, I would walk 500 miles/ and I would walk 500 more/To be the man who walked 1000 miles to fall down at your door.

The music. The wonderful songs that formed the soundtrack of my life—right now, it's Bob Dylan's 'Make You Feel My Love'.

Finally, my late maternal grandfather, Ramesh Jindal, for his Punjabi charm, flamboyance and inspiration. Nanu, you still make me smile, and wherever you are, I hope you don't have dhi *klostrol*!